D0378848

# TWELVE VOICES FROM GREECE AND ROME

# TWELVE VOICES FROM GREECE AND ROME

Ancient Ideas for Modern Times

Christopher Pelling
AND
Maria Wyke

OXFORD
UNIVERSITY PRESS

OXFORD
UNIVERSITY PRESS

Great Clarendon Street, Oxford, OX2 6DP,
United Kingdom

Oxford University Press is a department of the University of Oxford.
It furthers the University's objective of excellence in research, scholarship,
and education by publishing worldwide. Oxford is a registered trade mark of
Oxford University Press in the UK and in certain other countries

Published in the United States of America by Oxford University Press
198 Madison Avenue, New York, NY 10016, United States of America

British Library Cataloguing in Publication Data
Data available

Library of Congress Control Number: 2014940424

ISBN 978-0-19-959736-9

Printed in Great Britain by
Clays Ltd, St Ives plc

# CONTENTS

# PREFACE

Classical literature is a vehicle for thinking about our human condition—that was how the neuroscientist Susan Greenfield explained her lasting fascination with the plays of Euripides in a radio essay broadcast in 2008. Are we hapless pawns in the universe or accountable individuals? How does it feel to experience inner psychological conflict or to lose your mind completely? Within the same series, *The Essay: Greek and Latin Voices*, Seamus Heaney spoke movingly of the enduring appeal of Virgil. The Latin poet's sympathy with the world of nature (of frost and flowers and flocks of birds, of furrows opened under a shower of rain) and his disquieting reflections on the tears in our lives (the brutality of war, the reality of cruelty and bloodshed) might be grasped in a few lines that could then become your friends for life.

When we became involved with the BBC and the Open University in the development of that Radio 3 series, poets, novelists, satirists, journalists, scientists, and priests, as well as academics, all stepped up to talk of the excitement, the immediacy, the *consequence* of their particular engagements with the literature of ancient Greece and Rome. From that distant past (they agreed) come forceful and affecting voices to which we should still be listening and responding in the twenty-first century.

The enthusiasm of the participants in the series encouraged us to produce this book in which we explore the modern relevance of twelve Greek and Roman authors (or 'voices' as they became on the radio). The book, therefore, makes no claim to be a comprehensive guide to classical literature. It is designed to be suggestive; a palatable taster of what ancient literature and culture can do for us in the present day. Why twelve? Twelve seemed to us a neat enough number from among the huge clamour of possibilities—just enough variety while still allowing sufficient space to give an idea of what each author is offering to the modern world. Why *these* twelve? That has been a more difficult decision. Even if we had stuck to just a single letter of the alphabet, strong cases could have been made for the inclusion of Pindar, Plato, Plutarch, Plautus, Propertius, or Petronius. The classical world is rich in voices worth listening to. We have attempted to reflect the diversity of the literary genres of Greece and Rome, and the ideas and emotions they explore. Yet we have also selected authors whom we thought best suited to our approach or with whom (given the personal dimension of this book) we especially welcomed an opportunity to engage. That, ultimately, is our answer to the question why we picked these twelve in particular. They are all authors who have meant a great deal to us personally, whom we still find rewarding to teach with and to think about. We hope that readers of this book will find themselves sharing some of our enthusiasm.

It certainly isn't new to argue for the modern value of Greek and Roman literature. At the height of the First World War, the British classical scholar Sir Richard Livingstone wrote:

> The classics introduce us to modern problems. It is almost impossible to persuade those who do not know it, that classical literature is in any way modern; they think of it as something primitive and barbarous, and they will not believe that Euripides or Seneca have at

least as much in common with the twentieth century as Scott or
Thackeray. So I will give a few instances to indicate how the classics
teem with modern characters, situations, problems.

(A Defence of Classical Education (1916), 186)

However, in contrast to Livingstone, we are not claiming that
classical authors provide some kind of comfortable ancient sanction
for the elite British masculine self. We are not, as Livingstone does,
seeking from the ancients helpful lessons on how 'to govern people
who differ in race, language, temper and civilization' from ourselves. We suggest instead that there is available to us a more
complex, troubling (and, therefore, more valuable) engagement
with classical literature. One of our pervasive themes is the *danger*
rather than the satisfaction of assuming a neat equivalence of
experience between the ancient and the modern world. Another
theme is the attraction of thinking in a refreshingly different—
sometimes even startlingly alien—way about religion, say, or the
East, about happiness, sexuality, power, or the political role of
literature.

We are not looking for eternal 'truths' either: that is asking a lot
of any text. It is rather the idea of a 'conversation' that is important
to us—the ways in which texts speak to us and invite us to respond.
We do not mean a conversation on the grand scale envisioned in
1952 by the then President of the University of Chicago, Robert
M. Hutchins. Under the title 'The Great Conversation', he wrote a
passionate introduction to the first edition of the *Encyclopaedia
Britannica*'s vast series of *Great Books of the Western World*. The
carefully selected canon of Great Books was presented as a Great
Conversation between Great Thinkers 'about what is and should
be'. Americans were invited to participate in that conversation and

the 'Western Civilisation' it was supposed to articulate through reading the series. We here conceive our conversation with the ancients on a much smaller, more intimate—and more dynamic—scale. The texts of the ancient world can still speak, not just to us, but with us, and in a range of exhilarating and disturbing ways. They still matter, and what they talk about can still be fresh (whether empire, masculinity, nature, urbanity, madness, rationality, religious commitment and disbelief, family and friendship, desire, or death). The voices of ancient Greece and Rome can profoundly affect the individual lives (the thoughts, feelings, or even the actions) of those who actively converse with them.

We have not resisted writing about our own experience in this book, including the times when we first met these voices and their world; the Welsh grammar-school boy on his caravan holiday and the London convent-school girl reading furtively during break will both make their appearance. But most of the discussion touches on the experiences of others: we are not soldiers in the First World War trenches reading Homer at more or less the time that Livingstone was writing, nor ventriloquizing performers in operas on Dido or tragedies about Medea; nor are we very like five-star Pentagon generals pondering the relevance of Thucydides to modern strategy; nor Napoleons, mulling over Caesar's tactics and pronouncing on where he had gone wrong; and we are certainly not Nazis inspired by a reading or misreading of Tacitus' history of ancient Germania. Yet our classical authors have meant something to all these diverse groups, sometimes striking an emotional chord, sometimes stimulating thought and provoking argument, sometimes reassuring, sometimes discomfiting, often a mixture of all these; there is no reason to think that this will ever stop, with new readers always finding something different as the social and emotional baggage we bring to our conversations with the ancients changes.

One theme, indeed, is the way that these texts leave so much up to their readers. Because they are richly textured voices they are also equivocal. Cicero invites *you* to judge between opposing arguments for the existence of a supreme deity. Virgil forces you to weigh in the balance female against male and love against the chaos of war. Juvenal and Lucian press you to choose between the satirist and the targets of their abuse. Sappho challenges you to comprehend her erotic predicament and feel the nature of her pleasure or her pain. These voices urge you to respond, to open up a dialogue, to react—but not always in the same way on each encounter. So we hope that our own readers too will find new and different things in our texts and in the responses of others to them: hence the fullness of our suggestions for Further Reading. And we also hope that this short book might draw readers into exploring other voices from antiquity—because there are so many Greek or Roman authors who could easily have made it into 'the top twelve'—and to enter into conversations with them of your own.

We would like to thank the BBC and the Open University for their permission to develop the concept of 'Greek and Latin Voices' in a different direction, the BBC producers Beatrice Rubens and Tim Dee, James Robson at the Open University, and the other contributors to the original series from whom we often learned a great deal. For their advice, comment, and criticism, we are very grateful to: Susanna Braund, William Fitzgerald, Christine Hall, Jennie Kiesling, Fiachra Mac Góráin, Fiona Macintosh, Gesine Manuwald, Judith Mossman, Jennifer Ogilvie, David Oswell, Isobel Pinder, Naomi Setchell, Elizabeth Vandiver, Tim

Whitmarsh, and Jonathan Williams. Liz Sawyer kindly alerted us to the remarks of Livingstone and Hutchins that we have just quoted. A word of thanks is also due to Erica Martin at Oxford University Press for her resourceful pursuit of our illustrations, to Luciana O'Flaherty for her elegant editorial work on our text, to the OUP readers for their helpful suggestions and corrections, and to Matthew Cotton for his patience and diplomacy as we lingered over the composition of this book. It has been a considerable pleasure to write alongside and in exchange with each other.

CHRISTOPHER PELLING

MARIA WYKE

# LIST OF ILLUSTRATIONS

# I

# HOMER

'Homer' is the most mysterious figure among our authors. He—or 'they', as many think the *Iliad* and the *Odyssey* carry the stamp of two different master narrators—may well not have been writer(s) at all, but illiterate singer(s). We should think of an oral tradition, with poetry about Troy and other themes gradually crystallizing over centuries; probably something happened around 700–650 BCE to generate something close to our current *Iliad* and *Odyssey*; probably that 'something' was the activity of our great poet or poets. Some versions or parts of the poems may have immediately been written down, perhaps by dictation (though there is a question about the writing materials that could have been available), or a few generations may have intervened in which the poems were passed down orally. Maybe it was a bit of both. Early tradition cast Homer as a blind bard, capturing the notion that blindness may be compensated by the gods with brilliance or wisdom—a trade of sight for insight.

In the last days of the Second World War a young British soldier, seriously wounded in the final push towards Berlin, found a date in his father's handwriting in his copy of Homer. It stirred his thoughts, and he wrote to his father:

> When I was one, in Shillingstone
> June afternoon you spent
> In reading Homer; twenty now,
> Homer I read in Ghent.

> From Ghent to Shillingstone is far;
> 'Tis twenty years away.
> But clear-seen Ithaca is near;
> I'll meet you there today.

The image of Ithaca filled Odysseus' mind on the shore of Calypso's island, trapped with a beautiful goddess for seven years but still dreaming of the home he had left (*Odyssey* 1.58, 5.151–8). After witnessing far worse scenes, the soldier found that island of Ithaca more 'clear-seen'—a favourite Homeric adjective for Ithaca—than that memory of his own childhood.

Another twenty years later the soldier's brother wrote of the poem's 'unclouded purpose and confidence'. Perhaps it is indeed optimistic; perhaps it points to that world of fantasy that their reading allows the writer and his father to share, giving meaning to their lives even at a time like this. That may be why it is Ithaca, not Troy, that the poet yearns for. The carnage of the Trojan battlefield would be too gruesome, too close to the grimness of the Battle of the Bulge that the brother had fought through, and of the trenches in Flanders that the father had witnessed thirty years before. The domesticity of Ithaca offers hope. But the poem can be read very differently. Will it just be a daydream that frees the soldier's mind to fly away to Ithaca? Or might it be something worse, releasing the spirit just as the life-force left Homer's heroes as they died?

One thing is clear, and in many poems from the First World War as well: their memories of Homer could be so important as these young men struggled to make sense of what they faced. 'Stand in the trench, Achilles, Flame-capped, and shout for me!' wrote Patrick Shaw-Stewart, a brilliant young classicist, as he returned to action in

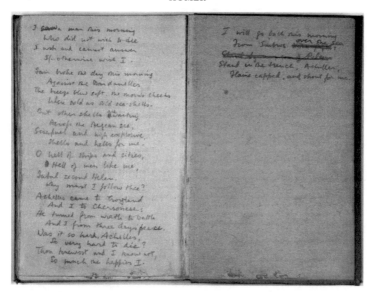

FIGURE 1.1. Manuscript of Patrick Shaw-Stewart's 'I saw a man this morning...', inscribed in his copy of Housman's *A Shropshire Lad* and found among his possessions after his death in 1917.

the Dardanelles in 1915: his poem was found inscribed in the fly-leaf of his copy of *A Shropshire Lad* after he had died (Figure 1.1). Those thoughts could be bright and uplifting: the First World War soldier in the trench was indeed a new Achilles, winning honour that would never die, or a Hector, prepared to give all to defend home and family. Or they could be more dispiriting, dwelling on the differences between that glittering distant world and the mutilation, the pain, the bodies exploded into nothingness.

Even if one saw continuity rather than difference, that could be bleak too.

> Say only this, 'They are dead'. Then add hereto
> 'Yet many a better one has died before'.

3

So wrote Charles Hamilton Sorley, dismissing the 'soft things as other men have said'. He was killed by a sniper's bullet in October 1915; the sonnet was found in his baggage. It quotes Achilles' words to Priam's son Lycaon, who is begging unsuccessfully for his life to be spared: 'Why do you weep so? Patroclus too has died, a much better man than you' (*Iliad* 21.106–7). True, this too may have offered some community across the centuries, in the knowledge that others had faced such things and thought such things before; there is an eerie human community even in the Homeric original, for Achilles addresses Lycaon, breathtakingly, as 'Friend'—a friend linked in the death which, we will see, Achilles knows he will himself face soon. But it is unlikely that anyone's loved ones, including Sorley's own, would find much relief in his stark words; any more than in Wilfred Owen's 'Strange Meeting', when he too imagines himself addressing the man he has killed as 'friend', and is so addressed in return.

Screaming shells, stinking corpses in no man's land, snow, rain, clinging mud, the surviving blind or limbless: all is so different from the clear air of Troy, where wounds are either immediately lethal or manageably mild and Hector returns home nightly to a warm bath. And yet Homer mattered so much, at least to some. The word 'conversation' is lame for a manner of thinking that was so fraught, but it introduces the theme of this book in an extraordinarily intense way. Why was it—why is it—such a good way to think about this modern world? How *could* it all be so meaningful still?

The question is sharper because it was Achilles who was so often in mind. For Homer's Achilles is special: the most special of special cases, different and extreme even among the characters of the *Iliad* itself; on the face of it, an extraordinarily difficult figure with which to relate. He can fight supremely well and run supremely fast—nothing there of the everyday likelihood that you might be out-fought by your enemy. In one way that is what we would expect, as his mother is a goddess—but there are other sons of gods and goddesses fighting around Troy, and none is as special as he.

If he had not been so special, there might never have been a problem. The trouble comes when the commander-in-chief Aga-memnon grudgingly accepts that he has to give up a slave-girl he has been given as a prize of war, but demands another girl in exchange. The quarrel briskly escalates, and within a few minutes it is not just any slave-girl he is demanding, it is Achilles' girl, Briseis. You're always doing this sort of thing, Achilles cries—that 'always' so familiar in quarrels. I've no quarrel myself with the Trojans, it's for you and your brother Menelaus that we're fighting this war . . .

And now you even threaten to take away my prize yourself. I laboured hard for it, and it was awarded me by the sons of the Achaeans. I never have a prize equal to yours, whenever the Achaeans sack some well-founded Trojan town. My hands bear the brunt of the battle's fury. But when the division comes, your prize is by far the larger, and I come back to the ships with something small but precious, when I have worn myself out in the fighting. Now I will leave for Phthia. It is a far better thing for me to return home with my beaked ships, and I have no mind to stay here heaping up riches and treasure for you and receiving no honour myself.

(*Iliad* 1.161–71)

So: Agamemnon takes the girl, Briseis; Achilles rages off to his tent, with the threat to go home ringing in the air. He does the lion's share of the work, but he does not get the appreciation he deserves.

Even Achilles' anger is anything but ordinary: that is why he is prepared to do something about all this. The word for this anger—the first word of the *Iliad*—is *mēnis*, often translated 'wrath'. It is a word that is nearly always used of a *god*'s rage. And the thing about gods is that they do not need to compromise, or to know when it is time to draw back. Once started on a course of action, they can just carry on. It is relevant again that he has a goddess-mother, so that the blood in his veins is semi-divine: the word for Achilles is often *dios*, 'godlike', and that is true in more senses than one.

But semi-divine: only semi-. Gods have no need to relent, for they have less to fear. In particular, they cannot die. Achilles can die, and he will: not within the poem itself, but we are left in no doubt that his actions, driven by that wrath, will eventually lead to his own death. When he celebrates the funeral of his friend Patroclus near the end of the poem, it is as if it is his own funeral too. In funeral games the dead man's possessions are given away as prizes, as he has no more need for them. Achilles gives away his own possessions as well.

Even his death is special for Achilles. His mother has told him something that ordinary mortals cannot know, something about that death.

> My mother, the silver-footed goddess Thetis, says that I have two fates that could carry me to the end of death. If I stay here and fight on round the Trojans' city, then gone is my homecoming, but my glory will never die: and if I come back to my dear native land, then gone is my great glory, but my life will stretch long and the end of death will not overtake me quickly. And I would advise the rest of you too to sail back home . . .
>
> (*Iliad* 9.410–18)

Achilles has a choice. For the moment, it is all clear to him. He will choose obscurity and length of years over an early death and lasting fame. But any audience will also know that he will change his mind, and this is not just because the very act of reading or hearing or talking about the poem shows that Achilles' glory 'never died', that he ended by winning that eternal fame that came with one of the two choices. By that point we have already seen enough of Achilles to know that the glorious battlefield, not the tranquil old age, is the choice for him. When three Greek envoys arrive at his tent to plead with him to return, they find him singing to the lyre, and his theme is 'the glorious deeds of men'. The battlefield is where he belongs.

So superhuman ability; superhuman rage; superhuman knowledge of his own destiny. Achilles' experience is something that only a very special person might have. But that 'choice' of his is still a version of a choice that faced those soldiers in the World Wars, just as it has faced so many generations of humans, especially men, in history. Do they go and fight, or do they not? Achilles may know that, if he goes into battle, he will die, and if he stays away he will live; ordinary mortals know only that they *may well* die in the one case and they *have a chance* of a long life in the other. ('Thou knewest, and I know not; so much the happier I', as Shaw-Stewart put it in the stanza before those 'Stand in the trench' lines). The everlasting renown that awaits Achilles is far more than the respect and honour that an everyday warrior can hope for. But these differences simply sharpen the dilemma, they do not fundamentally change it. We can already see here something that will recur with author after author in this book, the way that a story or an idea can be both firmly rooted in a specific time and society, one very different from our own, and still have resonance for our own experience. Of course we should not domesticate these texts, pretending that all the issues remain just the same three millennia later:

part of the business of reading them is to do what we can to re-enter the mindset of the original audience, reconstructing what they might find problematic or absorbing or bewildering and wondering whether those issues might be just as interesting as the ones we find ourselves; and we can make that effort while acknowledging that all such attempts are likely to over-simplify, and also that different readers and hearers must always have reacted in different ways. But one reason for making the effort is that this Other World is not always so Other as all that, and that these texts still have things to say that come very close to home.

If we do try to re-create how the first audiences of the poems would have reacted, it was probably not too different—whoever these were and whenever this was, and we saw in our initial summary that there is a good deal of mystery about that. In any case, we should surely think of the poems as *performed* orally, to audiences hanging on every word (Figure 1.2). Possibly an audience might be quite a grand one, at a wedding feast perhaps, or a festival for the gods; possibly it might be a more casual one, at whatever the village equivalent was of a coffee-shop or a tavern; probably it was sometimes more like the one and sometimes more like the other, and each performance could concertina in or out according to the time available and the hearers' reaction. We cannot even be sure that the poems were *ever* performed by 'Homer' in their present form, even if every line or scene were to go back in some way to him (or to them, if the two poems have different authors). But sure as can be, these were not audiences who were used to a world where the gods were often seen to come and mingle, nor where grand panhellenic expeditions were mounted for any reason, least of all to get back a woman whose beauty had launched a thousand ships. That world

FIGURE 1.2. Jean-Baptiste Auguste Leloir, *Homer and his Audience*, 1841. Doubtless any original performance was in less luscious a setting.

was already a distant one, yet part of the fascination would already be to see how, when so much was different, the human preoccupations were already very familiar ones: death, glory, love—and the loss of those one loved.

So how would those audiences—Greeks around 700 BCE, Great War soldiers, we today—reconstruct the values of that distant world? Honour of course matters greatly; one classic statement is made by the Lycian fighter Sarpedon, himself a son of a god (in his case Zeus himself). He is talking to his companion Glaucus: why are they here, fighting not even for their own country but for their ally Troy? That question leads only to another one:

> 'Why is it that we two are held in the highest honour in Lycia, with pride of place, the best of the meat, the wine-cup always full, and all look on us as gods, and we have a great cut of the finest land by the banks of the Xanthos, rich in vineyard and wheat-bearing plough-land? That is why we should now be taking our stand at the front of the Lycian lines and facing the sear of battle, so that among the heavy-armoured Lycians people will say: "These are no worthless men who rule over us in Lycia, these kings who eat our fat sheep and drink the choice of our honey-sweet wine. No, they have strength too and courage, since they fight at the front of the Lycian lines."
>
> Dear friend, if we were going to live for ever, ageless and immortal, if we survived this war, then I would not be fighting in the front ranks myself or urging you into the battle where men win glory. But as it is, whatever we do the fates of death stand over us in a thousand forms, and no mortal can run from them or escape them—so let us go, and either give triumph to another man, or he to us.'
>
> (*Iliad* 12.310–29)

There are two strands of thought there, linked by the theme of what people will say about the pair. The first concentrates on the present, what their own humbler countrymen may say: they have their privileges, and they must show that they deserve them. Still, this is not enough. The second acknowledges that, if they were going to live for ever, such worldly respect would not be enough to bring them to the front line. But they are going to die some time; the only sort of immortality is the glory that lives on, and it is in battle that 'men win glory'. This is an idea that one finds often enough in the *Iliad*, the memory of the 'undying fame' that the characters know, or hope, will be their lot.

Is that, though, enough? Achilles himself is unconvinced, at least once Agamemnon has taken away his prize of honour, Briseis. At first it barely seems to matter that she is a living, breathing girl; she might have been a tripod or a lump of iron—anything to show that he is properly appreciated. Even when Agamemnon climbs down and offers to make recompense, Achilles is not satisfied. Material goods matter in this world as a mark of one's status and honour, and Agamemnon offers plenty—perhaps too much, in fact: seven women, not just Briseis, and twenty more once Troy falls, and once they get home a daughter of his own in marriage (Achilles can pick which one) and seven cities to rule . . . Achilles, though, becomes more furious still: now he will sail home tomorrow, he is so enraged—though his stance softens a little as Agamemnon's envoys find better arguments to put to him.

So there is something wrong with Agamemnon's offer; it has just made things worse. Maybe it's that he doesn't come himself; at the end of the poem the Trojan king Priam does come himself to beg Achilles to release Hector's body, and he is successful even though the ransom he brings is far less than Agamemnon had offered. Or perhaps this just reflects a wider point, that Agamemnon's offer is *only* material. The goods are supposed to be emblems of genuine respect and appreciation of worth, and even though Agamemnon has by now accepted that he made a mistake (9.116–20), he failed to include that in his message to Achilles. Or maybe there is nothing anyway that Agamemnon could say, at least at this stage of Achilles' anger.

However exactly we explain it, I do not think that readers or hearers find Achilles' refusal hard to understand. We would find it more surprising if he accepted it—'seven girls, you say? Fair enough. Have them wrapped and sent round. Briseis will show them the ropes. See you tomorrow.' Yet people *in the poem* find it harder to make sense of it all. Even Ajax, the envoy who gets through to Achilles most by reminding him of 'the love of his companions, how we honoured him more than any other by the ships', just does not understand: it is

> all because of a girl, one girl—but now we are offering you seven, the very finest, and much more besides them.
>
> (*Iliad* 9.630–1, 638–9)

Nor is it difficult for us to understand him when he does come back to the fight, not then for immortal glory nor for the gifts (though he knows he will gain both) but more through a mix of anger, grief, and guilt, all because of Patroclus' death and all so intense as to drive him on to the death he knows must come (18.98–126). By now his human loves and affections are what matters most; his love for Patroclus, his guilt that he has let his own men down, his rage against Hector.

Even Briseis has come to matter; by the time Achilles receives the envoys she is no mere tripod, but a woman whom he is prepared to call his 'wife', whom he 'loved from my heart, slave-girl though she was' (9.342–3). But we might still feel that she does not matter *much*. Her own feelings in all this have been ignored. When she is finally allowed a voice, she laments—but for Patroclus; Achilles too is mentioned, but only because Patroclus had always been so good to her, even promising to get Achilles to marry her (19.282–300). That will not happen now. The other slave-girls echo her lament,

> professedly for Patroclus, and each of them wept over her own sorrows.
>
> (*Iliad* 19.302)

They do well to do so. No one else will weep for them.

Is this not, then, a profoundly, alienatingly masculine poem? Are not all these values so quintessentially male, even caricatures of childish masculinity: the carnage-stained glory, the desire to dominate, the self-centredness? And even the way everything starts from women—the war starting with Helen, the quarrel starting with Briseis—is that not a familiar male strategy, a woman's place being in the wrong?

Yes and no. Yes, it is certainly a masculine society, and we have to try to think our way into it if we are to understand what Achilles is so upset about. Yes, there are few women about. But those women are central, and not just because things start with them (and anyway what makes it all so deadly is not a point about the women but about the men, their competitiveness and aggressiveness once they take over). What the women say and stand for is to be taken seriously; it is through women that we see what war can mean. A formulaic adjective for battle is *kudianeira*, 'where men win glory', as in that speech of Sarpedon to Glaucus. For war, the adjectives are different: war is 'tearful' or 'chilling' or 'dread-sounding' or 'hateful' or 'full of misery' or just 'bad'. It is also 'the same for everyone', levelling even to the best, the most special. Hector's wife Andromache strives to keep him from the front line, trying to find the male-shaped arguments that might save him: the wall is weak just here, this is where you are needed (6.433–7). But it is no surprise when he deflects her:

> Go back to the house and see to your own work, the loom and the distaff, and tell your maids to set about their tasks. War will be the men's concern, all the men whose homeland is Troy, and mine above all.
>
> (*Iliad* 6.490–3)

Not easy words for a modern reader to find sympathetic; and yet in their context we—or most of us—may do so, as the closeness and tenderness of husband and wife has just been so strongly felt. Their young son is terrified by his father's helmet and shies from his embrace, and husband and wife share the light moment, Andromache 'laughing through her tears' (6.484). We do not see them together again. The *Iliad* ends with the laments for the dead Hector, as women mourn, not just the warrior and the prince, but the man they loved: Andromache his wife and the mother of his child, Hecabe his mother, then, strikingly, Helen—the woman whose beauty started it all, but who now simply mourns the man who was so gentle and civil to her. That loss is one part of what war really means; and, in this masculine world of brutal action, it is the women's voice that is heard at the end.

So this is not a simple poem—that is evident—and it is not a poem with a single world-view. There is not a single 'heroic code' here which the poem blazons or defends; there is not a single way of looking at war. There are multiple ways here of looking at complex issues. We are just never allowed to forget that they are complex, and, however distant, there are some aspects of its complexity—what's going on in Achilles' head, for instance, or the ways it could all seem so different to women—that later audiences can understand in ways that the men in the thick of it may not.

The *Odyssey* presents us with a different world, just as his journey home presented the battle-hardened Odysseus with a new set of predicaments. Violence is still there, an ever-present part of the background: memories of the sack of Troy, intruding on a pleasant dinner; the casual ruthlessness of Odysseus' own returning band— 'As I sailed from Troy the wind took me to Ismarus, the city of the Cicones: I sacked the city and killed its menfolk, and we divided up the women and the vast plunder...' (9.39–41); the brutish behaviour of the suitors for Odysseus' wife Penelope, culminating in a plan to ambush and murder his son Telemachus. But simple strokes of the sword will not now take one very far, for danger comes in different forms. It is a world where the talents of an Odysseus rather than an Achilles are needed—deviousness, trickery, patience, planning; a world where, usually, drawing back and biding one's time are the wise course. It is a world, too, where women play a different role. In the *Odyssey* women control a good deal more, and Odysseus often has to show his shrewdness in finding the right things to say to a woman. He is very good at it, however awkward the situation: when appearing, brine-covered and naked, from under a bush to surprise the young girls playing ball by the sea-shore, when most of them scatter but the princess Nausicaa remains; when the sorceress Circe changes his men into pigs, then tries and fails to do the same with Odysseus, then quickly suggests that they go to bed together; and when he finally gets home and tells Penelope of all his adventures—but is tactfully vague about the other women he has slept with, just mentioning 'Circe's trickery and subtlety' and saying that Calypso 'longed to' make him her husband but he always refused . . . (*Odyssey* 23.310–43). Nothing more than that. Wise man.

I was 16 when I first read the *Odyssey*, in the old Penguin translation of E. V. Rieu. It was on a family caravan holiday. I was getting a bit old by then for tales of one-eyed monsters—the Cyclopes—or witches turning humans into pigs, but it did not feel like the fairytales I had been reading ten years earlier: it was again that same feature, the way that in this distant and glamorous world one can still find so much that is instantly understandable. That 16-year-old could certainly find a lot that was uncomfortably close-to-home in the teenage Telemachus, who has his moments of gawky adolescence: the false sophistication towards the beginning, for instance, when the goddess Athena is visiting their palace in disguise, and pretends not to know who Telemachus is: can this really be Odysseus' son?

> 'My friend,' answered the courteous Telemachus, 'I will be honest too. My mother certainly says I am Odysseus' son; but for myself I cannot tell. No man can be certain who his father is . . . '
>
> (*Odyssey* 1.214–16)

Not quite the thing to say, and Athena tactfully leads the conversation in a different direction. Then the boy visits the court of Helen and Menelaus. The time comes for Telemachus to introduce himself, and Menelaus and Helen drop some gentle hints; Telemachus keeps missing his cue.

There are some other touches that that 16-year-old might not have been so quick to pick up. One is the way that Odysseus gets on with the goddess Athena. After Odysseus has landed back on Ithaca, he does a good line in elaborate cover-stories to explain why a stranger should suddenly have turned up on the island. On one occasion he wastes one of these stories on someone who is apparently a local, but turns out to be Athena in disguise. I am a refugee from Crete, he says; a Phoenician crew has just dropped me here, and must have sailed off when I was asleep . . .

> That was Odysseus' story. The bright-eyed goddess smiled at him and caressed him with her hand. She now wore the appearance of a woman, tall, beautiful and accomplished. Then she spoke, and her words winged their way to him. 'Anyone who met you, even a god, would have to be a consummate trickster to surpass you in subterfuge. You were always an obstinate, cunning, and irrepressible intriguer. So you don't propose, even in your own country, to drop the tricks and lying tales you love so much! But no more of this. We both know how to get our own way: in the world of men you have no rival in judgement and argument, while I am pre-eminent among the gods for ingenuity and ability to get what I want . . . '
>
> (*Odyssey* 13.287–99)

It takes one to know one: the goddess and the man understand one another. And the smile, the gentle caress, that tone of 'here you go again': not for the only time, it is almost flirtatious—just as the deference with which Odysseus speaks to her is sometimes tempered with just a touch of affectionate familiarity.

But *almost* flirtatious, *almost* erotic—almost, but not quite, and that almost-but-not-quite is important. One reason for the not-quite is because of Athena. She is a virgin, the most manly of the goddesses; she doesn't do that sort of thing. But another is because of Odysseus. On his journeys he has been faced by several women on whom, one way or another, the male imagination might dwell; Calypso, the goddess on her idyllic island, devoted to him, offering him immortality if he will stay; Nausicaa, the young princess, innocent but nubile, her thoughts beginning to be on marriage; the powerful, magical Circe, eying him up and down and suggesting immediate sex. But none of them will do, for none is Penelope, and this is not home. The Welsh, as that 16-year-old Cardiff boy knew, have a word for it: *hiraeth*, the yearning for the landscape and familiarity of one's own land when far away, the longing that the exile never loses. The first we saw of Odysseus was that scene when he was sitting on Calypso's shore, crying his eyes out, desperate to see even the smoke circling up from the chimneys of Ithaca. These are the words he speaks to Nausicaa:

> May the gods grant you your heart's desire; may they give you a husband and a home, and the blessing of harmony so much to be desired, since there is nothing better or finer than when two people of one heart and mind keep house as man and wife, a grief to their enemies and a joy to their friends, and they themselves know it best.

> (*Odyssey* 6.180–5)

Beautiful words.

When he gets there, though, home is not so serene. Violence returns to the forefront. He has 108 suitors to kill, and the old warrior techniques of the *Iliad* are necessary after all; and he needs the help of Athena in decidedly less flirtatious ways, as she first helps him to maintain his disguise and then plays a role in the combat itself. The world of the journeys may have been close to fairytale; this is starkly different. Nor is everything comfortable. These are not the routine impersonal killings of the end of a James Bond film, where the bloodshed does not count for very much. We may or may not feel for the suitors themselves; we may certainly feel—perhaps even that eighth- or seventh-century audience may have felt—for the slave-girls who slept with them, doubtless without much choice in the matter, and whom Odysseus first makes clear up the mess, then kills by hanging them all in a row

> to bring them to the most pitiable end. For a little while their feet twitched but not for very long.

(Odyssey 22.472–3)

That is too much for modern tastes. In a celebrated modern work taking its inspiration from the *Odyssey*, Derek Walcott makes Penelope step in here to stop the killing. It is a reminder that much as we try and easy as we find it to 'converse' with these poems, the world is still a distant one, and cannot always be brought so close.

Returning veterans do not always take easily to peacetime life, and even in our poem Odysseus is beginning to stumble. He is reunited with his father Laertes, but the meeting goes badly wrong. He spins yet another yarn, claiming that he is a visitor from afar, but yes, he might well have entertained someone like Odysseus five years ago ... Laertes collapses in distress, and Odysseus quickly tells him the truth. But why did he play this heartless trick in the first place? Maybe, as one critic has suggested, deception has simply become so ingrained, such a 'conditioned reflex', that he cannot be straightforward any more.

Perhaps indeed it is the *traveller*'s reintegration, not the veteran's, that may pose problems. C. P. Cavafy's *Ithaka* wishes his voyager a long and happy journey, full of bright summer mornings sailing into new harbours. Best that it should last for many years. The journey could not have happened without Ithaca, but when he reaches the island it will have nothing more to offer:

> Ithaca gave you the wondrous voyage.
> Without her you'd never have set out.
> But she has nothing to give you any more.
> If then you find her poor, Ithaca has not deceived you.
> As wise as you've become, with such experience, by now
> You will have come to know what Ithacas really mean.

But what *do* they mean? Simply the vision, 'clear-seen', that one needs to give purposefulness to the journey? Just the starting-point, a past that he will know has irretrievably gone? Or a final point of retreat, when the time has come to live contentedly with the memories? Maybe different things for different voyagers; 'Ithacas' is a telling plural. Maybe different brands of wisdom too.

So what will Odysseus' own brand be, and what sort of future awaits him? Perhaps it really will be a gentle old age, harmoniously shared with Penelope. But Tennyson saw the danger that it might all be too boring:

> It little profits that an idle king,
> By this still hearth, among these barren crags,
> Match'd with an aged wife, I mete and dole
> Unequal laws unto a savage race,
> That hoard, and sleep, and feed, and know not me.
> I cannot rest from travel; I will drink
> Life to the lees . . .

Or maybe he will go off again in search of new adventure,

> to strive, to seek, to find, and not to yield.
>
> (Tennyson, *Ulysses*)

We may well wonder. That is part of our own 'conversation' with the poem, as we too, like Cavafy and Tennyson, find our imagination stirred. There are hints in Homer's poem along those lines of looming discontent, but they are muted and few. On the whole, getting home is enough—getting home, and to Penelope. It is those beautiful words to Nausicaa that rest in the mind. They capture not merely an ideal, but also the human longing for that ideal—the *hiraeth*—clear in the mind even when so far away; just as Ithaca seemed so lovely and clear-seen to that young man in the trenches seventy years ago.

CP

# II

# SAPPHO

Most of the voices in this book are male: even when 'women' speak on the Greek stage, it is with the lines given them by male playwrights and spoken by male actors. Sappho—or Psappho, as she spelt it herself—is one of the few female authors whose works survive, and her personal voice is particularly haunting when she talks of one woman's love for another. We do not know very much about her life. She was born on the island of Lesbos in the second half of the seventh century, she had several brothers, and she perhaps went into exile in Sicily. She had a much-loved daughter called Cleis. Later, much later, she was pictured as having been slight of build and with a dark complexion. Most of what is said about her in antiquity seems to be based on inference from the poems—many more poems than we have today, of course, but with other literary figures we can often see that such inferences were wild ones.

> There are nine Muses, some say: how careless!
> Look—Sappho from Lesbos is number ten.
>
> (Epigram attributed to Plato, *Palatine Anthology* 9.16)

> The people of Mytilene honour Sappho, even though she was a woman.
>
> (Aristotle, *Rhetoric* 1398b)

A few years ago, a news story from the island of Lesbos hit the press. Three islanders were taking a gay rights group to court for using the word 'Lesbian' in its name. One of the plaintiffs was particularly indignant: the word 'Lesbian', he said, had only been used of gay women in the last few decades; the people of Lesbos had been there for thousands of years. 'My sister', he exclaimed, 'can't go round saying she's a Lesbian!' The news item ended by saying that the Homosexual and Lesbian Community of Greece could not be reached for comment. Probably just as well.

Whatever else that shows, it does suggest the lasting impact that the poems of Sappho, full as they are of passionate and delicate impressions of one woman's love for other women, have had—and still have today, two and a half thousand years after they were first written around 600 BCE. Any tourist today looking at the T-shirts on sale in the shops of Lesbos would not be in much doubt of that either—nor of the positive impact on the island's tourist economy of that reputation for female–female love. But it is true that those connotations of the word are largely modern ones, even if not quite so modern as the angry plaintiff claimed. (They are Victorian in origin, in fact, and it was doubtless originally a coy euphemism for a love that particularly engaged the imagination of that age (Figure 2.1); 'Sapphism' is found at around the same time.) True, there is a delightful little poem of another lyric poet, Anacreon, that might suggest something different, but I am not sure it does:

> Here it comes again—the purple ball
> Of golden-haired Love, and I'm being
> Called upon once more to play
> With the girl in the fancy sandals.
>
> But she comes from Lesbos, lovely Lesbos.
> She has no time for my hair, for it's grown grey.
> She has her eye on someone else, another . . .
> . . . girl.
>
> (Anacreon, fragment 358)

Figure 2.1. Simeon Solomon, *Sappho and Erinna in a Garden at Mytilene*, 1864.

Anacreon is laughing at himself there: boy, is he in the wrong movie. But the joke need not imply that *all* girls from Lesbos are like that. Anacreon is writing a couple of generations after Sappho, and he and his audience surely knew her poems. 'Lesbos' can be a pointer to Sappho, just Sappho. Perhaps this girl in the fancy sandals is, emblematically, Sappho herself; perhaps just someone who loves Sappho's verse and shares her tastes, sexual as well as poetic.

Just as important is Anacreon's tone. We need not see the 'bitterness' there that some modern critics have found: the joke is on him, as it often is when he writes about the signs of age, and it is wry, not bitter. Nor is it a barb at the girl's sexual tastes, nor a sneer, nor a lubricious leer. It is just that he is wasting his time.

Modern critics of Sappho have found her sexuality more difficult to take, and scholars and imitators have tiptoed, often clodhoppingly, around Sappho's female eroticism. One remarkable contribution came from probably the greatest classical scholar of all time, Ulrich von Wilamowitz-Moellendorf, writing just before the First World War. Sappho did not show him at his best. There is nothing homoerotic for Wilamowitz about Sappho's love: 'The openness with which she spoke of her love excludes any possibility of that "shameful love"—it is not worth spending another word on that.' Horace called her *mascula Sappho*, 'manly Sappho', but Wilamowitz insisted that this meant only that her poetry was a match for men. 'She would never have been a suffragette.' No, she was a school-mistress, or perhaps a cross between a music mistress and a priest-ess: local girls would be sent to her house—a 'girls' boarding school', he says—to be brought up properly. She was attached to them, of course: some of the affectionate songs were addressed to her girls as they left to be married. Nothing more than that. This is Sappho as Miss Jean Brodie.

The theory lingers on: the latest edition of a standard classical encyclopaedia, published in 2001, still calls it 'essentially plausible'. But it really isn't, even though like many pieces of wishful thinking it starts from a nugget that is true, or true enough. Greek thought *was* more ready to see an educational dimension in the relationship of an older and a younger lover, whether heterosexual or homosex-ual: that is clear enough from Plato's *Symposium*, and often else-where. But the tinges the theory is given in modern criticism go some way beyond that, even though Sappho's own surviving words have no reference to 'teaching' at all. The idea comes back even with those much more comfortable to admit the erotic aspects, indeed dwelling on them: '"tweedy" games mistresses' figure in a psycho-analytically directed article of 1970; another, very respected critic in 1983 turned the school's coursebook into something more like the Kama Sutra, with her pupils given 'enough understanding of Eros to bring their husbands pleasure...'. Her girls would be escorting a bride on her way to the wedding couch: 'Sappho taught them just what to do'. Not, I think, quite the prospectus to appeal to most Greek parents, then or now.

Yet of course criticism has changed, and in a big way. What was once a charge, an allegation of shamefulness, is now an essential part of Sappho's appeal. One very good modern treatment is titled *Lesbian Desire in the Lyrics of Sappho*—this is by Jane McIntosh Snyder—and dwells not just on the sex but also on, for instance, the creation of a strong female presence and persona in a world without clear male authority; on the presentation of loving relationships which are more equal and reciprocal than they might be in either a heterosexual world or one of male homosexuality; and, if we do turn to the sex, 'Sappho' (says Snyder) 'stands as one among few writers in the Western world who have presented the female body as a landscape for desire in an active sense, not merely as the passive object of male lust'. Every generation finds its own Sappho, and we ought to respect past generations' creations as well as our own—but this is one of those cases where our own generation has surely become more in tune with the things that mattered most to Sappho and her world.

Not that reconstructing that world is very easy. As we saw in the initial summary, most of what we hear about her seems to be based on simple reconstruction from her poems. That may not be valueless—those doing the reconstruction had much more of the poetry than we do now—but there was a tendency to take everything over-literally: that is something we will notice several times in this book. Yet even an 'I' cannot always be taken as autobiographical, as Sappho was writing at least some of her poems for others to perform, probably choirs of young girls. So we should think of her as songwriter as well as self-revelatory poet, and we would evidently go astray if, for instance, we assumed that Lennon and McCartney really envisaged holidays on the Isle of Wight when they were 64.

Yet that modern analogy does not wholly work, for she does sometimes talk of herself in much more personal ways. 'Who, Sappho, is wronging you?', asks Aphrodite in fragment 1; 'Sappho, why?' the poet asks herself, intriguingly, in a song that again goes on to mention Aphrodite (fragment 133b); 'Sappho, I don't want to be leaving you', says a girl in a third poem, one to which we will return in a moment (fragment 94). And the songs as a whole do create a coherent picture of a personality and a life, full of other names too—Anactoria, Atthis, Gongyla, and more—so that even cautious scholars find it easy to talk of 'Sappho's circle', though they picture it in different ways. If we do make that attempt to reconstruct that world, then we are only doing what the poems themselves invite us to do, reading them with their grain; we are at least dealing with 'Sappho', the constructed figure of the poems, with a strong likelihood that—at least most of the time—we are also dealing with Sappho, the flesh and blood human being talking about her real-life experience and loves.

We do not have much to go on. Only a very few poems survive in anything like a full form—probably only two that are complete or almost complete. We hear a little about her family, including her daughter, 'a beautiful child who is like golden flowers in form, darling Cleis', in exchange for whom she would not take all of Lydia (fragment 132). Gradually during the last century more have been discovered, mainly on papyrus fragments. One that is (probably, but more on this in a moment) almost complete was published only a few years ago, filling out a fragment that was already known in a much more damaged state from another papyrus. It is a charming piece on the way Sappho is growing old, and cannot dance with the young girls as freely as she did. Here it is in Martin West's translation. (There is uncertainty in the first two lines: it may be something like 'I, children, come bringing these...', drawing attention to the part that Sappho still plays as singer.)

> ...young girls...
> ...deep-bosomed Muses' lovely gifts
> ...clear melodious lyre.
>
> But as for me, old age has got my whole
> body, my hair is white that once was dark.
> ...my knees will not hold up
> ...to dance like the young fawns
> ...but what can I do?
> To stay untouched by age, that cannot be:
> a lesson, so they say, the goddess Dawn
> learned, when in her rose arms she bore Tithonus
> off to the world's east limit; still old age
> caught up with him...his immortal bride.
>
> (Fragment 58)

Tithonus was the husband of Dawn, who was granted her wish to make him immortal; but she forgot to ask for agelessness as well, so he and she had to watch him withering away, unable to die. The last line presumably conveyed something like '[he still had] his immortal bride': he could gaze on that beautiful young wife, just as Sappho can still gaze on the beautiful young girls, one generation after another. It is not difficult to find the emotions there resonating across the centuries; nor to add the extra thought that we, unlike Tithonus, will not have that eternal mix of the groans of ageing and delight in the presence of beauty. And is that for better or for worse? That implicit question is left hanging in the air.

But even here there is uncertainty. *Is* that the ending, in fact? There is a possibility that there were more lines, at least four: the recently published papyrus does clearly end the poem at this point, but the already-known more fragmentary papyrus goes on to include the extra lines and *may* have presented them as part of the same poem. Maybe both versions, the shorter and the longer, are authentic Sappho, and the choice between them would depend perhaps on the gathering where they were to be performed, perhaps simply on the taste of the performer. The first two of those four lines are almost lost, but they talked about the possibility that someone, presumably a god, might 'bestow' something: then

> My liking's for the gracious. Thus does love
> define my sunlight and my beautiful.

Or something like that: the Greek could also mean 'my lot is brilliance and beauty, and they come from desire for the sun', and that is the way they were taken by a later author who quotes the lines, Athenaeus. Perhaps the ambiguity is deliberate, and certainly the voice is recognizably Sappho's. 'The gracious' could also be translated as 'delicacy', the gentle softness of a life of leisure and some luxury, and this is one of her favourite words: she calls on 'the delicate Graces and the fair-tressed Muses' to come to her side, she has someone cosseting a loved one in 'delicate woollen cloths', she pictures 'delicate Andromache' on her wedding-day (fragments 128, 100, 44). If the lines do belong here, they presumably show Sappho consoling herself that she too, like Tithonus, is not dead yet, still loves to see the sunlight, and still has her sense for brilliance and beauty. On the one way of taking the Greek, that love for the daylight comes from living a life full of desire; on the other, that desire is now one to go on seeing that light, and this gives brilliance and beauty enough.

Well, perhaps. Both ways, it makes good, non-trivial sense. But some will feel that in this context either thought is too simple and obvious, too clumsily upbeat for what has gone before. If that is what the gathering required, then they had yet to know the joys of vinous melancholy. Leaving it with Tithonus makes better, lingering poetry, at least—but probably not only—for modern tastes.

So often the fragments are much more minute, giving us the sort of fascinating snatches that one hears from a distant, crackling radio station where the signal comes and goes. Take one of the scantiest and the most haunting.

> You will remember . . . for we too when we were young . . . did these
> things . . . many and beautiful things . . .
>
> (Fragment 24a)

What is that about? Is it that a couple are parting, reminding each other (and apparently others too, for the 'you' is plural) of the good times? We will see another poem like that in a moment. If so, notice that the couple were young *together*, and there is nothing of the schoolmistress and pupil here; nor is there the age-difference of the older pursuer and the younger pursued that was thought to typify male homosexual relationships. (We can see what the modern critic meant by that 'more equal relationship'.) But the Greek also has that tell-tale 'too': we *too* in our youth did these things. Perhaps she is chiding others, perhaps chiding herself, for being too censorious of the young, too forgetful that we too had our moments, and a lingering nostalgia for our own past blurs into the vicarious enjoyment of the pleasures that it is now the turn for the young people we care about to enjoy—very much the same emotion as in the poem on the creaking knees, in fact. Possibly there is something about reading any poetry that entices the reader or hearer into the free play of imagination, colouring all those white gaps around the short lines on the page, but—as Anne Carson suggests in the introduction to her own translation—all those gaps mean a greater than usual 'free space of imaginal adventure' as we do our best to read Sappho.

Memory is important in another, longer fragment too.

> Honestly, I wish I were dead.
> She was covered in tears as she went away,
>     left me, saying 'Oh, it's too bad!
>     How unlucky we are! I swear,
> Sappho, I don't want to be leaving you.'
>     This is what I replied to her:
>     'Go, be happy, and think of me.
> You remember how we looked after you;
>     or if not, let me remind
>         . . . . .
> all the lovely and beautiful times we had,
>     all the garlands of violets
>     and of roses and . . .
> and . . . that you've put on in my company,
>     all the delicate chains of flowers
>     that encircled your tender neck

. . . . .
. . . . .
  and the costly unguent with which
you anointed yourself, and the royal myrrh.
  On soft couches . . .
  tender . . .
you assuaged your longing . . .
  There was never a . . .
  or a shrine or a . . .
  . . . that we were not present at,
  no grove . . . no festive dance . . .

(Fragment 94a)

Memory, then: and the play of memory, in three different layers. Sappho is looking back at a parting: the girl was leaving her, and did not want to go. The moment of parting is one layer, a little in the past. But as they parted, as Sappho now tells us, she reminded the girl of a further layer of the more distant past, all the 'lovely and beautiful times we had'. That phrase is consoling, but it is also *correcting* the girl's tearful phrase 'How unlucky we are!'. Those past times, back in the more distant layer of memory, are indeed 'beautiful' in this description: the delicate soft bed, where 'you assuaged your longing', a phrase that gently but clearly points to the physical pleasures of sex (not, surely, just 'taking a nap', as Wilamowitz and others have thought); then we pass quickly to the 'shrine' and the 'grove' where they spent their time together— spiritually *their* space—and the 'dance' and the music that they also shared. Sappho was being, or at least projecting herself as being, so very mature as she reminded the girl of those beautiful times, so firmly embedded in their memories that they are now part of themselves. This is a time when we do feel that she is the older lover of the two.

But there is another aspect too. Remember the first line: 'Honestly, I wish I were dead'. We cannot be quite certain what is going on there, and it may be that this is already part of the dialogue that is recalled, something the younger woman was saying to her. But probably it is not, and this is Sappho herself speaking, something she says in the here-and-now. It was one thing to be restrained and mature when saying goodbye: now she is on her own, and the true devastation that she too feels can come out. In the Greek the 'honestly' is literally 'with no deceit'—almost 'no kidding', though the stylistic level is higher. Possibly it was a conversational cliché like this 'honestly', but if so Sappho gives it new point: there *was* a sort of 'deceit' in the fine, self-controlled words of the parting. It was not just the girl she was trying to persuade, but herself. Yesterday's Sappho is also in dialogue with today's, and today's is her truer voice.

How much does it matter that this love of Sappho's was same-sex love? Well, it clearly mattered to Sappho. It clearly mattered to Wilamowitz too, and in a different way it has clearly mattered to many women readers who have found in Sappho a rare voice from the past to echo their own desire and/or their own status as female poets. Perhaps it mattered to Anacreon, if our earlier reading of that poem was on the right lines. But it does not seem to have mattered so much to other earlier readers. When Sappho is mentioned in comedy, it was as a heterosexual figure, a woman courted by other poets, Archilochus and Hipponax; and the climax of her love, so legend went on to tell, was a tragic affair with a man, a certain Phaon, after which she leapt to her death from the white cliffs of Leucas. When people thought about Sappho, it mattered that she was *a woman*, certainly: a vase of *c*.440–430 BCE shows her reading to, interestingly, three women listeners, so she is

FIGURE 2.2. Sappho reading to three women listeners: red-figure vase, school of Polygnotus, 440–430 BCE.

already distinctively speaking *to* women, not just *of* women (Figure 2.2); but it was her sex, and her sexiness, that mattered, not her sexuality. (The same, incidentally, went for Lesbos as a whole: Lesbian girls were just generally known for, as Sir Kenneth Dover put it, 'sexual versatility and inventiveness', and *lesbiazein* could be used more specifically of heterosexual *fellatio*. That distinctive association with same-sex female love is not found till the second century CE.) We hear of songs of Sappho being sung at that very masculine institution, the symposium, where male drinkers would talk and drink and sing, with the prospect of sex before the evening was out, often heterosexual sex with courtesans or flute girls. Perhaps the historical Sappho was at home in such a symposium: already in antiquity some

35

wondered if Sappho—or at least *a* Sappho, one who might easily have been confused with the poet—was a courtesan herself, something which, one suspects, would not have made Wilamowitz any happier. But more likely it was simply her poems, and the sensuality they evoked, that came to belong in those parties, with men happy to sing them lustily, even if many of them had been written initially for performance in all-female gatherings. In one of her poems (16) Sappho finds memorable language to say that love is the most important thing in the world, more important than armies or navies or the chariots of Lydia: look at Helen... If a man sang such a thing late at night, it would be a conscious setting aside of the concerns of masculine achievement, armies and navies; and the singer might remember that, just for the moment, he was echoing a woman's words and a woman's view, and luxuriating in a world he took to be rather different from his own. After all, it was party time, time to let yourself go. You could always be a man again in the morning.

A different world, but not too different. In another of her most famous poems, Sappho describes the symptoms of passion—darts of heat, numbed flesh, a 'breaking' of the tongue, a drumming in the ears.

> He looks to me to be in heaven,
>   that man who sits across from you
> and listens near you to your soft speaking,
>   your lovely laughing: that, I vow,
>   makes the heart leap in my breast;
> for watching you a moment, speech fails me,
>   my tongue is paralysed, at once
>   a light fire runs beneath my skin,
> my eyes are blinded, and my ears drumming,
>   the sweat pours down me, and I shake
>   all over, sallower than grass:
> I feel as if I'm not far off dying.

But everything must be dared,
For...[?] even the poor man...

(Fragment 31)

And we do not know how it went on.

That again is something to move the imagination, to make us try
to write the story that is behind it. The Greek leaves it unclear
whether Sappho is talking of one particular man or is being more
general—any man who is lucky enough to enjoy the girl's company.
Wilamowitz took it as a particular man, and thought it was a
wedding poem addressed to a favourite pupil; in that case it is the
bridegroom who is so lucky. And what is the 'that' that has such an
effect on Sappho? Is 'that' just the sound of the girl's voice and
laughter? Or the whole sight of their relationship? How then are we
to take that final 'everything must be dared'—if that is what it
means? The Greek word (*tolmaton*) is indeed most naturally taken
in that sense, but it could also, just about, mean 'endure': Homer's
Odysseus, urging himself to put up in silence with the suitors'
outrageous behaviour, talks of the time in the Cyclops' cave when
he 'dared/endured'—*tolma* again—to bide his time until his wits
saved him (*Odyssey* 20.20). If 'dared', then it sounds as if Sappho
may be steeling herself for another attempt to claim, or reclaim,
the girl's affections; if 'endured', it is all just something that she knows
she has to accept. Perhaps the continuation would have made it clear,
but it is very hard to guess what that might have been. Even if those
last words, 'even the poor man...', are accurate (the Greek text
is not certain), the poem might have gone on 'is sometimes favoured
by Fortune and raised to the heights', or 'can be taught by life to be
accepting of what comes', or, really, almost any way at all.

So we have at least two possible stories we can tell here. Maybe Wilamowitz was right, at least in the sense that it was a wedding or a betrothal that inspired the poem (which is not to say that it was a 'wedding song' actually to be performed at the wedding itself). If so, 'that' is probably the whole relationship, and in the turmoil of Sappho's emotions there will be a larger element of jealousy—possibly even despair, especially if 'endured' is the right way of taking that crucial word. If it is more a matter of 'whoever it is', there is no reason for Sappho to despair, and probably the 'that' is now the sound of the girl's voice and laugh; her heart can be fluttering on wings of hope, not resignation; and why should she not 'dare', try again to take the man's place?

Perhaps the original audience would have known exactly what the situation was, and could have filled in the dots; or perhaps it was always going to be a piece for different performances and audiences who did not know the principals, and they were invited to make up the story, just as we have to. And they, like us, would never know if they had got it 'right', or if there was any 'right' answer at all, no matter how many other questions they might find to ask. If Sappho cannot speak—'my tongue is paralysed'—is writing conceived as all she can do? Or is this, as usual, to be spoken or sung aloud—and if so, by how many? If it is not a wedding poem, how regular would it be in this society for two unmarried lovers to speak and laugh together? Is part of the point that others too might find such behaviour shocking, but not for the same deeply personal reasons as Sappho? Is the girl envisaged as herself hearing or reading this poem, with Sappho making sure her feelings were known—so a sort of courtship poem? Is the man?

So there are several stories one can tell, immediately the imagination is allowed to roam. When the Roman poet Catullus wrote his own version (his poem 51), a final stanza developed the idea that he had too much time on his hands, too much leisure—something that had long ago brought down cities and kings. Perhaps Sappho had something similar, but we cannot know: it is equally likely that Catullus is breaking off from his reverie and adding words of his own. Get on with your life, Catullus. Stop mooning about like Sappho! That's girlie stuff, and never did anyone any good. Man up! Be Roman!

What is clear, though, is that Catullus is finding Sappho an interesting way to think about his own love, and in this case it is heterosexual love: he calls his girl 'Lesbia', indeed—a pseudonym, of course, but again expressive of all the sexiness that Sappho could suggest. Theocritus similarly echoes Sappho when a woman is dumbstruck by the sight of the one she loves crossing her threshold, and this time it is a man (*Idyll* 2.102–9). Horace also nods at Sappho's poem, and Catullus' too, in talking about his own jealous love for, once again, a girl: more on this later (Chapter X). And other passions too could be described with those Sapphic physical symptoms. Plutarch (*How to track one's own Progress in Virtue* 81d) and Lucian (*Nigrinus* 35: see Chapter XII) even echo the poem in describing a young man's feelings when he is first exposed to philosophy, perhaps not so regular an experience for the youthful. Elsewhere Plutarch tells the tale of a doctor summoned to treat an ailing Hellenistic prince, and realizing from the Sapphic flavour of his symptoms what the trouble was: or part of the trouble, anyway, as it complicated matters that the boy had fallen for his young stepmother

(*Demetrius* 38). So heterosexual love, again: there really is something universal about this.

Yet the last thing to do with Sappho is to diminish the importance of the specific and the particular. Like the girl she was parting from in that other poem, this girl too is, to her, special; the beautiful times they shared were their times, not ours; it could not have been just any girl, and it probably could not, for her, have been a man. Her same-sex desire is not just an alternative counterpart of the heterosexual love of the time: there is less thought of dominance, the parties are more equal, the affection more symmetrical. Aphrodite can console Sappho by telling her that the chased can swiftly become the chaser:

> 'Who is it this time that I must persuade
> To love you, Sappho? Who is wronging you?
> For though she flee, soon she'll be chasing;
> though she refuse gifts, she'll be giving;
> though she love not, she'll love despite herself.'
>
> (Fragment 1, lines 20–4)

But if a drunken and emotional male in a symposium could feel that the poetry spoke to him too, without finding it a particular barrier that it was female–female sex that was in point, that was not, or not just, a matter of insensitively reducing everything to fit his own heterosexual or male-homosexual model—anything but, for it was essential to the uninhibitedness of the evening that he was consciously adopting a woman's voice. It can also be a feeling that, ultimately, what all forms of love share is just as important as anything that marks them apart. This is not a preachy book; but if anything were worth preaching about, it would be that.

## Postscript

Two days before this book went to press, we heard that a new poem of Sappho had been found along with another much shorter fragment. Both are preserved on a papyrus, now in London, of around 200 CE: there does not seem any doubt about authenticity. The longer piece talks of her two brothers Charaxus and Larichus. Both names were already known, but not from any fragments where the text was certain; there is however one poem (5) praying that an unnamed brother should get home safely, 'atone for all his past wrongs' and cause us 'not a single misery'. Herodotus later tells of 'the poet Sappho's brother Charaxus' who was a traveller to Egypt and paid a vast sum to buy the famous courtesan Rhodopis, 'and when he got back to Mytilene Sappho wrote a poem roundly abusing him' (2.135). Similar stories surface in later writers too, with odd different or additional details (Charaxus as a wine-trader, for instance, or with the woman's name as Doricha instead of Rhodopis, or with Sappho abusing her instead of him). Larichus is mentioned by the much later writer Athenaeus as a young cup-bearer in Mytilene, and the object of Sappho's 'praise'. Some small papyrological scraps of biography mention a third brother Erigyius, and one of them adds that it was young Larichus who was Sappho's favourite.

A stanza or so seems to be lost from the beginning of the newly surfaced poem. The speaker, presumably Sappho herself, is addressing someone—we do not know who, but perhaps it was her mother or father—and is impatient at hearing the same old chatter:

> . . .
> Oh, not again—'Charaxus has arrived!
> His ship was full!' Well, that's for Zeus

And all the other gods to know.
　　Don't think of that;

But tell me, 'go and pour out many prayers
To Hera, and beseech the queen
That he should bring his ship back home
　　Safely to port,

And find us sound and healthy.' For the rest,
Let's simply leave it to the gods:
Great stormy blasts go by and soon
　　Give way to calm.

Sometimes a heavenly helper comes, if that's
The way Zeus wills, and guides a person round
To safety: and then blessedness and wealth
　　Become one's lot.

And us? If Larichus would raise his head,
If only he might one day be a man,
The deep and dreary draggings of our soul
　　We'd lift to joy.

That 'arrived' at the beginning could mean 'arrived here', and in that case Sappho will be weary of yet another rumour, doubtless false, that her brother has come to port. But it probably makes better sense to think of it as 'arrived there'—in Egypt, shall we say, with a lucrative ship-full of goods—while Sappho is still at home, with younger brother Larichus.

There is so much here of the Sappho of the other poems: the woman who was impatient with the masculine values of warfare is now not concerned with the profit, just with getting her brother home safely; the mother who so loved daughter Cleis has a soft spot for her brothers too, even the worrying young Larichus who always has his head down. We irresistibly think of a teenager always hunched over his smartphone, and we might wonder if the ancient equivalent is a head in a papyrus roll; but it is presumably more that Larichus' spirits are low, and his big sister shares them (it's an 'us' at the beginning of that stanza, and a 'we' at the end whose spirits might lift). Or perhaps he is dangerously ill, and physical survival to manhood is in the balance. I dare say that it is a poem to be sent to Charaxus, or at least one he is expected to see or hear, wishing him that safe return; maybe Larichus is to see it too, and sense the worried headshaking of his older siblings. It is an expression of love and concern, projecting family closeness to the brothers themselves as well as to anyone else who may read or hear it. And if some of the moralizing comes close to cliché, that is telling too: sometimes one is so worried that conventional wisdom is all there is to grasp. One of those clichés at least seemed insightful enough to be echoed: Horace too suggested 'leaving the rest to the gods', who calm the seething ocean once the winds have blown (*Odes* 1.9.9–11).

This book is full of ancient voices whose words ring clear. But there is a particular thrill in hearing a voice that sounds so intimate, and knowing that ours are the first ears to hear it for well over a thousand years.

CP

# III

# HERODOTUS

Herodotus is the first prose writer in our collection; his work is indeed the earliest Greek prose work of any length to survive, though it was not the earliest to be written. It is normally thought to have reached its present state around 425 BCE, and that is probably about right, though the evidence is not wholly clear. 'Publication' was in any case a more continuous process in antiquity than it is today, and his work will by then have been reaching audiences for some time, partly doubtless through oral performance. His own life-experience will have brought him into contact with both Greeks and non-Greeks from many parts of the world: he came from Halicarnassus (the modern Bodrum) in Southern Asia Minor, a Greek city but one on the edge of the great Persian empire; then in 443 he took part in the colonization of Thurii in Southern Italy, a remarkable panhellenic enterprise which contrasted with the single-city colonies that were the norm. He also travelled extensively: at least he says he did, and even if he sometimes exaggerates there is no reason to doubt that he got to many of the places he mentions. He died at Thurii. The *Historiai*—more broadly 'Enquiries' than our own word 'Histories' would suggest—range widely over all the 'marvels' of the known world, but a connecting theme is the Persian expansion which culminated in the attacks on Greece in 490 and 480–79 and their repulse.

In 2005 the British Museum staged an exhibition called *Forgotten Empire: The World of Ancient Persia*. The title makes the point: a leading theme was the way that westerners had been over-dismissive of the Persian empire and its achievement, and how this all went back to the Greeks. The name of Herodotus figured prominently among those Greeks who had started the rot. This provoked an interesting debate in the *Guardian*. One article argued that 'the West' had fundamentally been right, that the Persian artistic achievement was nothing compared with Greek art, and that if Herodotus was dismissive he was on the right lines. Several very distinguished and very indignant Iranian archaeologists replied to that: Herodotus was Greek, they said, and so of course he was biased. They clearly won on the artistic side, but there was only one little letter questioning whether Herodotus was so biased and so simple as all that.

Such issues, then, continue to stir passions, especially in this modern world where west and east still find it anything but straightforward to appreciate each other's cultures. It tells a tale that the 2000s saw a lengthy wrangle in the American courts over whether tablets from Persepolis, similar to those on display in that British Museum exhibition, could be impounded to allow plaintiffs to claim damages from the Islamic Republic of Iran for their relatives' deaths in a terrorist attack. Britain also had its own controversy, this time on whether the Cyrus Cylinder (Figure 3.1), a prize exhibit in *Forgotten Empire*, should be sent to Iran on loan; after some delay, it did go on display in Tehran for four months in 2010–11.

Such modern sensitivities seem a long way from Herodotus, but it may indeed be that the path starts with him. In his influential book *Orientalism* Edward Saïd argued that western observers have taken under-differentiated views of 'the East', and he highlighted the role of fifth-century Greek culture in initiating such western prejudices (though in fact he put more weight on Greek tragedy). In some ways that is fair enough: we can indeed see Herodotus, together with Aeschylus' *Persians*, as providing a foundational text for such 'Orientalism' along with a self-congratulatory view of Greek cultural

FIGURE **3.1.** The 'Cyrus cylinder', recording in cuneiform script the achievements of Cyrus, discovered in Babylon in 1879 and currently in the British Museum.

superiority. We can also sometimes see such triumphalism in the vase-painting of the time (Figure 3.2), with a fancily-dressed Persian cringing as the Greek prepares to deliver the death-stroke. Yet it is equally possible to see both Herodotus and Aeschylus as providing a foundational *critique* of 'Orientalism' too, as giving their readers and listeners plenty of material to make them uneasy about their own complacencies. This is a very complex text indeed.

Its complexity goes with the vast range of material it covers. The first words tell us what to expect, and it is a lot.

> Here are presented the results of the enquiry carried out by Herodotus of Halicarnassus. The purpose is to prevent the traces of things that originate from humans from being erased by time, and to preserve the fame of the important and marvellous achievements produced by both Greeks and non-Greeks; among the matters covered is, in particular, the explanation how Greeks and non-Greeks came to war with one another.
>
> (Proem tr. R. Waterfield, adapted)

FIGURE 3.2. Fifth-century vase-painting of a Greek hoplite killing a Persian, both in distinctive dress.

So both 'Greeks' and 'non-Greeks'—in the original, the word is *barbaroi*, 'barbarians'—are going to figure here, and 'important and marvellous achievements' are going to be produced by both, by Them as well as Us. Not every Greek was so open-minded: five centuries later Plutarch was going to dub Herodotus a *philobarbaros*, a 'barbarian-lover'. It soon becomes clear that Herodotus particularly has the 'non-Greeks' of the East in view; room will be found in the *Histories* for northern and southern peoples too, but that 'war' between Greeks and non-Greeks is the one between Greece and Persia at the beginning of the fifth century BCE, and that was a conflict of East and West. The first few chapters semi-playfully discuss whether its origins should be traced back to a series of abductions of women, starting with the Phoenicians' abduction of Io from Greece, then going on to the Greeks' abduction of the Phoenician Europa and then of the Colchian Medea, and finally to the climactic Trojan War over the easterner Paris and his abduction of Helen. That is soon abandoned, and Herodotus moves on quickly to aggression much nearer his own time; but not before he has made the important geopolitical point that

> Ever since the Trojan War the Persians have regarded the Greeks as their enemies. They think of Asia and the non-Greek peoples living there as their own, but regard Europe and the Greeks as separate from themselves.

> (1.4.4)

And, we might add, the other side thinks pretty similarly, regarding 'Greeks' as something distinctive and special and 'non-Greeks', *barbaroi*, as separate. But it is *we* who might add that; Herodotus does not, and even that beginning with the Persians' view of it all may nudge his audience into looking at things from an unusual perspective.

So East and West are blazoned at the beginning as an important theme, particularly 'how they came to war with one another'. But this is only part of what Herodotus will cover. The brief he gives himself is very broad, all these 'things that originate from humans': that phrasing can include 'things' such as the Pyramids of Egypt, for instance, or the remarkable walls of Babylon, with a parapet broad enough for a four-horse chariot (1.179); it can embrace other things that 'humans' do as well, the Scythians' habit of smoking hemp in their sealed tents, say, something which oddly enough seems to make them rather happy (4.75). There is no better book to read on a train or a plane than Herodotus: there is always something to refocus your mind on a new and fascinating item after your concentration has been interrupted by a tunnel or a food-trolley. Everything is fair game, provided only that it is … *marvellous*, a key-word in that proem, and one that will come up repeatedly in what follows. The work is full of marvels, things to wonder at, things drawn from any part of the world that Herodotus may know about and that you, his audience, may not.

There is another key-word too, right at the beginning of that passage: this is to be Herodotus' 'enquiry', and the Greek word is *historiē*, the word from which our 'history' comes. History is curiosity: history is asking questions, and as Herodotus toured the world he was always full of questions. He talks of travel in Egypt, for instance, and putting lots of enquiries there to temple-priests. And some of the questions were ones he would simply put to himself. He was interested in the silting phenomenon of the Nile—again, we can see how wide the range of *historiē*, at least his *historiē*, can be. And his language is strangely emphatic, with a spot of dismissiveness.

> Even someone—a person of intelligence, at any rate—who has not already heard about it, but just uses his eyes, can easily see that the Egypt to which the Greeks sail is new land which the Egyptians have gained as a gift from the river. … The physical geography of Egypt is such that as you approach the country by sea, if you let down a sounding-line when you are still a day's journey away from land, you will bring up mud in eleven fathoms of water. This shows that there is silt this far out.
>
> (2.5)

This is something Herodotus did not need to be told by any priest. He had been primed before his arrival: that notion of the Egyptian coast as reclaimed land, 'the gift of the river', was one that was going around before Herodotus' day, and the phrase was in fact used by one of his intellectual predecessors, Hecataeus of Miletus, who at the beginning of the fifth century had written a two-book *Guide Around the World* which catalogued the places to be found. That emphatic tone is making a point: you don't need to have 'already heard about' this silting, it's perfectly obvious if you just use your eyes, and Hecataeus was just being ridiculous when he made so much of it. And we can picture too Herodotus dropping a sounding-line when he is still a day's voyage from shore. He just cannot wait to get that 'enquiry' started.

There is a lot for him to 'marvel' at, and to ask questions about, once he gets into the description of Egypt itself. There are the strange habits—they do everything in reverse over there, with the men sitting down to urinate and the women standing up; there are sheep pulling carts; there are the pyramids; there is the labyrinth. A little further on there is an even more miraculous thing, an island in the middle of a lake, which, so the Egyptians say, is a *floating* island. But

> I myself never saw it floating or moving, and I wondered, when I was told that it was a floating island, whether it really was.

> (2.156.2)

It is a lovely picture, Herodotus sitting there on his stool, eyes peeled as he watched intently all day—and '*I* never saw it move'.

All this seems a long way from Marathon, Thermopylae, and the Persian Wars, the themes that will fill his later books. And it is: there is no need to look for a single, unified topic in a work that takes as its theme 'the things originating from humans', whatever they may be.

But there is a resonance there that has implications for Greece, and for Persia too. It is partly a matter of putting that war and those civilizations in their place: in their place *in space*, with a feeling for the vastness of the world, including spaces so vast and civilizations so strange—the nomadic Scythians, for instance—that even the Persians have not been able to deal with them; in their place in time too, for Herodotus stresses that Egyptian civilization has been around for far longer than either the Greeks or the Persians. In one temple he was shown statues of priests that went back for 345 human generations: so much for any Greek unwise enough to claim a divine ancestor only a few generations ago, and this time he names Hecataeus as the person who was discomfited when he claimed exactly that on his visit to the same place. Hecataeus had in fact written a second work, the *Genealogies*, as well as his geographical book, and Herodotus may be nodding at that work here; though it is unlikely that Hecataeus told the tale himself, as not many Greek authors tell that sort of story against themselves.

Herodotus puts the Greeks in their *moral* place as well, and this is where we return to those questions of Greek triumphalism and complacency. Sometimes it is just a matter of reminding his audience that Greek is not always or necessarily best, that in this world of extraordinary customs Greek practices are just one among many. He tells a story of the Persian king Darius:

> During Darius' reign, he invited some Greeks who were present to a conference, and asked them how much money it would take for them to be prepared to eat the corpses of their fathers; they replied that they would not do that for any amount of money. Next, Darius summoned some members of the Indian tribe known as Callatiae, who eat their parents, and asked them in the presence of the Greeks, with an interpreter present so that they could understand what was

being said, how much money it would take for them to be willing to cremate their fathers' corpses; they cried out in horror and told him not to say such appalling things. So these practices have become enshrined as customs just as they are, and I think Pindar was right to have said in his poem that custom is king of all.

(3.38)

Had he wished, Herodotus could have made this an example to show how primitive those Indians were in comparison with the morally sophisticated Greeks, and how Darius was not much better if he failed to realize that; but Herodotus is clearly on Darius' side, as he is using the story to demonstrate that all peoples think their own customs best, and 'only a madman' would scoff at what others do (3.38.2). The context makes a subtler point too, for this comes at the end of a sequence where Darius' predecessor Cambyses was indeed showing himself a 'madman', mocking Egyptian religious practices so spectacularly that he even killed the bull Apis, an animal which the Egyptians held particularly sacred (3.29). That is a point in the narrative when his Greek listeners and readers might feel particularly superior at the expense of those brutal domineering Persians. And yet it is here that we see this other Persian, Darius, showing himself much more sensitive to cultural differences than the Greeks in the story were themselves, and for that matter than the audience, who would largely have shared that horror at the Indian practices. It is the Persian who emerges as the man with cultural insight, not the Greek, and nothing could make it plainer that these johnny-foreigners—even these tyrannical johnny-foreigners—are *not* all the same.

There are plenty of stories too of Greeks behaving badly. One that he tells of Egypt concerns Helen of Troy, making her second appearance after that mention among those early abductions—except that it is *not* Helen 'of Troy', for Helen never got there. Paris was running away with her, Herodotus explains, after taking her from her home in Sparta and her husband Menelaus. On their journey they stopped in Egypt, where the local king was appalled at Paris's behaviour.

> You're lucky that I think it important not to take the lives of visitors. Otherwise, you scum, on behalf of the Greek I would make you pay for what you have done—for the terrible crime you have committed after accepting his hospitality. You made advances to the wife of your host. As if that were not enough, you gave her the wings to flee with you when you left. But you didn't even leave it at that: you also plundered your host's house before coming here.
>
> (Proteus at 2.115.4)

So he gives Paris three days to get out, and insists on impounding Helen in his own custody along with all the valuables Paris has taken. When the Greeks get to Troy and demand Helen back, the Trojans have to say that they just haven't got her. It is only when the ten years have passed and the Greeks take the city that they discover a notable absence of Helen. Rather sheepishly, they call in at Egypt on the way back, and pick up Helen there. And now it is not just the Trojans who abuse hospitality; Menelaus, anxious to set sail on the last lap of his journey and delayed by adverse winds, seizes a couple of children from local Egyptian families and sacrifices them, just as ten years before his brother Agamemnon sacrificed a child at Aulis. Evidently, it is what Greeks do—at least these Greeks. Both the Trojan Paris and the Greek Menelaus behave appallingly: the moral hero is the Egyptian. So much for any self-satisfied Greek talk of superior civilization.

Admittedly, there is something a bit odd about this. Herodotus says that this is a story he got from the Egyptian priests; yet this notion of Helen staying in Egypt and never getting to Troy is one that we find in Greek literature too, and some time before Herodotus. It is one that Euripides goes on to use in his *Helen*, though in that play it is the Egyptian king who behaves shockingly to guests, with a practice of killing any Greeks he finds arriving at his shore. It is highly unlikely to be a native Egyptian tale of the sort Herodotus claims. So what has happened? Is he just making up those Egyptian sources, claiming that it comes from Egypt when in fact it is a Greek tale? Or do we here get a glimpse of what his 'enquiries' might really be like? 'Tell me, what do you think of this story I've heard? Does that sound to you right?' 'Well, perhaps, though I think you'll find that Egyptian kings would never be cruel to their guests, and in fact they'd be appalled to hear what Paris, so you tell me, had done in Sparta . . . ' Most classicists don't like the idea of that sort of enquiry, and there is a lot of eyebrow-raising at the thought of 'leading questions'—perhaps a hint at how many scholars, at least in the old days, were brought up in a world of judges and barristers. My own background was different, and that might equally be predisposing me to find that picture all too believable. My father was a sports journalist, and I often heard him interviewing sportsmen who weren't very good with words. 'Would you say, Len, that you just caught the ball perfectly on the volley, and that it dipped just under the cross-bar and inside the far post?' 'Yes, Reg, that was how it was . . . '—and all of that duly appeared in next day's paper as a verbatim quote from Len. It is not the worst crime in the world.

If Greeks are being put in their place, it is not so inglorious a place as all that, and it has plenty of marvels of its own. The biggest marvel of all was that triumph over Persia once the two sides had 'come to war with one another'. Let us pick up the action in 498 BCE. The Ionians—that is, many of the states of what is now Western Turkey—are in revolt from the Persian empire, which by now extends over a vast swathe of land from the Hellespont to India and from the Caucasus to Egypt. The Athenians are helping the rebels, and King Darius has just heard that Sardis, the capital of what had once been the kingdom of Lydia, has been burnt to the ground.

> News reached King Darius of the Athenian and Ionian capture and burning of Sardis. It is said that his first reaction to the news was to discount the Ionians, because he was confident of punishing them for their rebellion, and to ask who the Athenians were. On hearing the answer, he is said to have asked for his bow; he took hold of it, notched an arrow, and shot it up towards the sky. And as he fired it into the air, he said, 'Lord Zeus, make it possible for me to punish the Athenians.' Then he ordered one of his attendants to repeat to him three times, every time a meal was being served, 'Master, remember the Athenians'.

> (5.105)

Darius did indeed remember the Athenians, launching a punitive expedition against them eight years later. But it went wrong. The Persian army faced their enemy at Marathon. As the Persians prepared for battle, they suddenly saw a sight that amazed them.

> When their battle lines were drawn up and the omens from the sacrifices were favourable, the Athenians were released, and they charged the invaders *at a run*. The distance between the two armies was no less than a mile. When the Persians saw the Athenians running towards them...they thought the Athenians must be mad—mad enough to bring about their utter destruction—because they could see how few of them there were, and that their charge was

unsupported by either cavalry or archers.... They were the first Greeks known to charge enemy forces at a run, and the first to endure the sight of Persian dress and the men wearing it. Up until then even the word 'Persian' had been a source of fear in Greece.

(6.112.2–3)

The Persians lost, and that really was a marvel.

More marvellous still was what happened ten years after that, when the Persian king—by now Darius' son Xerxes—launched a much bigger expedition, so big that people talked of rivers being drunk dry as the millions marched by. Doubtless the force was not as big as that, but it was still vast. A large number of Greek states united to face the threat (and that unity was a further marvel, really, given their usual propensity to quarrel). First the Spartans checked the Persian advance by their heroic stand at Thermopylae; then the Greeks won two decisive battles, first the sea-battle at Salamis in 480 BCE, then a year later the land-battle at Plataea. The threat of conquest had passed, and Greece remained free.

Free: another key-word. Freedom is what they were fighting for; and, to an extent, freedom explains why they won.

While the Athenians were ruled by tyrants, they were no better at warfare than any of their neighbours, but once they had got rid of the tyrants they became vastly superior. This goes to show that while they were under an oppressive regime they fought below their best because they were working for a master, whereas as free men each individual wanted to achieve something for himself.

(5.78)

That attraction of freedom—freedom for everyone, not just for the powerful—is something that the Persians just don't understand. As Xerxes is on the march, he is deep in conversation with Demaretus, an exiled Spartan king who has wound up in his entourage. We'll be outnumbering them, he says, maybe by as much as a thousand to one: what hope can they possibly have?

> 'If they had a single leader in the Persian mould, fear of him might make them excel themselves and, urged on by the whip, they might attack a numerically superior force, but all this is out of the question if they're allowed their freedom.'

> (Xerxes at 7.103.4)

But Demaretus has his answer:

> 'Although they're free, they're not entirely free: their master is the law, and they're far more afraid of this than your men are of you. At any rate, they do whatever the law commands, and its command never changes: it is that they should not turn tail in battle no matter how many men are ranged against them.'

> (Demaretus at 7.104.4–5)

And Xerxes laughed. A few months later he will meet the Spartan three hundred at Thermopylae. He will not be laughing then.

There are other passages too which encourage a similar rosy-eyed view of freedom: a time, for instance, when some Spartan ambassadors to the Persian capital are entertained en route by Hydarnes, Xerxes' commander of the Ionian coast. Hydarnes cannot understand why they are so reluctant to become the King's friends; why, each of them might as a result become a ruler in Greece. The reply is firm:

> 'Hydarnes, you have only half the picture. Although you know what it's like to be a slave, you have never experienced freedom and you have no idea whether or not it's a pleasant state. If you had experienced it, you'd be advising us to wield not spears, but even battleaxes in its defence.'

> (Spartan envoys at 7.135.3)

It is easy enough, too, to find scenes where despotism shows its nastiest sides, scenes where courtiers do not dare to say a word of opposition, scenes of arbitrary whimsicality or brutal punishment: King Cambyses shooting a courtier's son through the heart to show that he shoots so well that he cannot possibly be mad, whatever people may say (3.35.3–4); Xerxes himself so annoyed when a loyal nobleman tries to beg one of his five sons off the expedition that he has the boy sliced in two and marches his army between the two halves (7.38–9).

The gulf of understanding between the two sides is often clear too. When the Persians hear that the Greeks are celebrating the Olympic Games, that might seem odd enough, with such mortal danger hanging over them. It is even odder when someone asks what they are competing for:

> They told him about the garland of olive that was given as a prize. At this, Tritantaichmes the son of Artabanus made a remark that showed his quality—but one which the king viewed as the mark of a coward. When Tritantaichmes heard that no money was at stake, but a garland, he could not stop himself blurting out in front of everyone, 'Well, Mardonius, what sort of men are these that you have brought us to fight? They make excellence rather than money the reason for a contest!' That was what Tritantaichmes said.
>
> (8.26.2–27.1)

So any Greek then, any westerner now, who felt complacent about the superior glories of freedom could find plenty of appropriate mood music in this text: a 'foundational text of Orientalism', indeed.

But of course there is more to it. That remark of Tritantaichmes may again show how the Persians just don't understand what makes Greeks tick; but Tritantaichmes himself has not understood fully either, if he thinks that they really care so little about money. There are plenty of moments during the war itself where we see money being very effective, with gold securing Persian sympathizers in the Greek cities; Themistocles, the architect of the Greek victory at Salamis, manages to get a massive bribe of thirty talents from his own countrymen in Euboea, and keeps the greater part for himself (8.4.2–5). If debate at the Persian court is flawed, then Greek debate is flawed too, even though it is in a tellingly different way: Greeks are certainly not deterred from speaking out, but their discussions easily collapse into a bad-tempered shouting match, as they do in the fraught debate before the battle of Salamis (8.59–64). Nor is the inspirational power of freedom as compulsive as all that. Many Greek states choose the safer path of submitting to the king, and it is hard to blame them. The alternative could so easily be the end of their cities completely, with entire populations forcibly transferred to deep within the Persian empire. It is even 'folly' to fight on against so overwhelming an enemy (6.10), and the Greek word is a strong one, pointing to a failure to get one's thinking and understanding into order: glorious folly, no doubt, admirable folly, but folly all the same.

That takes us back to that exchange of Demaretus and Xerxes, for Xerxes is not talking nonsense. Free men are . . . free, free to go their own way if they choose: the Persians have the cohesion that comes from unquestioned one-man rule, but there is a perpetual danger that the Greek alliance will break up. There is squabble after squabble, and when they cannot agree it sometimes descends to a total military shambles; the battle of Plataea begins with a fierce argument between Spartan commanders on whether they should shift their ground or not, with the junior commander simply refusing to obey orders, and meanwhile their Athenian allies just do not trust them at all (9.53–7). It is often the worst elements of freedom, not the best, that paradoxically contribute most to the final victory: the way that the close neighbours Athens and Aegina are at each other's throats, and so Athens builds the big fleet that can then fight the invader (7.144); or the way that Themistocles can threaten that the Athenians would just sail away if the others refuse to fight at Salamis, and readily be believed (8.62). The Greeks win in the end, but only just, and that only-just-ness matters too. It is perhaps the biggest marvel of them all.

Are the Greeks always so different from the Persians anyway? One delightful story towards the end takes an unexpected turn. The battle of Plataea has been fought and won, and the Greeks are exploring the Persian camp. The victorious Spartan general Pausanias finds the sumptuous banqueting paraphernalia that the Persian Mardonius had been using.

> The story goes that when Pausanias saw all these things, fitted out with gold and silver and embroidered hangings, he told Mardonius' bakers and chefs to prepare the kind of meal they had made for Mardonius. They did so, and then, when he saw the gold and silver couches with their fine coverings, the gold and silver tables, and the magnificent feast, he was amazed at all the good things spread out there, and, for a joke, he told his own servants to prepare a typical Spartan meal. When the food was ready, Pausanias was amused to see the huge difference between the two meals, and he sent for the Greek commanders. Once they were all there, he pointed to the two meals...
>
> (Herodotus 9.82)

And surely we know what he is going to say: no wonder we won—we hard men fighting all those bloated softies! But in fact he says something quite different:

'Men of Greece, my purpose in asking you all here is to show you just how stupid the Persian king is. Look at the way he lives, and then consider that he invaded our country to rob us of our meagre portions!'

*Why did he bother?* Surely not for the dubious pleasure of eating meals like this? Pausanias is clearly not impervious to the appeal of a little luxury, not so Spartan in temperament as all that.

Herodotus' audience would be able to fill in some other parts of Pausanias' story too, the way he was later suspected of Medism and treason and met a sorry end in disgrace, a tale which Thucydides would find the space to tell (1.128–35). Herodotus himself refers twice to aspects of these later activities (5.32, 8.3.2), in an oblique and knowing style that suggests an audience familiar with the scandal. There are further hints too in the final books of what will come after the Persians go home. Much of that story will be one of Greek against Greek: free once more, they will resume their usual round of inter-city quarrelling. There will be a new empire too, that of Athens, gradually filling the gap in the Aegean that the Persian defeat has left; there are a few mentions of the war that it all led up to, the Peloponnesian War of Athens and Sparta (431–404) that was being fought as Herodotus' work took its final form, and which we will hear a lot more about when we turn to Thucydides. Is Athens, then, the new Persia? If so, is the text to be seen as a warning, telling the Athenians that they will finally lose, foundering just as the Persians foundered? Or might the Athenians win, and if so are there reasons to be detected why they are *not* the new Persia, why there may be something in the Greek or Athenian mould to explain why things might be different? If so, what might that be? Might that too be something to do with freedom? Or even with democracy, that new experiment at Athens that brought them such spectacular success once they were free of the tyrants (5.78, quoted above)—though Herodotus has no illusions about the flaws of democracy too, given that it is so much easier to hoodwink an assembly of 30,000 people than just one man (5.97)?

All those are good questions, and scholars give different answers. Perhaps the most convincing emphasizes that Herodotus could not know who would win the Peloponnesian War, though many of his later readers would if he was successful in that aspiration 'to prevent the traces of things that originate from humans from being erased by time'. Whatever the outcome would have turned out to be, those readers could find material in Herodotus' treatment of the past to help them to understand it. Maybe it would be a story of Athenian failure, as they fell into the Persian pattern of aggressive, over-confident imperialism; or maybe success, and something distinct-ively Greek would have made the difference. But whatever those readers found, they might also be sensitive enough to find indica-tions that it wasn't necessarily so; that this outcome could so easily have been different, just as that earlier struggle between freedom and tyranny could have gone the other way.

The classical voices we are hearing in this book are all remark-able, in their way. They are all authors that repay reading, indeed repay a lifetime of reading. But Herodotus conveys the liveliest and the most attractive personality of them all. That infectious curiosity, that open-mindedness, that readiness to believe that there may well be a marvel around every new corner, that interest in every part of the world—this is the person that, of them all, I would most like to be like.

CP

# IV

# THUCYDIDES

Thucydides' own life was fundamentally affected by the great war that he describes, that between Sparta and Athens from 431 to 404 BCE. He fell sick with the great Athenian plague in the early 420s but survived. Then in 424 he held a command in northern Greece, but failed to protect the city of Amphipolis from the gifted Spartan commander Brasidas, and was punished by exile. He moved to his family estate in Thrace and spent the next twenty years there: clearly absorbed by the war, he comments that this exile allowed him to hear versions of events from both sides. His history was doubtless taking shape gradually over these decades, but some important parts were clearly written once the fighting had finished and its outcome was known. In contrast to the broad scope of Herodotus' history, Thucydides' focus is sharply on the war, and many generations have particularly admired and learned from his penetrating analysis of human behaviour in warfare. His concentration on political and military matters reflects only one strand in ancient historical writing and again contrasts with the broader interests of Herodotus, but it does often make him seem very 'modern' to those used to the preoccupations of more recent historiography, and this has contributed greatly to his enduring appeal.

> Thucydides of Athens wrote this history of the war fought against each other by the Peloponnesians and Athenians.
> He began his work right at the outbreak, reckoning that this would be a major war and more momentous than any previous conflict. There were two grounds for this belief: both sides were at the full height of their power and their resource for war, and he saw the rest of the Greeks taking one side or the other, either immediately or in intent.

This was in fact the greatest disturbance to affect the Greek and a good part of the non-Greek world, one might even say the majority of mankind . . .

(Thucydides 1.1.1–2, tr. M. Hammond)

That is how Thucydides begins his history of what we call the Peloponnesian War. He goes on to argue in detail for the view that this was the most 'momentous' war of them all—more momentous even than that glamorous war against the Persian invaders fought fifty years before, the war that Herodotus had described. Thucydides' war is the one between Athens and Sparta that broke out in 431 BCE, and lasted a full generation, twenty-seven years, until 404—the war that was happening at the time when Herodotus' work reached its final form, and during which many of Euripides' plays were performed. It split into several phases. The first ten years were more or less a draw, and in a sense that meant an Athenian victory: Sparta and the rest were fighting to stop Athens, and ten years on Athens had not been stopped. The Athenians had even won some spectacular victories, especially one when they had taken alive and imprisoned some 400 Spartans on the island of Sphacteria off the Peloponnesian coast, a success that Sparta found particularly humiliating and (given their low population of full citizens) worrying. A captured shield that the Athenians inscribed in celebration still survives (Figure 4.1).

After a peace treaty in 421 there was an uneasy peace for a few years, but it was more cold war than peace. Then everything burst out again in 415, and in an odd way. The Athenians were persuaded to launch a great overseas expedition, to go to Sicily, and take on a *potential* threat there. It was a pre-emptive strike. Athens decided to do it in force, thinking this would make it more risk-free, but it didn't.

FIGURE **4.1**. A shield captured from the Spartans at Pylos in 425/4 BCE and triumphantly displayed at Athens. It is inscribed 'the Athenians took this from the Spartans at Pylos'.

Two years later, in 413, there was a massive defeat. That did not end the war: it went on for nine further years to 404, with Athens showing surprising resilience in one way but a great lack of self-belief in another (they even gave up the democracy of which they were so proud for some months in 411). Eventually, though, it came to total defeat in 404. Spartan ships sailed into the Athenian harbour at Piraeus; and the walls of Athens were dismantled, to the sound of flutes, as Greeks rejoiced at the end of the Athenian empire.

Thucydides' narrative breaks off some years before the end of the war, but he lived to see the end of it, and there are various ways in which he makes it clear how the war is shaping towards that final conclusion. And what a narrative it is. This is how he describes the climactic battle in Sicily, the sea-battle fought within the Great Harbour of Syracuse:

> When one ship was bearing down on another, the men on the decks kept up a constant barrage of javelins, arrows, and stones; and when the two closed, the marines fought hand to hand in an effort to board the other. In many areas of the battle there was so little room that a ship which had rammed an enemy in one direction would find itself rammed from another, with the consequence that one ship would have two or sometimes even more ships entangled round it, and the captains were faced with the need to defend or attack against the enemy not just one at a time, but in multiples from all sides. And all the while the great din of so many ships crashing into one another both terrified the crews and made it impossible for them to hear the orders shouted by the coxswains. . . . While the sea-battle hung in the balance the two land armies on the shore shared the tension and thoughts and feelings of the combatants, with the local troops rooting for yet further triumph and the invaders terrified of ending up in a situation even worse than the present . . . The action was quite close in front of their eyes, and they were not all looking at the same arena. So if some saw their own side winning in their particular part of the battle, they would take instant encouragement and begin calling on the gods not to deprive them of this hope of salvation; others who had witnessed an area of defeat turned to loud cries of lament, and from the mere sight of what was happening were in more abject terror than the actual combatants. Yet others, focused on a part of the battle which was evenly balanced, went through all the agonies of suspense: as the conflict lasted on and on without decisive result, their acute anxiety had them actually replicating with the movement of their bodies the rise and fall of their hopes—at any moment throughout they were either on the point of escape or on the point of destruction. And as long as the battle at sea remained in the balance you could hear across the Athenian ranks a mixture of every sort of response, groans, cheers, 'we're winning', 'we're losing', and all the various involuntary cries let out by a great army in great danger.

(7.70.5–71.4)

That is some battle, and that is some description. We tend today to think of Thucydides as the super-analyst, the penetrating critic, probing beneath the surface to explain why things happen, and that is absolutely right: more of that later. But he is a brilliant story-teller as well. Notice in that case how much is seen through the eyes of the people lining the shore, straining to make out what is happening, living every blow, with even their bodies twitching with involuntary striking and dodging movements. It almost makes us into eye-witnesses too. And those observers know, just as we know, how much turns upon the fighting. A little while later, with the battle lost, the Athenian general Nicias does his best to encourage his men, and ends by reminding them of the greatness of Athens, a greatness which even now they may be able to revive: for 'it is men that make a city—not walls, not ships without the men to fill them' (7.77.7). The destruction of these fighting men indeed spells doom for their city too, even if it will take those extra nine years before it happens.

Still, it is not just Athens that suffers; it is not even Athens that suffers most. Remember those words at the beginning: 'this was the greatest *disturbance* to affect the Greek and a good part of the non-Greek world, one might even say the majority of mankind'. Exaggeration, certainly, even when one takes into account that vast numbers of 'mankind' were not yet within the European compass. But it is exaggeration with a purpose, and that word 'disturbance' is crucial. The Greek is *kinesis*, 'movement', the word from which 'kinetic' and 'cinema' are derived: and what the war sets in motion, what it causes, becomes a dominant theme. War, says Thucydides, is a 'violent schoolmaster': it brutalizes the temper of those involved in it.

In peace and prosperous times both states and individuals observe a higher morality, when there is no forced descent into hardship: but war, which removes the comforts of daily life, runs a violent school and in most men brings out passions that reflect their condition.

So then civil war spread among the cities, and those who came to it later took lessons, it seems, from the precedents and progressed to new and far greater extremes in the ingenuity of their machinations and the atrocity of their reprisals.... To lay a plot and succeed was clever: smarter still to detect another's plot.... In short, the currency of approval was damage done—either the pre-emptive strike before an opponent could do his own intended damage, or the instigation of those who otherwise had no thought of doing harm. And indeed family became less close a tie than party, as partisans were more prepared to do the deeds without question.... Revenge was more important than avoidance of the original injury.... The citizens who had remained neutral fell victim to both parties: they were destroyed for failing to join the cause, or out of resentment at their survival.

(3.82)

Notice, first, that Thucydides is here talking about civil war—war between two factions within a single city—in Corcyra, the modern Corfu. That island plays a curious role in the war. It is some distance from Athens and the Peloponnese, way out to the west, and yet it was here that it all started, in the mid 430s. It blew up because of an even smaller town, Epidamnus, the modern Durrës in Albania. There was civil war within that town too, and the popular party drove out the men of power; when the exiles continued to attack and plunder, those in the city sought help from Corcyra, and when they did not get it turned to Corinth. It is all a matter of colonies and mother-cities, for Corcyra had originally been founded as a colonial settlement from Corinth, and Epidamnus had in its turn been founded from Corcyra. Things escalated; Corcyra and Corinth were soon at war; Athens was sucked into it, because they could not allow their enemy Corinth to crush Corcyra and acquire another fleet. So things start with the little people, the relatively powerless, but they become really shattering when the big powers like Athens and Sparta are drawn in.

When we were talking about Homer we noticed that there too things started with the relatively powerless, in that case the women, Helen or Briseis or Chryseis (Chapter I). They escalate when the big men, Achilles and Agamemnon, take over; but they have a way of coming back on the women too, so that the real impact of the war is seen most clearly in what it means for the women, especially the widowed Andromache, but also Helen herself, who (as we saw) has almost the final words in the poem as she laments for Hector. In Thucydides too it is the involvement of the big powers that means that everything becomes devastating; but once again things come full circle, and the little states are the ones that suffer worst. Corcyra, the start of it all, is where war, running that 'violent school', eventually teaches the most scarring lesson.

It is interesting too that it is *civil* war where everything is seen at its bloodiest. When the war breaks out, it looks as if it might be a more formal, more old-fashioned war. It begins with an exchange of heralds between Athens and Sparta, with the final messenger proclaiming that 'this day will be the beginning of much evil for the Greeks' (2.12.3); then there is a full-dress invasion of Athenian territory by the Spartan king Archidamus, ravaging the fields in the traditional manner. But in fact it is not going to be that kind of war, or not only that kind of war. So much of it is going to be what we see at Corcyra, the knife-in-the-back-in-the-middle-of-the-night sort of war. The persons you really have to fear are not an enemy king at the head of an army, they are those who live next door,

71

perhaps even your own family. And so many of the themes that Thucydides identifies at Corcyra are seen at the larger, inter-state level as well: there too he traces a world of pre-emptive strikes, as the Athenians or Spartans decide that their best course is to get their retaliation in first; there too there is disingenuous use of language; there too it is the people in the middle—the little people, or those who try to stay neutral—who suffer particularly badly. We will see that later in the case of the tiny island of Melos. But civil war is the prism that shows up these themes at their starkest and most murderous.

Why? Because it is there that passion flares strongest. Thucydides is often now portrayed as a 'realist' thinker, one who presents humans as reaching their decisions on pragmatic grounds of expediency, pursuing their own interests without concern for any altruistic 'morality'. There is something in that, though Thucydides' speakers in fact have quite a lot to say about morality and justice. But talk of 'expediency' is lazy: expedient *for what?* All too often, it is expedient for the pursuit of passion, especially hatred: if people are calculating, they are calculating how to do down the people they loathe. The closer it comes to home, the more they hate: 'hate thy neighbour'. It may be one's close inter-state neighbours, the way Thebes hates Plataea, just down the road; it may be one's inter-state 'family', the way the colony Corcyra is at odds with its mother-city Corinth. The biggest hatred of all is the hatred one feels for one's enemies in one's own city. Sometimes we see the big powers trying to act as a moderating force: Athens tries to do that at Corcyra, and it is when an Athenian force pulls out that the real bloodshed starts. But it is the presence of the superpowers that creates the conditions where things can escalate so drastically, and there is not much they can do about it except get drawn in.

A good deal of this will sound awfully familiar today. For a modern audience, Thucydides comes very close to home. It is no coincidence that Thucydides should be the classical author most read in contemporary political science and military programmes. The US Naval War College's current 'Strategy and Policy' syllabus tells the students that Thucydides' text is worth an entire library in exploring such themes as 'strategic leadership, homeland security, the disruptive effects on society and politics of a biological catastrophe, how and when to mount joint and combined operations, generating and sustaining domestic and international support in a long war, confronting an adversary with asymmetric capabilities', and so forth. Political scientists have indeed focused so sharply on this text that one has written on 'why International Relations theorists should stop reading Thucydides', given that his world and the ways he had of conceptualizing that world were so very different from our own.

Thucydides himself would doubtless have been gratified to know that this would be his fate, but he might not have been too surprised. At the beginning of that Corcyrean chapter he described those phenomena of civil strife as 'things that happened then and will for ever continue to happen, as long as human nature remains the same, with more or less severity and taking different forms as dictated by each new permutation of circumstances' (3.82.1). He says something similar at the end of his introduction:

> It may be that the lack of a mythical element in my history will make it less of a pleasure to the ear: but I shall be content if it is judged useful by those who will want to have a clear understanding of what happened—and, such is the human condition, will happen again at some time in the same or a similar pattern. It was composed as a possession for ever more than as a showpiece for a single hearing.

> (1.22.4)

The same things come back, in ways that are similar enough—he thinks—for lessons to be learnt. And what lessons there are to be drawn from this 'possession for ever', and particularly whether we can learn enough to avoid reliving the catastrophes of the past, is a very good question indeed.

Why, then, did the Peloponnesian War happen? Many things were said at the time, as both sides aired their grievances; but there was something deeper, says Thucydides.

> The truest cause is one that emerges least clearly in what people said: it was that the Athenians were becoming great and caused the Spartans to be fearful, and this left them no choice but to fight.
>
> (1.23.6)

The Spartans were *fearful* of the Athenians, and they *hoped* to be able to stop them: otherwise they would not have fought. And both fear and hope keep coming back in Thucydides' narrative, massive emotions that are particularly thought-provoking as we look for lessons to learn—lessons for Thucydides' contemporaries, perhaps lessons still for today. Rationality is all very well, and politicians, theorists, and historians cannot do without it; but emotions cry out for analysis too.

First, fear. It is extraordinary how many of the crucial actions in Thucydides' war, and in the peace before it, were driven by fear, by simple anxiety about one's own physical security. Athens did not want a war in the first place, Sparta did not want a war either. But there were various developments that made both sides nervous, and persuaded them that they just had to act. The first set of incidents in Thucydides is the one already mentioned, when Corcyra asks Athens to come in on her side against Corinth. The Athenians don't want to do anything to bring on the war, but they are persuaded that the war is going to happen anyway, and they feel that they cannot afford to let Corinth win this exchange. So Athens gets involved, though it tries to minimize its own military part in the fighting: that turns out to be impractical too, and the Athenians on the spot feel they have no alternative but to get more and more involved. Corinth loses, and is furious: and the Athenians have found themselves driven by their own fear to take the actions which bring on the thing they are most frightened of, a war which threatens their national security.

Fear is most interesting, though, in what would seem the rashest enterprise of all, that expedition of the Athenians to Sicily in 415 that ends so disastrously. On the face of it, that does not seem driven by fear: it seems rather to be the consequence of blithe over-optimism, the feeling that Athenians are so fear-free by now that they can go on a great adventure overseas. That is indeed one strand in Thucydides' portrayal. But there is another strand too, and that, again, is Athenian fear. Those in favour of the expedition play on it (6.6.2): there's a big danger, they say, that unless you strike first Syracuse will start moving against you: look how aggressive they're being against their fellow-Sicilians! And fear cuts in even more a little later. The Athenians have already voted to send the expedition, but the person who has been most opposed, the politician Nicias, reopens the issue. He tries to be clever about it. If you're going to do this, he says, do it properly, and don't take any risks: you need to go in greater force—double (or almost double) the numbers of ships, infantry, everything: make sure that there are enough back-up people as well... (6.20–3). And Nicias has got it wrong. He thinks this scaremongering will put people off, as they realize the scale of what is involved: in fact they jump at it, they immediately vote to send as much as he wants, and are now confident that it will be risk-free—especially as they now decide to send Nicias himself, Mr Hesitant, Mr Oh-I-Don't-Think-So, to temper the exuberance of the other two generals, the military man Lamachus (Mr Up-And-At-Them) and the diplomat Alcibiades (Mr Silver-Tongue-Smooth-Talk). The Athenians are playing for *caution*: it is the caution as much as the impetuousness that Thucydides stresses. And that ups the stakes. If the expedition had been smaller, failure might have been less catastrophic: Nicias increases rather than decreases the risks: and it comes back on his own head, and those of his men, who are destroyed so miserably at the end.

In other Greek authors—in Greek tragedy, perhaps—that pattern could have been left at that. The bigger you are, the more likely you are to fall; and that would have something to do with the way the gods work. Thucydides presents us with a world without gods, and that is very striking for Greek culture; that indeed is one of the aspects that may seem to make his narrative so modern and so close to the ways in which international relations experts look at events today. One of the most moving passages in his narrative comes when the pious Nicias expresses his confidence that the gods will come to their aid even when their plight is desperate (7.77); but we know already, and soon see confirmed, how pathetically far from the truth he is. Instead of the gods, Thucydides gives us a number of very secular ideas to explain why it turned out that way. One important theme is the way that the Athenians' fear became others' fear: they arrived in Sicily with such tremendous might that the towns that should have been on their side took fright. The Athenians were confident that they would find allies on the spot: Syracuse had made enough enemies. But even the traditional allies of Athens and even the recent enemies of Syracuse were afraid of them: the Athenians relied on their allies on the spot at least to provide them with food—they would pay for it—but even so they found this hard to come by. Athens always knew it could not do without allies, but may not have realized how crucial they would become: they were important not so much for providing manpower, but for providing bases, resources, food—and, when the going got really tough, for providing a place the Athenians could head off to. And by then there was nowhere to go. Had the Athenians gone in smaller numbers, had they relied on diplomacy rather than terror, they might well have done better.

'We have nothing to fear but fear itself', a wise Athenian might have said, but in a different sense from the way that would normally be taken. So Thucydides himself, so often regarded as a 'realist' thinker, is actually bringing out how unrealistic these 'realist thinkers' can often be—a point that ought to be taken more on board than it is by those neo-realist experts who appeal to his authority to justify massive military interventions. To trust to overwhelming power, to try too hard to make oneself safe, can be deeply counterproductive.

What about hope? Sadly, it fares little better. If fear tends to be catastrophic, so does hope, but it tends to be the fear felt by the great and the hope felt by the tiny. Quite early in the war Athens is debating what to do about one of her allies, Mytilene on the island of Lesbos, which has had the temerity to 'revolt': it is interesting that by then their choice can so casually be put in those terms, as the Athenian alliance has by now become empire. The revolt has been crushed, though not easily. What should now be done with the Mytileneans? The issue is whether to execute all the males and enslave all the women and children, or do something milder—and eventually the milder course is taken, though it is not as mild as all that and one thousand men are executed. The hard-liner in the debate is the populist demagogue Cleon, arguing that an example needs to be set: once other states have seen how tough Athens can be, that will teach them not to act the same way, and it will give Athens so much less to fear: fear, yet again. He is opposed by the more moderate Diodotus, who argues that that sort of example-setting just does not work: for hope is not like that.

> In the cities of Greece the death penalty is prescribed for many offences less serious than this and bearing no comparison to it. Even so, hope still induces men to take the risks, and no one has ever embarked on a dangerous scheme in the conviction that he will not survive it. And what rebel city has ever made its move believing that its own forces, with or without allied help, were inadequate for the attempt? . . . So either we must find some still more powerful deterrent than death, or at least recognize that this deterrent has no effect. Poverty leading through sheer necessity to the courage of desperation; power leading through presumptuous pride to the greed for more; these and the other conditions of life which hold men in the grip of particular passions drive them with an irresistible and overmastering force into dangerous risks. Hope and desire are always ingredients. Where desire leads, hope follows; desire develops the plan, and hope suggests that fortune will be generous; and both can be ruinous, as their invisible influence is more powerful than the dangers in plain sight. . . . In short, when human nature is set on a determined course of action, it is impossible—and very naïve to think otherwise—to impose any restraint through force of law or any other deterrent.
>
> (3.45)

So, when people care enough about an issue, they will always be led on by hope, no matter how senseless and unrealistic that hope will be. They will never accept that resistance is, literally, hopeless.

The sequel proves Diodotus' predictions to be, if not totally right, at least right on this. A crucial stage here comes eleven years later, in 416, in one of Thucydides' most famous and most moving passages: the Melian Dialogue (5.84–113). This is still in the period of cold war, just before the Athenians move on to Sicily. Melos is another case of the tinies: a small island, not too far from the mainland coast, which at first tries to be neutral, but Athens will not allow that. Athenian bullying and aggression then leads them to 'revolt'. Athens moves against them, but first they summon the Melian magistrates to a secret meeting—secret, so that both sides can talk frankly. Thucydides' narrative, most unexpectedly, moves into dialogue form, and that startling and isolated feature itself marks the tension of the moment.

The Athenians are frank about the way the discussion should go:

> ATH: We shall not bulk out our argument with lofty language, claiming that our defeat of the Persians gives us the right to rule or that we are now seeking retribution for some wrong done to us. That would not convince you. Similarly we do not expect you to think there is any persuasive power in protestations that though you are a Spartan colony you have never joined their campaigns, or that you have not done us any harm. So keep this discussion practical, within the limits of what we both really think. You know as well as we do that when we are talking on the human plane questions of justice only arise when there is equal power to compel: in terms of practicality the dominant exact what they can and the weak concede what they must.
>
> (5.89)

Brutal language: the 'realist' Thucydides, indeed, though again we should not assume he necessarily thinks the Athenians are *right*, either morally or practically. But they also want the Melians to save themselves:

ATH. We are here in the interests of our own empire, yes, but
what we shall say is designed to save your own city. Our desire is to
take you under our rule without unpleasantness: it is in both
our interests that you should survive.

MEL: And how could it be in our interest to be your slaves? How does
that compare with your interest in being our masters?

ATH: Because submission offers you the alternative to a much more
terrible fate: and because we gain by not destroying you.

MEL: So can we not be friends rather than enemies? Would you not
accept our inactive neutrality?

ATH: Your friendship is more dangerous to us than your hostility. To
our subjects friendship indicates a weakness on our part, but
hatred is a sign of our strength.

(5.91–5)

And so it goes on. Every point the Melians put—that the gods will
save them, that war is unpredictable, that the Spartans will come to
their rescue—the Athenians counter. *Don't make us do this.* Yet the
Melians go on hoping; they and the Athenians are just not talking
the same language, and the Athenians seem genuinely surprised
when they go on fighting for their homeland even when, surely,
anyone can see it is hopeless. So they do make the Athenians do it;
and they lose, though it takes longer than expected. The men are
executed, the women and children enslaved. That harder line that
was rejected at Mytilene has now become the norm. And, yet again,
the Athenians feel they have no choice: they just cannot afford to let
a little state defy them, otherwise they will have to fear for their
whole empire. It is fear again that drives them, that same fear which
in the next section of narrative will drive them on to Sicily. Once
again more religious contemporaries would have found a cosmic,
god-driven pattern in the relation of Melos and Sicily: Athens is
beastly to the little people, and then gets her own come-uppance as

punishment. Thucydides sees the pattern, but explains it differently, and once again stresses fear. But it is not just fear that does the damage, it is hope as well. Hope is a terribly dangerous thing, for the little people; fear, insecurity—that is dangerous too, but paradoxically for the big ones.

Thucydides is about power; Thucydides' Athens is about power. One of its most cited passages is the praise of Athens in Pericles' funeral speech in honour of the dead of the war's first year (2.35–46); but Pericles says nothing about culture, nothing about Aeschylus or Sophocles or Euripides or the Parthenon. Athens is an 'education to Greece', says Pericles—but an education in power and self-belief. Thucydides mentions the buildings of Athens only once: if, he says, visitors from a later generation came to Athens and then to Sparta, they would infer that Athens was much more powerful than it really is and Sparta very much weaker, because in each case the buildings give a misleading impression. So glorious architecture is just a pointer, and a misleading one, to what matters most—power. Those are the terms in which his characters think too. When Pericles, in almost the last words he utters in Thucydides' text, looks forward to what later generations will think of Athens, this is how he puts it:

> You should recognize that Athens has the greatest name among all men because she does not yield to adversity, but has made the greatest sacrifice of lives and labour in war, and has acquired the greatest power of any city in history to the present time. Future generations will retain in perpetuity the memory of this power. All things must wane, and we may have to give a little ground too, but posterity will remember that we had the widest empire of Greeks over Greeks, that we have held firm in the greatest wars against their combined or separate forces, and that we have lived in the richest and greatest city of all.

> (2.64.3)

Yet—is that what Athens is remembered for? There had been great powers before, and there would be much greater powers a little later, Macedon and then Rome. I do not know whether Thucydides himself would agree with what he has here made Pericles say. But it is hard for a reader today to be comfortable with the idea that a people's greatness, least of all the greatness of Athens, is simply defined by its power.

CP

# V

# EURIPIDES

Aeschylus, Sophocles, Euripides: the three great Athenian tragedians are always listed in that order, although Sophocles and Euripides were virtually contemporaries. There may be several reasons for that, but it reflects a broader stereotype of Euripides as the *enfant terrible*, boldly pressing on the boundaries of art and ideas established by the other two. The contrast of the turbulent Euripides and the tranquil Sophocles is as old as Aristophanes' *Frogs*, but ignores important features of both: Sophocles can be deeply disturbing and Euripides is often very traditional. Euripides first competed in the tragic festival in 455, and so was presumably born around 480. He wrote some ninety plays; eighteen survive, half of them by a curious chance of the medieval manuscript tradition, whereas we have only (probably) six by Aeschylus and seven by Sophocles. Prizes were awarded to the winning plays each year, and Euripides won only four in his lifetime, far fewer than Aeschylus or Sophocles: the frequency with which he figures in Aristophanes' comedies confirms that he was a controversial figure and a favourite talking-point. He died in 407–406, and the story goes that in the 406 festival Sophocles dressed his chorus in mourning for his great competitor. Sophocles himself died a few months later.

Euripides, so the story went, was not a man who liked company. He so loathed his fellow-humans that he lived in a 'foul and wretched cave' on the island of Salamis, writing his plays to the accompaniment of the sound of the sea. And, again so the story went, his looks were melancholy, thoughtful, and severe: he hated laughter and he hated women. And he was probably an atheist too.

There is no need to think that stories like this are true: people made up such things to explain a poet's work. 'The sound of the sea', for instance, probably reflects the way in which so many of Euripides' plays use images drawn from the shimmering waves and the rolling torrent and the call of the seagulls. But that is what makes such stories interesting, as they point to the features in the work that people thought needed explanation. In these stories it is the fact that Euripides is so grumpy, so misanthropic; and, in particular, so at odds with women. Other tales dwelt on the same things. When he realized his first wife was unfaithful, they said, he wrote the *Hippolytus*, which exposed women's immorality. His second wife was unfaithful too, they said, so he was even more inclined to slander women. So the women planned to kill him and launch an attack on his cave . . .

That last bit is clearly based on Aristophanes' play *The Women at the Thesmophoria*. The Thesmophoria was a women-only festival, exactly the sort of thing to stimulate intrigued curiosity in a male; one version of this particular story had them attacking Euripides at the festival itself. What Aristophanes makes one of his women characters say in that play is itself interesting enough:

> For a long time now, I have been fed up when I see how you're rubbished by Euripides, that son of a greengroceress. The dreadful things he says about you! He's been attacking you wherever he can find spectators and actors and choruses, saying that we're adulteresses, man-chasers, drunks, traitresses, chatterboxes, scabs, curses on men. So whenever they come back from the theatre, they give us a suspicious look, and hunt around to see whether we've got a lover hidden anywhere in the house. We can't get away with any of the things we used to . . .

(Aristophanes, *Women at the Thesmophoria* 384–99)

That makes good comedy, especially when the next speaker, sticking up for Euripides, goes through all the worse things Euripides might have said if he'd chosen: 'how we get bonked by the slaves and the muleteers', for instance, if there is no one else around, or how we chew on garlic after a naughty night with our lovers to stop our husbands smelling anything amiss.

Yet modern readers—and directors—of Euripides do not always read him in that misogynistic way. Gilbert Murray, the great scholar and translator of the early twentieth century, saw him very differently: 'To us', said Murray, 'he seems an aggressive champion of women'. So how could it be that such different things are said about the same plays, even if Aristophanes' side of it need not have been meant so earnestly as Murray's? Can it be so difficult to tell whether a work of literature is misogynist or feminist?

It is easy to see what sort of thing Murray had in mind. Let's take the *Medea*. Jason owes a lot to Medea: it was she who helped him to return home victorious with the Golden Fleece, and she had killed her own brother to help him escape. They married: they came to Corinth; they have children. Yet now the chance has come along for Jason to dump Medea and marry the Corinthian princess instead. He jumps at it; he even has the effrontery to say that he is doing it in the children's interest. That is not the view the local women of Corinth take. They have arrived to express their sympathy, and Medea comes out of the house—the marital house that Jason has betrayed—to address them:

> Women of Corinth, I have come out of the house, so that you may not find fault with me...I never expected this blow, and it has destroyed me. There is no pleasure in life. Dear friends, I want to

die. He was everything to me, I know that well; and now he has turned out the worst of men, this man, my husband.

Of every creature that has life and wit, we women are the most miserable breed. First we must pay a fortune to buy a husband—and, even more painful evil, a master for our bodies. And that is the critical question, whether he is good or bad. For divorce is not respectable for a woman, and one cannot refuse a husband.... And if we do our tasks well and have a good husband, life is enviable. Otherwise, death is better. A man, when bored with life at home, goes out and refreshes himself elsewhere; but we must look to that one single soul. They tell us that we have a safe life there at home while they do the fighting in the battle-line. They are wrong: I would sooner stand three times in battle than bear one child.

(Euripides, *Medea* 214–15, 225–37, 241–51)

This is breathtaking. That last part is talking of not merely fighting, but *hoplite*-fighting: standing arm to arm with one's comrades in the front line, thought of as the highest form both of courage and of male bonding. It is shocking, especially to a male audience—and most, perhaps all, of that audience would have been male. But it is stirring too. No wonder that speech was read out at suffragette rallies only a few years before Gilbert Murray was writing, in a cause that was close to Murray's heart.

It is a particular sort of 'shocking', too. Tragedy often challenges its audience by putting prejudices up for examination: airing the idea, say, that democracy has flaws as well as strengths, and can easily be exploited or perverted; that Greeks may not be so much better than, or even so very different from, barbarians. But by now these have become pretty *comfortable* challenges, the sorts of home truth that we are all aware of, but have got so used to that we can live with them. It is a type of challenge-fatigue. And if the Athenian man-in-the-street ever really worried about the strengths of democracy or the merits of

86

Greek civilization, he would have at least some idea of what might be said in their defence. This is different. These challenges are not so familiar, and it is not nearly so easy to see how one would argue against them. Medea's points about double standards might just about be laughed down, if a man was sufficiently prejudiced. But that final point about fighting and childbirth is certainly no laughing matter, especially in a world where death in childbirth may well have been a bigger statistical danger for women than death in the front line was for men. And there is nothing one can say back.

Still, there is more to think about before we start regarding Euripides as a crusading proto-feminist. The very topic of 'childbirth' is all too raw a theme in this play: Medea is going to kill her own children as a way of getting back at Jason. It is true that Jason has behaved appallingly; true too that Medea may retain some audience sympathy all the way through, as part of the tragedy is that she *loves* these children and she is destroying an important part of herself when she kills them. But it is still hard to think that she is a positive model. Most of the audience may begin by feeling for Medea when she is so badly treated, but at the end the most uncomfortable thing may be the thought of *what they have been brought to sympathize with* during the previous hour or so, and how it has all turned out. It is not so much that Euripides is 'challenging' audience prejudices, he is pulling them apart.

Nor is this the only time that the audience will be sitting uneasily on their seats as the sun shines down on them. That 'sun', so visible in the clear Greek sky, is disquieting too: that sun is the god Helios, Medea is his granddaughter, and at the end of the play he sends her a chariot to carry her away to a new home. Heaven—the gods—are giving their stamp of approval; and that new home will be in

Athens, so the audience's own city will be drawn into giving protection to the murderess. And what about Jason? Before Euripides he had been a Greek hero. Now, to quote Gilbert Murray again, 'when Jason had to defend an obviously shabby case, no gentleman cared to hear him; but Euripides insisted on his speaking.' No Greek 'gentleman' would be comfortable either with what he goes on to hear, as Jason smugly says that the greatest benefit he has given Medea is to bring her to Greece, the home of civilization. Civilized behaviour? This? Great to be a male; great to be a Greek; great to be an Athenian. Euripides takes all those complacent audience assumptions one after another, and yes, he pulls them apart.

By now we can see why Aristophanes could have fun with Euripides in one direction, and why Murray could admire him in an apparently opposite way. Perhaps, though, they are not so different after all. He is showing a woman doing dreadful things, far more dreadful than those minor offences which Aristophanes' women were protesting that he had exposed—adultery, gossip, drunkenness, and so on. But as he does so he also asks *why*. The two things go together. He forces his audience to think themselves into Medea's head, and to work out how a loving mother could do such a thing. That is going way outside any comfort zone, and it is taking a woman's mind very seriously indeed.

Take another play, the *Hippolytus*, perhaps the same *Hippolytus* as people said Euripides wrote in a bad mood after his first wife had been unfaithful. Once again we have a woman, Phaedra, who does something dreadful. Aphrodite, goddess of sexual passion, has something to answer for, certainly: she delivers the prologue, and makes it clear that she is orchestrating matters to secure revenge on Hippolytus, the young man who has so totally rejected all the goddess stands for. But most of the interest falls on the human level. Hippolytus is Phaedra's stepson, the son of her husband Theseus, and Phaedra falls for him. Such things can happen; they are all the more understandable in a world where wives would often be the best part of a generation younger than their husbands. Hippolytus, with his aversion to all things sexual, naturally has an even bigger aversion to this. Phaedra is humiliated and terrified that the truth about her passion may come out, and she kills herself—but not before writing a letter to Theseus accusing Hippolytus of raping her. Theseus believes her, understandably enough: as he says, her corpse, lying there, is an irresistibly persuasive silent witness. He curses Hippolytus, and Hippolytus dies, most horribly.

In all this Hippolytus' own, rather creepy psychological make-up is one source of interest, but far more involving, once again, is the mind of the woman. The person who persuades Phaedra into allowing an approach to Hippolytus is the Nurse—her own Nurse? Her children's Nurse? Perhaps both. That approach is quite evidently a very bad idea. Hippolytus is never going to say, 'Phaedra? My stepmother? Yes, splendid. Let's say 3 o'clock tomorrow. I'll clear my desk.' So what makes Phaedra play along? In the crucial scene the Nurse has a long speech saying how unreasonable Phaedra is to resist love. The arguments are transparently weak, but Phaedra clearly finds them attractive.

PHAEDRA: In the name of the gods, please, no—for what you are saying is well said, but bad—please go no further: for I'm so well worked over by love—if you say bad things well, I shall be spent on the very thing I am trying to avoid.

NURSE: Well—if that's what you want. . . . I have some love charms at home (I have just remembered): these will heal your disease, with no shame and no harm to your mind—provided you are brave. But we must have something from the man you want, some token, a lock of hair or something from his clothes, so as to weld together one joy from the two.

PHAEDRA: This charm—is it to be rubbed on, or drunk?

NURSE: I do not know. My child, you should want the benefit of it, not to know what it is.

PHAEDRA: I'm afraid you may turn out all too clever for me.

NURSE: Oh, you'd be afraid of anything! What do you fear?

PHAEDRA: That you might reveal something of this to Theseus's son.

NURSE: Let things be, my child. I will take care of it.

(Euripides, *Hippolytus* 503-7, 509-21)

What is going on here? Phaedra clearly suspects that there's more to this soothing talk of 'a love charm' than the Nurse is letting on: she is afraid that she will 'reveal something of this to Theseus's son'—and it of course sounds much more likely that the charm is meant to work on him than on her. Yet she does not stop the Nurse. Is that because Phaedra is just so weak, for she is literally lovesick, and has been carried on stage on a litter? Is she being ground down by a stronger character, one who is being peculiarly brutal to her? ('It's not fair words you need,' the Nurse has said; 'it's the man.') Or is there a part of her that really wants the approach to be made, persuades herself it's not hopeless after all? She is, after all, so 'well-worked over by love', as she says. There is no clear answer to that, but this is the sort of question an audience will ask, once again being drawn into that uncomfortable zone of trying to understand why a woman can do such terrible things.

This is not the only time where Euripides rubs his audience's noses into subjects they might have preferred not to think about at all. Take *The Trojan Women* of spring, 415 BCE. The setting is the plain outside Troy, and the city has just fallen. The first scene belongs to the gods: Athena and Poseidon agree that the Greeks face sufferings ahead, punished on their return voyage for various acts of sacrilege they have committed as they sacked the city. That looming fate for the bullying victors hangs in the air through all the following scenes. Still, the emphasis falls on the other side, as we see what defeat means for the captive Trojan women, one after another. In many ways this is more of what we have already seen in the *Iliad* (Chapter I), with women showing what war really means: but the voice of suffering is here even more agonized, as each in turn falls to the worst possible captor as a prize. Cassandra, the virgin princess, goes to the lustful Agamemnon; Andromache, the dutiful and loving wife, is taken by the son of Achilles, the killer of her husband; Hecuba, widow of the dead king Priam and mother of Hector, falls to Odysseus, whose skilled and ruthless rhetoric has caused so many of her woes. The play builds to a double climax. The worst moment, almost unbearable for any parent or grandparent, is when the child Astyanax is torn from his mother Andromache to be thrown, on Odysseus' orders, from a high tower. Andromache is carted off before she is even able to care for him in his death; his grandmother Hecuba has to wash the small bloodsoaked and broken body.

Telling, though, in a different way is a venomous exchange between Hecuba and Helen, the woman all the Trojan captives hate as the one who started it all. It is a sort of trial, with the victorious Menelaus, now reunited with his errant wife, standing as judge. Hecuba urges him to kill the woman, Helen pleads for her life. The arguments are fascinating, and bring out how complex and elusive any moral truth can be; but even more telling is how little it all matters. Getting rid of the hate-figure is not going to do the Trojan women much good; but will the argument work anyway? For the moment, Menelaus is convinced, and pronounces the death-sentence: take her away to the ships... He is clearly going to take her home before killing her, and one suspects that he has in mind another use for her first. *Don't take her on the same ship*, Hecuba cries: her thoughts are presumably along similar lines, with a realistic insight of what use Helen might make of such an interlude. 'Why?' asks Menelaus; 'has she put on weight while she's been away?' (1050)–perhaps the only joke in Greek tragedy, and one that falls chillingly amid so much passionate hatred. In fact he agrees, and she will go on a separate ship, but we know that the women's fears are well-founded. 'You'd taken Troy and she was your captive,' says the furious old Peleus in another play, 'but you did not kill her: one glimpse of her breast, and you dropped your sword and kissed her' (*Andromache* 627–30)–a moment of extraordinary emasculation of a heroic warrior, captured beautifully also in the vase-painting here (Figure 5.1). Any reader of the *Odyssey* would have known that Helen and Menelaus have some home-life together to come. However fiercely sensed the rights and wrongs may be, they do not matter much: not by now, and not in war.

Spring, 415. That is a thought-provoking date for a play that makes so much of the horrors of war. In the last chapter we heard a lot about the devastation of Melos during the long-running Peloponnesian War: the massacres and enslavements on the island had ended only a few months earlier, in mid-December 416. At almost exactly this time–the precise dates are unclear, but it is unlikely that there were more than a few weeks between the two–the Athenians were also taking their fateful decision to go to Sicily, with all those consequences that we saw in the previous chapter. Maybe we should be cautious about taking the play as too direct a comment on those two actions of imperialist aggression, Melos and Sicily. They loom

FIGURE 5.1. Menelaus is about to strike Helen, but drops his sword at the sight of her. Aphrodite (left) and a flying Eros look on. Attic red-figure, *c*.450 BCE.

heavily in our own awareness because of Thucydides, but Melos was only one of several such atrocities during the war, and Euripides would have been working on the play during all the winter of 416–15: he could not have known that the Sicilian issues would come to the boil so close to the time of the dramatic festival. But certainly war was in the air, and all that war entailed.

Is Euripides, then, warning the Athenians? Perhaps he is. That indication that the Greeks in the play will get their come-uppance might well give the audience some pause: true, those Greeks will be punished for their sacrilege rather than their brutality, but everyone will have known how readily the one went with the other, how often fighting men trampled on sacred ground. Thucydides' Melians too had cautioned the Athenians that they might be storing up future trouble for themselves if they established this ruthless pattern; his Athenian ambassadors wave the argument away (Thuc. 5.90–1), but not all their countrymen and women will have been so sanguine. Whatever they may or may not have feared for themselves, they are anyway brought to see with stark honesty what warfare means—what they are doing to other humans if not to themselves, creating more widows and more slaves, killing more children, destroying more lives, with any morality floating away into nothingness. If war is what the audience want, then they should be clear what they are wishing for. Here again there is nothing comfortable, then or now.

Greek tragedies deal with timeless issues. If that first audience of 415 BCE would have thought particularly about events like Melos and decisions like that to attack Sicily, it is no surprise that modern producers have turned to this play and nudged their audiences to think of modern counterparts. Unsurprisingly, there has been a burst of productions since the Iraq invasion of 2003—the database of Oxford's Archive for the Performances of Greek and Roman Drama lists 26 different productions in 2003–4 alone, especially in the UK and USA but also in Belgium, Latvia, Austria, the Netherlands, Australia, and Japan—and they have sometimes trowelled on the contemporary resonances: mock-ups of a CNN report, costumes of modern desert battledress. It is hard to think that such obviousness is needed. Michael Cacoyannis' film version of 1971 used no such ploys, and a team of distinguished female actors—Katharine Hepburn as Hecuba, Vanessa Redgrave as Andromache, Geneviève

Bujold as Cassandra, Irene Papas as Helen—did harrowing justice to this play that so memorably explores female anguish in and at war.

The Peloponnesian War had eleven years still to run; the last play of Euripides that we have, the *Bacchae*, was put on in 405, just a year before the war's end. That too explores psychology, both female—there is plenty of interest in the women followers of Dionysus, sometimes known as 'maenads' in order to capture a brand of madness (*mainesthai, mania*) in their exhilaration—and male, as we look closely at the young Theban king Pentheus. It takes an exciting religious notion: a new god has arrived on the block. This is Dionysus, freshly arrived in Greece with his women followers from the East; but in an important sense he is coming home, for his father was Zeus but his mother was the Theban Semele. His birth was admittedly a rather unusual one, and we will hear more on this when we turn to Lucian in our final chapter. But what matters here is that he is a local god made good, and that the locality does not know what to make of him.

It has sometimes been thought that this story preserves the memory of something historical, the expansion of the Olympian pantheon to include a new arrival whose characteristics owe something to Near Eastern models. We should not make too much of that, as we can trace Dionysus' presence from very early times: a second-millennium BCE Linear B tablet from Pylos has the word DI-WO-NI-SO-JO. What the 'newness' captures is something else, the way that Dionysus reflects something rather different in experience from most of the Olympians, the likes of Athena or Apollo or Artemis. Not wholly different, perhaps: we have seen in *Hippolytus* the devastating effect that Aphrodite can have on a human mind, and that takes us in a similar direction. But Dionysus correlates even more with something outside one's normal self, the exhilaration of breaking through the limits of one's usual personality. His Roman equivalent was Bacchus, and we will hear more about his wild inspiration when we reach Horace in Chapter IX.

With both Dionysus and Bacchus, drink is an easy and frequent way of capturing some of that experience:

> Next (after Demeter) came Semele's son Dionysus, introducing to mortals the liquid drink of the vine, a counterpart to Demeter's grain: it releases poor humans from grief, filled with the flow of the grape, and gives sleep and forgetfulness of the evils of the day; nor is there any other remedy for suffering.
>
> (Teiresias, at *Bacchae* 278–83)

But drink is only a part of it, often only a small part. As E. R. Dodds, Gilbert Murray's successor in his Oxford chair, put it, it is 'not only the liquid fire in the grape, but the sap thrusting in a young tree, the blood pounding in the veins of a young animal, all the mysterious and uncontrollable tides that ebb and flow in the life of nature'. Those who can let themselves go with such a tide can find a harmony with nature that, once again, goes beyond normal experience. That is how the chorus of *Bacchae* sing as they enter:

> Earth runs with milk, with wine, with the honey of bees. And the Bacchic god holds up the blazing flame of the pine torch, smoking as if with Syrian frankincense, and rushes with his fennel rod, exciting his wanderers with running and dance and stirring them with cries, throwing his luxuriant curls to the sky. 'On, Bacchants! On Bacchants!... To the mountain! To the mountain!'
>
> (*Bacchae* 143–61)

Later we hear how the women of Thebes have rushed to those mountains; one struck a rock, and pure water sprang up; another struck the ground, and this time it was wine; a third scratched the earth, and milk spurted and honey dripped from the ivy rods. The women revellers, the god, nature itself—all are as one.

Such exhilaration is not something to reject lightly. But it is also hard to get one's head round, and even those in Thebes who sympathize do not find it straightforward. One person does not even try, and that is King Pentheus. For him, if it isn't just a matter of wine, that's only because it is sex as well:

> I hear that our women have left their homes for some fake Bacchism, and are rushing around in the shaded mountains, worshipping this new god Dionysus—whoever that is—with their dances; that there are brimming wine-bowls in the middle of their bands, and they're slipping off one by one into the wild to service the men. The excuse is that they are worshipping Bacchants, but it's Aphrodite they care about, not Dionysus.
>
> (*Bacchae* 217–25)

A messenger from the mountains tries, bravely, to put him right:

> They were lying there among oak leaves, letting their heads drift down to the ground: it was all very proper, and it was not at all what you said, women drunk from the wine and music and prowling for Aphrodite in the desertion of the woods.
>
> (*Bacchae* 685–8)

But Pentheus will not take telling. He comes face to face with Dionysus, in a series of extremely eerie scenes. Dionysus, the god who presides over so much wildness and ecstasy, is the one figure who stays serenely calm throughout, even when he has orchestrated an earthquake that has reduced the palace to rubble. Pentheus issues a torrent of threats and abuse, and calls for weapons to shut the stranger's mouth. Then, suddenly, just a monosyllable, the same sound in the Greek as in English:

DIONYSUS: Ah!
Do you want to see them as they cluster on the mountains?
PENTHEUS: Oh yes, more than anything. I'd give a vast weight of
  gold for that!

(*Bacchae* 810–11)

And from then on the king is Dionysus' toy. The god persuades him
to put on female dress, in another bizarre scene where he helps the
mortal with his wardrobe, arranging the pleats of the dress and
putting a lock of his hair back into place. It is to be his death kit.
Once he reaches the mountains, the women see him and grab him.
Even before he left, he did not know what he was seeing—'I seem to
see a double sun, and a double city of Thebes' (918–19); they do not
see properly either, and mistake him for a fawn. In a travesty of
Dionysiac ritual, they tear their victim apart (Figure 5.2). It is
Pentheus' mother Agave who leads the murder and comes back
on stage holding her son's severed head, still not recognizing it;
Pentheus' grandfather Cadmus, devastated, brings her round slowly
and delicately to see what she has done. That revelry of the ladies of
Thebes might initially have seemed to recapture the joys of that
chorus from the east, but it has turned out to be something else, a
peculiar and intense and horrific version.

This is another play, then, which shows Euripides exploring
psychology, this time male psychology too, with that peculiar
form of psychic invasion and that uncanny power that the god
exercises. Once again, it is hard to think that Euripides' audience
is going to find this dramatic experience cosy. Pentheus may have
got what he deserved, but there are also factors that may elicit some
sympathy too; he is several times described as 'the young man', for
instance, and old Cadmus tells us how the youth always took care of

FIGURE 5.2. The Bacchants tear Pentheus apart. Attic red-figure vase, *c.*480 BCE.

his grandfather (admittedly with a continued hint of the bully-boy: tell me who's causing you trouble, and I'll take care of them, 1310–22). But more important is sympathy for others: for Agave, helpless after Dionysus' parallel psychic takeover of her; and particularly, perhaps, for Cadmus, left as the family's grieving relic. He must go into exile, and eventually (as the play foretells) be changed, along with his wife, into a snake. Even then his troubles will not be at an end: even when sailing down to Hades he will have no peace (1330–62). He has done his best throughout; he did not deserve this.

Becoming a snake is cruel, it is bizarre—yet not inappropriate. The 'Cadmeans' in myth had sprung from a dragon's teeth in the soil; now Cadmus himself will return to the ground. Even the total fragmentation of the family somehow fits. It was his own people, the ruling house of Thebes, that rejected Dionysus. Now that family pays for it, all of them. The god had earlier destroyed the house literally, with that miraculous earthquake; now he destroys it figuratively as well, scattering its members across the earth.

It makes a horrid sort of sense: 'justly, but too much', as Cadmus himself says to Agave. He makes the same point courageously to Dionysus himself: we know we have done wrong, but you are punishing us too much, and 'it is not fitting for gods to have tempers like humans' (*Bacchae* 1348). Something similar was said in the *Hippolytus*, when a wise servant begged Aphrodite not to be too hard on the young man: 'for gods ought to be wiser than humans' (*Hippolytus* 120). 'Ought to be': the nuance of the Greek (*chrē*) is subtly different from 'must be', and the servant does not sound any more confident than Cadmus that the gods would do what, by Cadmus' mortal standards, was 'fitting'. Indeed, the Aphrodite of the *Hippolytus* was just as ruthless as Dionysus is here, in that case destroying the high-principled Phaedra as collateral damage in her determination to punish Hippolytus for dishonouring her.

Gods like this are beings to fear, but hardly to love. What is an audience to make of them? What are *we* to make of them, if we are indeed to have a 'conversation' with these plays and find something still meaningful for us?

Given all Euripides' interest in human psychology, one tempting way is to take them, or at least some of them, not so much as personalized beings but as some impersonal or supra-personal 'force' that operates on human minds. One can see that it would not be easy to bring a disembodied 'Sex' on stage; so might Euripides be using 'Aphrodite' to explore something general about human emotions? Some lines almost suggest as much:

So Aphrodite is no god after all, but some force greater than a god,
who has destroyed Phaedra and me and the house.

(The Nurse, at *Hippolytus* 359–61)

And Dionysus might stand for those 'mysterious and uncontrollable tides that ebb and flow in the life of nature', especially in exhilarating, ecstatic, not-one's-normal-self emotions. There is something in this; and yet it is too easy a way to make sense of Greek gods. They may certainly have particular *connections* with 'forces': Aphrodite links with sex and Dionysus with exhilaration just as Poseidon links with the sea or Hades with death. Understandably, too, those aspects are reflected in the ways that gods bring down those whom they wish to destroy, fitting their lethal methods also to the peculiarities of their victims. Aphrodite uses sex, and Phaedra, a woman whose family has a tradition of irregular and catastrophic sexuality, is especially vulnerable; Dionysus uses Pentheus' prurient fascination with what the women might be getting up to in the wild; Poseidon sends from the sea a bull, that emblem of rampant sexuality, to destroy the young, sex-denying horseman Hippolytus. But this does not mean that the gods *are* those forces. They are personalities as well, just as their Homeric versions showed human personal characteristics to the highest degree. Remember that it is a particular affront to Dionysus that he has been rejected by his own family: Pentheus is his cousin. One cannot be cousin to a 'force'.

What one must not expect from these gods is anything very loving or protective, even for those whom they like. Hippolytus himself is Artemis' favourite, and she can do nothing to save him, just promise to destroy one of Aphrodite's golden boys in return (*Hippolytus* 1420–2). When we do see signs of divine protection for those the gods care about, that is not reassuring either: remember the Sun, whisking Medea away in that chariot. To those more used to Christian ideas of divine love, that is quite a jump; these gods may seem very bleak and comfortless beings. Nor is it just modern or Christian ideas that are distant; we are some way too from the providential notion that 'humans are dearer to the gods than they are to themselves' that we will find in Juvenal (Chapter XI). Yet there *is* some comfort here. Things are not as bad as all that: one must not forget the good aspects of Dionysus as well, this god who is 'most dread, but most gentle to mortals' (*Bacchae* 861). When the joys and the exhilaration come, let us make the most of them. People who refuse such pleasures are not enviable, even when their fates are not so dramatically dreadful as those of Hippolytus and Pentheus. But the good times are never anything you can count on, and you might as well know where you stand. You may well end up as collateral damage, just like Phaedra or Cadmus or Agave or Medea's children. Even in cases like that, you can understand all those catastrophes that vengeful gods have brought: that is the way that gods behave, just as gods who work with natural forces send earthquakes and volcanoes and plagues that bring down all sorts of people who do not deserve it—and, for that matter, just as the ordinary people of Melos did not do much to deserve their fate. That is the way things are, and you might as well know how you stand. Handle it. Often enough, humans have had to.

Maybe, indeed, humans are at their greatest when accepting their fragility, and Greek tragedy can suggest as much. That is why the end of Sophocles' *King Oedipus* is a good deal less depressing than one would expect after seeing a great, intelligent, dutiful king brought low. Euripides is a very varied writer, and some of his own plays can be read or seen like that: his *Heracles*, perhaps. But most of them cannot, and no one wholly likes being as uncomfortable as Euripides' audiences often would feel. Frankness and clarity are often not joyful; most of us are not made of the same stuff as Oedipus, so admirably determined to find out the truth about himself when others urge him to stop. That is surely why those stories made Euripides out to be so grumpy, so unfriendly to his fellow-humans, so atheistic. But Aristotle called Euripides 'the most tragic' of the poets; and you don't, or you shouldn't, go to tragedies to feel comfortable.

CP

# VI

# CAESAR

For many ancient authors, scarcely any information is available about their participation in public life. But Julius Caesar is a major player on the stage of ancient history, and certainly the most famous Roman of them all. From contemporary evidence we glean a great deal about him as a man of extraordinary talent, charisma, and drive: a cultured member of the Roman elite who liked to indulge his sophisticated tastes, a lively orator, a shrewd and energetic general, a writer of great clarity, an astute politician, a ruthless dictator, and, finally, the target of assassination. Later writers shaped him into a quasi-mythic figure—most memorably Plutarch in his biography and, drawing upon Plutarch, Shakespeare in his Elizabethan tragedy. Caesar vastly extended the boundaries of the Roman empire with his conquest of Gaul in the 50s BCE. He then provoked a civil war, usurped power, and established a permanent dictatorship. He was murdered by his fellow Roman senators on the Ides of March 44 BCE for his autocratic rule and his aspiration to kingship. Both Caesar's war commentaries (seven books recording his campaigns to conquer Gaul from 58 to 52 BCE; three books on the civil war that followed his rebellious march on Rome in 49 BCE) were written to serve immediate political ends at a time of anarchy for the dying Roman Republic.

Julius Caesar provides an apt opening for the Latin segment of our book and our selection of six Latin voices. That is not to say that Latin literature begins with Caesar's two records of his military achievements. Epic, drama, philosophy, historiography, personal poetry—these are already well-developed genres at Rome by the middle of the first century BCE. But Caesar's voice is good to start with here because it exposes the political power of classical literature, is masterfully manipulative, and, for century after century, was absorbed not just by emperors, kings, and generals but also by children. For most of the last two millennia, Caesar's *Gallic War* and (to a lesser degree) his *Civil War* were the first points of entry into the excitements of the Roman world.

Caesar's Latin is crystal-clear. It comprises a noticeably limited and repetitive vocabulary of some 1,300 words. Adjectives are mainly functional. They categorize and evaluate. Verbs are generally practical. They describe troop movements, communications, military planning and action. The arrangement of words into phrases, clauses, and sentences is easily grasped because strictly obedient to the rules of Latin grammar. Sentences are most often brief and declarative. Narrative is linear. So Caesar's writings always used to be the first proper Latin to be placed in the hands of a beginner, myself included. Thus my Latin teacher in the early 1970s found herself needing, bizarrely, to enthuse about Roman warfare in order to sustain her girls' interest in the ancient language: the hierarchies of command (legionaries, centurions, military tribunes, legates, and, above them all, the *imperator* or commander-in-chief), the equipment (eagle standards, shields, swords, and javelins), the tactics (marching columns, fortified encampments, cavalry manoeuvres, besieged cities) and the strategy (speed, audacity, attack). And life as a classroom soldier recruited into Caesar's Latin legions did indeed seem wonderfully alien, dangerous, masculine, and adult.

Often Caesar has been not just the beginning of Latin but also of British history. In Books 4 and 5 of *The Gallic War*, the Roman general presents his two brief incursions into Britain in 55 and 54 BCE as strategic necessities and as extensions of Rome's empire beyond the edges of the known world. Caesar's touch, in many histories of Britain, at last brought to our soil civilization, nationhood, and empire. The significance of the 'Landing of Julius Caesar' was captured in stirring, patriotic illustrations—such as that in Walter Hutchinson's four-volume *Story of the British Nations: A Glorious and Vivid Panorama of the Mightiest Empire in History—One Quarter of the Earth*, published in the 1920s (Figure 6.1). Similar illustrations still find a place in primary school histories of the Romans in Britain, although the accompanying narrative is now mostly stripped of imperialist fervour. And Caesar's voice has become somewhat muted in the study of Latin at schools. But as Julius Caesar fades from the British curriculum, so we have come to understand that his Latin prose is anyway too powerful, too

FIGURE 6.1. 'The Landing of Julius Caesar', lithograph by W. P. Caton Woodville to illustrate *Hutchinson's Story of the British Nations, c.*1920.

dangerous, too calculated—and too fascinating—to have been left in the hands of children for so long.

Caesar's *commentarii* or war commentaries constitute a highly potent cohesion of word and action. They were once a 'bible' for military officers on bellicosity, breath-taking daring, fearless resolve, personal intervention, and—above all—extraordinary speed of execution. Outside military academies, they are now more often exploited metaphorically as lessons for leaders in the art of corporate war. But Caesar also wrote in the same manner as he fought, and on occasion (as the ancient anecdotes have it) even at the same time. Like his campaigns, Caesar's accounts of them are brief, tightly organized, forceful, and 'winged with fire'. And, in addition to such matters as dynamic leadership and lucid composition, *The Gallic War* and *The Civil War* also deliver master classes in how to influence people.

When Caesar composed the seven books of *The Gallic War* (whether as year-by-year despatches from the field, or as a rounded narrative toward the end of the 50s BCE), he was looking beyond military command to the next stage of his career. Caesar needed to place himself in the public eye even though absent on campaign, avoid prosecution by his opponents for multiple illegalities, and win both popular and elite support for his further political advancement. After 49, when Caesar began work on *The Civil War*, he needed to justify the military conflict he had instigated against his rival Pompey, win opponents over to fight on his side, and mobilize support for the continuation of his supreme authority into the future. Thus, in both *commentarii*, Julius Caesar fashions himself as an ideal Roman general and dutiful servant of the state. He sculpts these self-serving portraits using a bare style that is both graceful and carefully contrived. He invites his contemporary readers to draw conclusions at which the texts merely hint, to participate in the construction and the progress of Caesar's story, to advance his political authority, to become one of Caesar's men. We, now, can engage with these literary strategies and admire (or, at times, condemn) their extraordinary skill, ever aware of their historic consequences.

Caesar's narratives, therefore, are highly partisan. Or, in much stronger formulations, they are considered deformations of history, even pure propaganda. They are also momentous. They do not just tell Roman history, they are designed to make it. Plutarch later analyses that history in terms of how poor government in Republican Rome enabled a charismatic man, endowed with both astonishing talent and an intense ambition for pre-eminence, to destroy it. The Greek biographer fills in for us the psychological motivations Caesar's works fail to provide. Shakespeare gives us an especially memorable and influential version of the bloody death that awaits their soldier-author. We cannot now approach the war commentaries without remembering as we read them that Julius Caesar was assassinated by his friends on the Ides of March 44 BCE because of the ambition for power which drove him. These works, then, are commanding literary events: instruments of a turbulent European history; agents in the destruction of the Roman Republic and the formation of an imperial monarchy.

Between 58 and 52 BCE, Julius Caesar fought an extremely aggressive, bloody, and cruel war of expansion that eventually subjugated to Roman authority vast territories stretching across most of modern-day France and Belgium, and into the Netherlands and Switzerland. The general also broke through two frontiers to attack the

Roman Empire's most distant foes (respectively crossing the Rhine into Germany and the English Channel into Britain). War would bring to the commander-in-chief wealth, a loyal army, and the equally great advantage of being able to write home about his performance of Rome's supreme virtue—military distinction. This was no mean task since a large proportion of his readers back in the city feared or hated him. Yet *The Gallic War* contains no dedication, preface, or explanation and opens instead with the description: 'All Gaul is divided into three parts' (1.1). How banal is that? This famous beginning, however, contains so much more than some basic geography. It indicates to us a number of important things. Because Gaul is a whole, partial conquest will not be enough. Because Gaul has clear boundaries, reaching them will complete the task of conquest. Because Gaul is already and variously divided (the author claims further that it is inhabited by three nations with three different sets of languages, customs, and laws), it will be easy to subjugate. Because Caesar has already mastered the territory intellectually, his physical mastery of it will follow just as surely.

The first appearance of the Roman general in his account of the war is equally carefully contrived: 'When it was reported to Caesar that they [the migrating tribe of the Helvetii] were attempting to make their route through our Province he hastens to set out from the city, and, by as great marches as he can, proceeds to Further Gaul, and arrives at Geneva' (1.7). 'It was reported to Caesar.' Caesar here is not the subject of the sentence and, therefore, not the instigator of a self-serving war of expansion, but the newly appointed, quickly responsive governor of Rome's threatened province in the south-east. 'Our Province.' Caesar is fond of using the first person plural possessive to identify our army, our province, our empire, our way of life. 'Our'—mine and yours—gives Caesar ownership of all these aspects of Rome's power and draws in his readers to applaud the many ways in which he protects and enhances what also belongs (and is precious) to them. Similarly: 'He hastens. He proceeds. He arrives.' The general stands in for the activities of his troops, giving their rapid march a neat shape and taking all the credit. Yet much more remarkable than any of these features is the way that Julius Caesar refers to himself here and throughout both war commentaries in the third person even though they are both closely focused on him. Instead of using the first person to describe his own achievements as a general, he gives us a narrator who is nameless (although readers will be aware that this is 'I-Caesar' the writer). That narrator sees, hears, and comprehends all, and can best demonstrate how 'he-Caesar' the character brings order and civilization to the barbaric lands beyond Rome's borders. What a perfect mechanism for making us feel that we are reading an independent, objective, *self-evidently true* description of Julius Caesar's accomplishments.

When the Helvetii still try to pass through Caesar's Roman province on their way to establish new settlements in the west, the narrator tells us that the general responded with hostility because he recalled how that Celtic tribe had once killed a Roman consul and humiliated his army. When the Helvetii then attempt to cross westward through the lands of Rome's Gallic allies, Caesar attacks and kills those of their forces bringing up the rear. The narrator concludes: 'Thus, whether by chance, or by the design of the immortal gods, that part of the Helvetian state which had brought a signal calamity upon the Roman people, was the first to pay the penalty' (1.12). So Julius Caesar fashions a picture of himself as a general who cares for 'the Roman people' (the narrator is very fond of the phrase *populus Romanus*). Caesar is the upholder of their honour, the avenger of their defeats, even the agent of their gods. He is also the avenger of a private wrong, we are told, because this same group of Helvetians had once killed a distant relative of his. Caesar is full of Roman virtue: dutiful to gods, country, and family.

Across the first few books of *The Gallic War*, the Roman general is gradually brought deeper and deeper into the fray. In Shakespeare's *Julius Caesar*, Antony stirs the Roman people to seek revenge for Caesar's murder by revealing to them the mutilated corpse lying pitiably in the Forum. He points out how the cruel dagger thrusts have penetrated through the very mantle their noble leader first put on one summer's evening, 'that day he overcame the Nervii' (*JC*, 3.2.175). And it is in combat against the remote Nervii (the fiercest of the ferocious Belgian tribes) that the narrator of the war commentary endows Caesar with the prowess of a Homeric hero. The legions are entrenching their camp for the night on a slope above the river Sabis, when the Nervii and their allies, suddenly emerging from the marshes and woodland on the other side, wade across and charge swiftly up at them. Taken by surprise and outnumbered, it is the commander-in-chief who must seize immediate and total control (any contribution that might have been made by his officer corps is suppressed at this point):

> Caesar had everything to do at one time: the standard to be displayed, which was the sign when it was necessary to run to arms; the signal to be given by the trumpet; the soldiers to be called off from the works; those who had proceeded some distance for the purpose of seeking materials for the rampart, to be summoned; the order of battle to be formed; the soldiers to be encouraged; the watchword to

be given. A great part of these arrangements was prevented by the shortness of time and the sudden approach and charge of the enemy.

(*Gallic War* 2.20; tr. McDevitte and Bohn)

The Roman general's perception of the developing crisis and what it requires of him is instant and extensive. In one long and swiftly flowing movement, he grasps the complex and deteriorating situation and makes a quick and daring intervention:

Caesar *proceeded*, after encouraging the tenth legion, to the right wing; where he *perceived* that his men were hard pressed, and that in consequence of the standards of the twelfth legion being collected together in one place, the crowded soldiers were a hindrance to themselves in the fight; that all the centurions of the fourth cohort were slain, and the standard-bearer killed, the standard itself lost, almost all the centurions of the other cohorts either wounded or slain, and among them the chief centurion of the legion P. Sextius Baculus, a very valiant man, who was so exhausted by many and severe wounds, that he was already unable to support himself; he likewise *perceived* that the rest were slackening their efforts, and that some, deserted by those in the rear, were retiring from the battle and avoiding the weapons; that the enemy on the other hand though advancing from the lower ground, were not relaxing in front, and were at the same time pressing hard on both flanks; he also *perceived* that the affair was at a crisis, and that there was not any reserve which could be brought up, having therefore snatched a shield from one of the soldiers in the rear (for he himself had come without a shield), he *advanced* to the front of the line, and addressing the centurions by name, and encouraging the rest of the soldiers, he *ordered* them to carry forward the standards, and extend the companies, that they might the more easily use their swords.

(*Gallic War* 2.25; tr. McDevitte and Bohn)

The narrator puts his protagonist into energetic performance under a heroizing spotlight. There 'Caesar' enacts brilliantly the qualities associated with the ideal military commander: strategic and tactical understanding, authority, bravery, and leadership from the front. We can appreciate the fabulous extent of their effectiveness not only because we are told immediately that Caesar's soldiers are now filled with hope and courage in his vicinity, but also because the narrator concludes both Book 2 and the campaigning season of 57 BCE so decisively: all Gaul has been pacified, the fame of this war has spread, even nations on the other side of the Rhine are promising to obey the general's commands, and back in Rome an unprecedented fifteen days of thanksgiving have been decreed (2.35).

Setbacks, however, soon follow. And across the subsequent books of *The Gallic War*, political stakes and literary expressiveness intensify together. The narrator depicts Caesar's antagonists as gradually mimicking the Romans in technological skill and military acumen, but failing to capture their humanity. Making a last collective effort to win back their ancestral freedoms in the seventh and final book, the Gauls have become a greater menace and, therefore, a greater prize. There Caesar also confronts his most difficult and most richly characterized adversary—the Arvernian chieftain Vercingetorix (whose calls for national liberty are presented as a treacherous ploy masking his personal pursuit of kingship). The two generals stalk each other across the book's first half. The final showdown takes place below the fortified hilltop town of Alesia (modern Alise-Sainte-Reine) which Caesar encircles with highly elaborate siege works to protect his soldiers as they fight inwards against the besieged and outwards against the Gallic relief forces they expect to arrive imminently. The scene is set for another theme of epic poetry like the hero's battlefield exploits—the capture of the enemy city.

The narrator provides substantial details about what happens within Alesia that Julius Caesar could have neither seen nor heard.

Gallic reinforcements have not yet arrived. The corn is all consumed. An assembly is convened to decide on sally or surrender. Critognatus, an Arvernian of high birth and considerable influence, intervenes in direct speech with another option:

> 'What, therefore, is my design? To do as our ancestors did in the war against the Cimbri and Teutones, which was by no means equally momentous who, when driven into their towns, and oppressed by similar privations, supported life by the corpses of those who appeared useless for war on account of their age, and did not surrender to the enemy: and even if we had not a precedent for such cruel conduct, still I should consider it most glorious that one should be established, and delivered to posterity. For in what was that war like this? The Cimbri, after laying Gaul waste, and inflicting great calamities, at length departed from our country, and sought other lands; they left us our rights, laws, lands, and liberty. But what other motive or wish have the Romans, than, induced by envy, to settle in the lands and states of those whom they have learned by fame to be noble and powerful in war, and impose on them perpetual slavery? For they never have carried on wars on any other terms. But if you know not these things which are going on in distant countries, look to the neighbouring Gaul, which being reduced to the form of a province, stripped of its rights and laws, and subjected to Roman despotism, is oppressed by perpetual slavery.'
>
> (*Gallic War* 7.77; tr. McDevitte and Bohn)

Critognatus is permitted to play out a rousing rejection of servitude (*servitus*) and a stirring appeal for Gallic liberty (*libertas*) utilizing a panoply of rhetorical devices that might make a Roman senator proud, such as multiple direct questions, historical exempla (prior Germanic invasion and Roman conquest), alliteration (paralleled in this English translation by 'laws, lands, liberty'), antithesis (cruel/glorious, distant/neighbouring, liberty/slavery), and emphasis through variation (reduced, stripped, subjected, oppressed). Yet the high moral tone is conveniently undermined by his advocacy of cannibalism. Just in case this demonstration of Gallic barbarity is insufficiently clear to Julius Caesar's readers, the speech is introduced as one of 'singular and detestable cruelty'.

When the Romans fight the concluding battle at Alesia under attack from both sides, Caesar is (as always) master of all manoeuvres. And, at the denouement, the spotlight again falls on him joining in the fight, immediately recognizable in the scarlet cloak of the commander-in-chief (7.88). The final stages are clinically executed. In the blunt words of the narrator, 'great slaughter ensues' (*fit magna caedes*). A few more sentences, and Caesar is sitting out at the front of his camp. Before him the Gallic chieftains are surrendering Vercingetorix and laying down their arms.

This is not the end of war in Gaul, but it is almost the end of *The Gallic War*. Although two more years of fighting were needed for total subjugation to be achieved, a sense of narrative closure is arrived at here with the end of the campaigning season and the text's return to Rome—where a thanksgiving of twenty days is decreed. The capture of Alesia and the submission of the leader of all the Gauls were triumphant enough for Julius Caesar's immediate political purposes (one of his officers completes the account of the war in an eighth book published after Caesar's assassination). He also wanted his conquest of Gaul to be remembered in the longer term, as is evident from coins he had minted a few years later (Figure 6.2, a silver denarius of approx. 46–45 BCE showing Caesar's ancestral goddess Venus on the obverse, and on the reverse a trophy of Gallic weapons with a bound male and a grieving female seated underneath it on either side). *The Gallic War* is even designed to celebrate Caesar's fame for posterity, that is for the likes of us. Yet

FIGURE 6.2. Coin of Caesar depicting the conquest of Gaul, *c.*46–45 BCE.

we may find ourselves seeing only poignancy in Caesar's triumphant coinage and siding rather with the judgement of the elder Pliny, who remarked that this 'great slaughter' in Gaul was in truth a great wrong done to the human race (*Natural History* 7.92).

*The Civil War* deals with turbulent events: from January 49 BCE when Caesar crossed into Italy seditiously with his troops because his political advancement was being blocked by traditionalist members of the Senate, through to victory in battle against his rival Pompey in the summer of 48, and on to Pompey's death in Egypt and the commencement of war in Alexandria later that autumn. Like *The Gallic War*, this narrative is incomplete, but rather more disjointed. It manifests the same kind of brisk, plain reportage but strains to deliver it on subject matter that, for its original audience, would have been more disconcerting and more intimate. How do you laud Caesar's virtue when it is being brought to bear violently on fellow Romans? Since many potential readers would have participated in the events narrated, it is more a delicate question of selection, omission, tone, and emphasis than falsification or sheer invention. Both the vocabulary of 'our' and 'their' and the morality of 'victory' have to be translated to a new, unsettling context. Carried over from *The Gallic War*, the deployment of the possessive 'our' (as in our soldiers and our army) again aligns Caesar with the might of Rome and the best interests of the Roman people. He is Rome's embodiment, but this time against the claims of other Romans. 'They'—the Pompeians—are categorized as un-Roman: at best inept, self-interested criminals, at worst cruel barbarians. Caesar's victory is rendered the better outcome of civil war when it is achieved at the expense of opponents like that. Nonetheless, the narrator describes only a few of the Pompeians by name, because Julius Caesar needs some of 'them' to join up with 'us' and cooperate in the anticipated post-war reconstruction. And the deployment of 'we' and 'our' also helps draw readers of *The Civil War* over to Caesar's rather than Pompey's side. If Caesar's army is 'our' army (both Rome's and the reader's), then in reading the text we have already been brought within the reach of his supreme command.

The narrative of *The Civil War* opens with the Roman Senate in turmoil. The Pompeian faction is obstructing the presentation of a letter from Caesar containing only the most reasonable of proposals. They prevent proper debate. The moderate majority are subjected to threats and menaced by the proximity of Pompey's troops. They vote under duress. The Senate is summoned to meet with Pompey at night outside the city where all have to submit to his orders as if they were not senators but subordinate soldiers. Pompey's chief supporters are motivated not by the interests of the Republic (that is *res publicae* or public matters), we are told, but by their own. The narrator provides a substantial and damning list including enmity, resentment, debt, greed, ambition, fear of prosecution, love of luxury, and desire for adulation. While, spurred on by Caesar's enemies and unable to countenance a rival, Pompey has betrayed their former friendship, already exploited scandalous military means to bolster his power, and is eager for war. Grave and extraordinary decrees are passed. The vetoes of the tribunes of the people are unconstitutionally defied, and they are forced to flee from Italy to Caesar for their physical safety. Violating chronology, the narrator puts the loss of due republican process and the destruction of senatorial government first. The laws of god and man have been overturned. Chaos reigns. Consequently, although Caesar prefers peace (according to this account), he must now come to the rescue of the troubled Roman Republic.

Just beyond the border of Italy, Caesar delivers a rousing speech to his troops in which he presents again the injustices that have been inflicted upon him and thus instigated civil war:

> These things being made known to Caesar, he harangued his soldiers; he reminded them of the wrongs done to him at all times by his enemies, and complained that Pompey had been alienated from him and led astray by them through envy and a malicious opposition to his glory, though he had always favoured and promoted Pompey's honour and dignity... He exhorted them to defend from the malice of his enemies the reputation and honour of that general under whose command they had for nine years most successfully supported the state; fought many successful battles, and subdued all Gaul and Germany. The soldiers of the thirteenth legion, which was present (for in the beginning of the disturbances he had called it out, his other legions not having yet arrived), all cry out that they are ready to defend their general, and the tribunes of the commons, from all injuries.
>
> Having made himself acquainted with the disposition of his soldiers, Caesar set off with that legion to Ariminum, and there met the tribunes, who had fled to him for protection; he called his other legions from winter quarters; and ordered them to follow him.
>
> (*Civil War* 1.7–8; tr. McDevitte and Bohn)

Caesar appeals to his soldiers to defend from assault not only the constitutional authority of the tribunes but also his own reputation (*existimatio*) and honour (*dignitas*). The claim that Caesar's personal standing must be protected from injury gains a seemingly natural legitimacy from the context in which the claim is made. Roman soldiers must be loyal to their general. His standing is based on their military conduct. They too (and at great risk) have served the state; therefore they too have been slighted. Thucydides (as we have seen earlier in this book) engages his readers viscerally with the horrors and brutality of civil war when he positions them watching from shore with anguished Greek soldiers, as a brutal sea-battle between Athenians and Spartans progresses right before their eyes. Here, in contrast, readers are positioned among the soldiers of the devoted thirteenth legion, crying out their support, willing Caesar to lead them into civil war. Caesar sets off, as the narrative would have it, in response to his soldiers' will. The narrator conveniently fails to mention that, in doing so, the general has crossed the river Rubicon, entered Italy while still in command of his troops, and, therefore, acted treasonably against both the Senate and the people of Rome.

While the first and second books of *The Civil War* between them contrast what the future might look like after a Caesarian or a Pompeian victory (respectively, order and clemency versus barbarism and cruelty), most of the third book is taken up with the campaign in Greece, and culminates with Caesar's crucial victory over Pompey at Pharsalus in the summer of 48 BCE. Like the audience of a Greek tragedy, readers of the war commentary possess foreknowledge of the outcome. Dark, tragic irony pervades the presentation of Pompey's self-confidence, his hopes and promises for the future. His poor judgement is set against Caesar's far-sighted understanding. Pompey even abandons the field and his men before the battle is completely lost and returns to camp—despite being observed earlier pledging that he would do so only if victorious. Caesar's men swiftly break in (just as, according to the account of Herodotus we touched on in Chapter 3, the Greeks had penetrated into the luxurious Persian camp after the battle of Plataea). The apparently innocent sketch of what the Caesarians find operates simultaneously as acute moral condemnation:

> In Pompey's camp you might see arbours in which tables were laid, a large quantity of plate set out, the floors of the tents covered with fresh sods, the tents of Lucius Lentulus and others shaded with ivy, and many other things which were proofs of excessive luxury, and a confidence of victory, so that it might readily be inferred that they had no apprehensions of the issue of the day, as they indulged themselves in unnecessary pleasures, and yet upbraided with luxury Caesar's army, distressed and long-suffering troops, who had always been in want of common necessaries.
>
> (*Civil War* 3.96; tr. McDevitte and Bohn)

The point of view is that of Caesar's veterans. The initial absence of connectives (arbours, plate, floors, tents) mimics the speed with which they make their shocking discoveries. The Latin text, unusually, adds exotic colouring with the introduction of the Greek word *trichila*: here translated 'arbours', other English translations include 'gazebos' or 'cabanas'. The luxury of which Caesar's men find all this to be evidence is a moral charge (alongside effeminacy) that was regularly levelled against Eastern monarchs. The moral truth is out: it is the hubristic Pompeians who have conducted themselves like soft, despotic barbarians; while the extensive deprivations Caesar's army is said to have suffered marks them as hard, virile men of the good old Republic.

Next, the point of view shifts abruptly:

> Pompey, as soon as our men had forced the trenches, mounting his horse, and stripping off his general's habit, went hastily out of the back gate of the camp, and galloped with all speed to Larissa. Nor did he stop there, but with the same dispatch, collecting a few of his flying troops, and halting neither day nor night, he arrived at the seaside, attended by only thirty horse, and went on board a victualing barque, often complaining, as we have been told, that he had been so deceived in his expectation, that he was almost persuaded that he had been betrayed by those from whom he had expected victory, as they began the fight.

> *(Civil War* 3.96; tr. McDevitte and Bohn)

The change of perspective from Caesar's triumphant soldiers to the defeated enemy commander again detaches the nameless narrator from the general Julius Caesar. Mustn't the narrator be omniscient (perhaps even impartial) if he can accompany Pompey as he flees? That Pompey strips off his general's habit completes physically what has happened to him morally in the course of *The Civil War*. He has been swayed by his officers and tolerated their bickering. His tactics have been poor and his predictions of victory mistaken. He leaves his men behind on the battlefield, departs by the back gate of the camp in haste and in disguise, and sails off in a supply boat. And then has the gall to accuse *his* men of betrayal. Finally, in death, Pompey is stripped of the very last shreds of greatness (and, therefore, of legitimacy): murdered in a small rowboat, by distant Egyptian shores, at the hands of those who once supported him.

*The Civil War* ends abruptly with Caesar in Alexandria, the war not yet over, and the surviving Pompeians still fighting in various quarters of the Mediterranean. Three anonymous commentaries survive on the campaigns Julius Caesar continued to fight until

45 BCE in Egypt, Africa, and Spain, but he wrote nothing about them. Why is that? Suggestions include that he may not have published *The Civil War* in his lifetime and stopped writing it because it ceased to work as a potential means of self-justification. In the war commentary, Caesar is represented as a devoted servant of the Republic, and as a protector of its traditions of government and its citizenry. Yet, as the civil war progressed, the general's powers became in contrast more and more autocratic and the honours he accrued became dangerously regal and divine—until they became intolerable.

The historical figure Julius Caesar has exerted an extraordinary influence on Western culture in quite diverse ways ever since his assassination. The voice of Caesar that emerges from *The Gallic War* and *The Civil War* has also had its own periods of particular popularity. In the early nineteenth century, for example, when in exile, the French Emperor Napoleon Bonaparte dictated an analysis of the war commentaries as a fitting conclusion to a lifelong engagement with *being* Caesar (and *better* than Caesar). Caesar provided Napoleon with models for military strategy and leadership, the seizure of power, and the establishment of both charismatic military rule and empire. No wonder Caesar is not fit for children. His voice may be pure and lucid in form, but it is dark and blood-stained in content. Yet that is all the more reason for us to listen to it and respond.

MW

# VII

# CICERO

Cicero contributed to Rome's political community through his skill at speaking and writing. His words were his life. He did not start out with the advantages of Julius Caesar; he was born some way from Rome, had no particular aptitude for soldiering, and suffered the drawback of being a 'new man'—the first from his family to enter the Senate. Yet the period from the 80s to the 40s BCE is commonly known as 'the age of Cicero' because three-quarters of its surviving literature is by him. It is an astonishingly diverse and vast corpus of published speeches, poetry, letters, and treatises that reflect not only on politics but also on morality, justice, community, humanity, and the supernatural. Egotistical and conservative, Cicero has nonetheless become a symbol of commitment to civic life and resistance to tyranny. Senator, orator, and author in the midst of violent factionalism, he achieved the consulship in 63 BCE. Controversially, he responded as consul to a conspiracy led by the Roman senator Catiline with the execution of some of the co-conspirators. For this controversial act, he was later briefly exiled. On return, he passionately advocated the preservation of republican government. Cicero was murdered in 43 BCE by agents of Mark Antony, heir to Caesar's autocratic power.

Cicero was killed for the eloquence of his speeches, the incisive-ness of his writings and his resistance to tyranny. The ancient details of his murder vary, but they are cumulatively horrific. On 7 December 43 BCE, assassins sent by Mark Antony (who was eager to inherit Julius Caesar's autocratic powers) broke down the doors of Cicero's country retreat. But the Roman senator was not there. They ran after him as he was escaping down a path that led to the sea. Cicero saw them coming and ordered his litter to be set down. Although he was covered in dust and wasted by anxiety, he gazed steadfastly out at his killers. As he stretched his neck out for them, they slit his throat. Then they hacked off his head and hands. They carried back the severed extremities to an exultant Antony in Rome and, on his orders, put them on display high up in the Forum where Cicero had so often and so courageously spoken out against self-interested political ambition. But not before Antony's wife had set the head on her lap, opened its mouth, pulled out its tongue, and stabbed it repeatedly with a hairpin as vengeance for the persuasive power that it had—until recently—possessed. The early nineteenth-century Italian artist, Bartolomeo Pinelli, included a vivid depiction of this dreadful domestic scene as a key event in his illustrated history of ancient Rome (Figure 7.1).

FIGURE 7.1. Mark Antony's wife Fulvia stabs Cicero's tongue with her hairpin, etching by Bartolomeo Pinelli in *L'Istoria Romana*, 1818–19.

From our great distance, we cannot know quite which details of this story are true. Not least because Cicero's death quickly became the stuff of legend—for its horror, its bravery, and its political significance. Roman boys were allocated the moment of the murder as a classroom exercise. Argue a case with Cicero—should he accept a terrible death and the mutilation of his corpse to save Rome from tyranny or should he burn his speeches to save himself? Which is the greater good: love of country or of life? With the silencing of Cicero, Rome had lost not just a great orator, writer, and politician but also—according to some—liberty itself and the freedom of speech liberty permits. I start with the murder of Cicero because, in retrospect for us too, it adds to his voice a profoundly symbolic and modern resonance. And it makes of the time before his murder a period when government was still by the voice (and the pen) of its citizens, and not by the sword of its generals or the daggers of their henchmen.

Marcus Tullius Cicero speaks, writes, and acts at the centre of a world that is deeply and protractedly disturbed. He bears witness to extreme political violence and factionalism. He ascends triumphantly to the pinnacle of public office and suffers the tragic fall of exile. He endures the rise of autocracy, and seeks to prevent the complete destruction of republican government and the creation of permanent one-man rule. His writings are themselves designed as a mode of political and ethical *action*. The word is put in service to the civic community. The peculiarities of Roman life give the word such potent force. Women, slaves, and foreigners are deprived of public expression and standing, but an ambitious male citizen conducts most of his life as an intensely competitive public performance. Speaking to persuade is an integral part of that performance (whether prosecuting or defending a court case before a jury, electioneering, legislating, or policy-making before the Senate or the Roman people), and a route by which to win fame and advance your career. Voice and gesture can make or break you (not least when, like Cicero, you cannot substitute the authority that accrues from noble birth, great wealth, or military prowess). You need to hone your skills at inventing arguments, arranging topics, choosing the most appropriate style and techniques for your delivery, and committing all your finely chosen words to memory. There were no autocues in antiquity.

In our era of social media, political sound bites, pithy headlines, and the microscopic analysis of material forensic evidence, we none-theless still need on occasion to persuade others of our view through sustained, affecting speech, and Cicero still offers extraordinary, exuberant lessons in the art of eloquence:

> The very thing that was most to be desired, members of the jury, the one thing that will have most effect in reducing the hatred felt towards your order and restoring the tarnished reputation of the courts, this it is which, in the current political crisis, has been granted and presented to you; and this opportunity has come about not, it would appear, by human planning, but virtually by the gift of the gods. For a belief, disastrous for the state and dangerous for you, has become widespread, and has been increasingly talked about not only among ourselves but among foreign peoples as well—the belief that, in these courts as they are currently constituted, it is impossible for a man with money, no matter how guilty he may be, to be convicted. Now, at this moment of reckoning for your order and your courts, when people are ready to use public meetings and legislation to stoke up this hatred of the senate, a defendant has been put on trial—Gaius Verres, a man already convicted, according to universal public opin-ion, by his character and actions, but already acquitted, according to his own hopes and assertions, by his immense wealth.

I have taken on this prosecution, gentlemen, with the complete support and confidence of the Roman people, not because I want to increase the hatred felt towards your order, but in order to mend the tarnished reputation which we both share.

(*Against Verres*, 1.1–2; tr. D. H. Berry)

Here Cicero is introducing the first of a series of speeches he had prepared in the prosecution of Verres, the outgoing governor of Sicily, who was being brought to trial in August 70 BCE for the corruption and extortion in which he had indulged throughout his ruthless administration. Sufficiently captured in this English translation are the Roman orator's sonorous rhetorical strategies of repetition, variation, exaggeration, and emphasis. It is not just Verres that he puts on trial. The verdict of guilt or innocence will reflect inversely upon the fairness of the law courts, the integrity of the political order of the Senate (to which at this point membership of juries had been controversially limited), and the international reputation of Rome. Cicero aligns himself emotionally both with the jury (*ourselves*, a tarnished reputation which *we both share*) and against it (*your* order, *your* courts). They are the hated Senate, he the prosecutor supported confidently by the people. And, thus, climactically, it is Cicero himself who is positioned as the giver of the desired, opportune, heaven-sent gift that will stem the current crisis and rescue the reputation of the courts, the Senate, even the whole state (namely the submission of evidence to justify a verdict of the ex-governor's guilt and, consequently, the Senate's innocence).

Cicero's speeches are valued for their exceptional prose style, legal and political expertise, and persuasive power (most critics think only this first of the prosecution speeches was actually delivered for, disheartened, Verres absented himself from court soon after it and then of his own accord fled into exile). Yet they have also been admired for their admixture of eloquence and a 'conceptual inventiveness' or contemplative intelligence almost always directed at the well-being of the body politic. It was characterized as Cicero's 'wisdom' in the Renaissance. In the case of the speeches against Verres, for example, the Roman advocate reflects upon non-citizen rights and freedoms, honesty, justice, and fair government. Cicero's speeches were published as contemporary self-advertisements, lessons for future orators, contributions to literature, and lasting articulations of issues that should concern us all. What makes a good citizen? What constitutes justice? Is there a law of nature? Do we have an inner conscience that can torment us? What is the best form of government? In what does our shared humanity consist? What might make us humane or happy? Is the universe meaningful? Should we fear death?

Such questions as these are addressed more directly in Cicero's essays, where he sought from philosophy a practical guide to the right kind of civic life. During the dictatorship of Julius Caesar (in the period 45 to 44 BCE), Cicero found in philosophical writing a fragile consolation for the recent death of his daughter Tullia and another way to work for the good of the state when the courts were suspended, the Senate no longer properly autonomous, and access to the assembly of the Roman people obstructed. But what kind of educational mischief was afoot when, at my London convent school, we were prescribed one of these treatises—*On the Nature of the Gods*—as a Latin text for study? From late antiquity, its second book had been exhibited as a handy refutation of pagan religion and defence of Christian doctrine:

And in truth, if you see some great and beautiful building, would you infer, because the architect is not immediately visible, that it must have been built by mice and weasels? It is the same with all the splendour of the world, all the multitudinous beauty of the heavens, all the power and glory over land and sea. Can anyone among us be so mad as to imagine that we can claim to be the lords and masters of these dwelling-places of almighty God? And do we not even understand that what is higher is always better? The earth however lies low and is surrounded by a dense atmosphere: and just as we see it happen in some towns and districts that the minds of the inhabitants are dulled by the heaviness of the air, so it happens also in some degree to the whole human race, because they are earthbound at the misty bottom of the universe. But even from our natural wit, such as it is, we may infer the existence of some divine intelligence more powerful than our own.

(*On the Nature of the Gods*, 2.17; tr. J. M. Ross)

When I pick up the Latin text now, almost forty years later, I find that we had clearly been far too busy analysing Cicero's long, elaborately composed sentences, the musical rhythms of his phrasing, his mastery of rhetorical figures (ranging from anaphora to wordplay), to pick up on the dialogic structure of his narrative. It turns out that we were like the poor, dull residents of that murky town situated at the lowest point of the mist-bound earth at the very bottom of the bright universe. For this argument for the existence of a supreme deity based on the beauty of nature is not presented as Cicero's own and is challenged by a more sceptical speaker in the third book. By the end of the work, religion is not overthrown nor deity denied (all men, we learn, are animated by a divine spark that connects them to the universe and to each other and obliges them to care for the world and for their fellow men). Instead, we find a sceptic's recognition of the difficulties attached to the formulation of a rational theology. There can be no certainties. The dialogue form permits the exposition of conflicting doctrines and invites the reader to judge which of them is most reasonable. The approach is pleasingly disputatious and one that I would have welcomed when faced with the monologic sermons and dogmatism of my own Catholic education. It seems that our priests and nuns were more obedient disciples of the early Church father Tertullian than of the Roman sceptic Cicero: 'Once we have Jesus Christ, we need no further curiosity; once we have the gospel, no further inquiry' (Tertullian, *The Prescription against Heretics* 7).

In the last, most violent phase of the Roman republic, when the governing classes were competing ever more ferociously among themselves for the greatest power, public speaking took on renewed importance. So, after Julius Caesar was assassinated on the Ides of March 44 BCE, when Mark Antony was intimidating Roman citizens with a huge bodyguard of the dictator's veterans, when the assassins Brutus and Cassius had already left the city, it was through speeches (both spoken and written) that Cicero repeatedly attempted to change the course of events—to save Rome from yet another (perhaps more tyrannical) dictatorship, to restore her to the traditional order of republican government.

It was Cicero himself who first cast a heroic mantle over the speeches that would bring about his death (fourteen survive, more may have been in circulation in antiquity). He suggested for them the title 'Philippics'. *Philippics*: to imply that Mark Antony was as dangerous to republican Rome as Philip, King of Macedon, had once been to democratic Athens. *Philippics*: to elevate Cicero to the level of the great statesman Demosthenes, who had attacked King Philip so fluently three centuries earlier. Cicero began their delivery on 2 September 44 BCE, with a relatively reasoned yet defiant and forceful appeal to Antony—full of references to 'respect' and 'friendship'—advising him not to exceed the powers he had been granted by the state and instead to serve the Republic. Within days, Antony denounced to the Senate both Cicero's character and his career. Even though Cicero was not present to hear Antony's tirade, he wrote his second *Philippic* as if he had replied there and then, face to face. It remains one of his most famous works.

After first defending his own prestige, Cicero turns on Antony and demolishes *his* with an assault on his morals. Cicero begins with the private life of his opponent conducted scandalously from the moment he became a youth and right through his adulthood:

> Then you assumed the toga of manhood—and immediately turned it into a toga of womanhood. First you were a common prostitute: you had a fixed rate for your shameful services, and not a low one either. But soon Curio appeared on the scene. He saved you from having to support yourself as a prostitute, fitted you out in the dress of a married lady, as it were, and settled you in good, steady wedlock. No slave boy bought for sexual gratification was ever as much in his master's power as you were in Curio's. How many times did his father throw you out of his house! How many times did he post guards to stop you crossing his threshold! But you, with night to aid you, lust to drive you, and the prospect of payment to compel you, had yourself lowered in through the roof-tiles.
>
> (*Philippic* 2.44–5; tr. D. H. Berry)

We might find this personalizing of politics vicious and improper. But in ancient Rome, invective was a very common means of political debate. You take the moral high ground and, in colourful, witty turns of phrase, you attack your opponent where it hurts Romans the most: (if you can) foreign ancestors, servile birth, unpleasant appearance, (otherwise, or in addition) sexual and gender perversion, dissipation, extravagance, indebtedness, cowardice. So what is remarkable here is not that Cicero mocks Antony, but *how* he does it. Antony begins life as an effeminate prostitute (and a pretty good one at that) and then is promoted to wife. The process is depicted brilliantly as a ridiculous perversion of a Roman wedding, where the bride is brought solemnly into the house of her husband. The vivid plot twists—the angry father, the locked door, the guards, and the tenacious lover—are all borrowed from the comic stage. The detailed anecdote climaxes with three hierarchical impulsions (night aids, lust drives, *the prospect of payment* compels) and re-entry over the roof tiles. Would you trust government to a 'man' who is mastered by his sex drive?

Cicero then attacks with equal venom the ways in which Antony's immorality has disrupted his public life:

> You with that gullet of yours, that chest, that gladiator's physique downed such a quantity of wine at Hippias' wedding that you were forced to throw up in full view of the Roman people—the next day. What a disgusting sight—disgusting even to hear of! Had this happened to you at dinner, as you knocked back bottle after bottle, is there anyone who would not have thought it outrageous? But at a gathering of the Roman people, while conducting public business, as Master of the Horse, when a mere belch would have been shocking, he vomited, filling his lap and the whole platform with morsels of food stinking of wine!
>
> (*Philippic* 2.63; tr. D. H. Berry)

Cicero strives to bring an intensely repugnant scene before his readers' eyes. He first stresses Antony's misdirected bodily capacities; the gullet, the chest, the physique fit for a gladiator not a Roman soldier. He emphasizes that Antony had not even recovered THE NEXT DAY. He exaggerates heavily. Antony *fills* his lap and the *whole* speakers' platform. And he ends with a description to repel our senses of sight, sound, and smell—those wine-reeking bits of vomit drenching the centre of government. Roman invective works to strip its targets of their various identities as a noble (*nobilis*), a citizen (*civis*), a man (*vir*) and a human being (*homo*). To be labelled a woman or a gladiator is to be radically diminished in status and disenfranchised from Roman civil society. Soon Cicero will attempt to dehumanize and demonize his opponent too.

In September 44 BCE, Mark Antony was the highest elected magistrate of Rome—a consul and a commander of legions. Yet with his second *Philippic* (and, possibly, the frankness afforded by private circulation), Cicero managed to ridicule him, diminish his moral authority, and exhibit him as unsuitable to govern Rome. When, soon after, Antony left the city, Cicero radically changed the strategy of his remaining speeches. To convince the largely unsympathetic senators and people not to send an embassy to negotiate with Antony, to push them away from appeasement and into a declaration of war against a fellow Roman, he now uses a sharper weapon, namely the invective of monstrosity:

> But this most hideous monster, who can endure him or how? What is there in Antony save lust, cruelty, insolence, audacity? He is entirely made up of these vices glued together. No trace in him of gentlemanly feeling, of moderation, of self-respect, of modesty. Therefore, since it has now come to this critical question, whether he pays his penalty to the Republic or we become slaves, by the Immortal Gods!, members of the Senate, let us at last take our fathers' heart and courage, resolving to regain the freedom that belongs to the Roman race and name or to prefer death to slavery.
>
> (*Philippic* 3.28–9; tr. G. Manuwald)

Antony is composed from vices. He lacks any of the virtues that give a man substance. He is a physically and morally repellent monster or beast (*belua*). You cannot negotiate with a beast, but you do have the human resources to beat it in a fight. Here Cicero also draws on and positions himself within the commanding rhetoric of national crisis: the situation is critical; we must marshal the resolve of our ancestors; the freedom of the Romans is at stake. And he utilizes a rousing 'disjunctive mode' as he so often does as the *Philippics* proceed. There is no middle course, no appeasement, no third way: the decision is between the monster's punishment and our enslavement; the struggle is over slavery (*servitus*) or freedom (*libertas*); the preference over slavery is for death.

Later on, in January 43, Cicero incarnates the Roman Republic as a combative entity:

> Therefore, members of the senate, in my judgement no mention should be made of envoys. I think things should be put in hand without any delay and prosecuted at once. I say that a state of civil war should be recognized, suspension of business proclaimed, military cloaks donned and a levy held with no exemptions in the city and in the whole of Italy . . . If these measures are adopted, the mere opinion and report of our sternness will crush the felonious gladiator's madness. He will realize that he has taken up arms against the Republic; he will feel the sinews and strength of a united Senate.
>
> (*Philippic* 5.31–2; tr. G. Manuwald)

The Senate is envisaged as a corporeal adversary, strong enough to retaliate and crush the mad gladiator. By now Antony has been branded more tyrannical than the early kings of Rome, and crueller than Rome's worst foreign foes. He is no true Roman, but an enemy of the state (a *hostis*). And always this moment is critical.

This moment requires immediate action. This moment calls for all-out war.

The series of *Philippics* ended with an all too cursory moment of political success for Cicero—Antony was defeated in battle but only temporarily; later still he would be declared a public enemy but not in time to save Cicero. While Cicero constructed in his speeches a vision of himself as political hero, critic of autocracy and protector of traditional republican liberties, many modern scholars have countered that he not only failed to match up to that vision but was in fact instrumental in the Republic's ruin. Against the auto-cratic aspirations of Antony, he foolishly praised and even collab-orated with Caesar's heir, Octavian—later known as Augustus and as first emperor of Rome. At worst, as a politician Cicero emerges from this revisionary perspective as inept, compromised, vain, and con-stantly vacillating. Not a crusader against autocrats, then, but their dancing puppet. However, to those of us unmoved by Cicero's commitment to aristocratic rule and pragmatic conservatism, these failings can form part of his modern appeal as an instance of human fragility in the corrupting atmosphere of politics.

To the voice of Cicero the public speaker and philosopher-statesman, his hundreds and hundreds of surviving letters add many more expressive tones. Although carefully composed, and most fre-quently concerned with political and social dealings between men of the Roman elite, most do not appear to have been designed for widespread or lasting distribution (although, towards the end of his life, Cicero seems to have contemplated their selective publication). So, when we read them now, some seem uniquely to draw us right inside the ways of thinking and feeling of the ancient world. Here is Cicero writing to his wife Terentia on 29 April 58 BCE. Some fifteen years before his noble assaults on Antony, Cicero has been sentenced to exile (the supreme punishment Rome could inflict upon its citizens) for the controversial decision he had made during his consulship to execute conspirators against the state. He is thus travelling away from the city into anticipated disgrace, poverty, and near death:

> Poor me, I am ruined, and in dire straits! What am I to do? Beg you to join me, when you are a sick woman, prostrated in body and mind? Or should I *not* beg you, and as a result be without you? This is the course, I think, that I shall follow: if there is a prospect of my return, you must strengthen and assist the process. But if, as I myself fear, the door is closed on me, then join me in any way you can. Be assured of this one fact: so long as I have you, I shall not regard myself as utterly lost. But what will become of my fond Tullia? You must together look to this, for I have no counsel to offer. However the situation develops, the poor girl's marriage and fair name at any rate must be safeguarded. Then again, what is to become of my Cicero? I cannot write more on this now, for I am choked with grief.
>
> (*Letters to Friends*, 14.4.3; tr. P. G. Walsh)

Little other literature from ancient Rome presents us with the marital passion and familial affection expressed here so pitifully. The husband is all too aware that he has damaged his wife's domestic security, endangered the marriage prospects of his beloved daughter, and destroyed the future career of his young son. A sudden exclamation of grief. An agonized set of questions. Concern for his wife's health holds him back from asking her to join him, whilst love impels him to do just that. In a tragic paradox, hope would mean separation, fear reunion. Companionship in suffering provides great comfort, but consideration of the plight of his two children leads on to grief and an expressive interruption of writing.

In contrast, a boastful, unpleasant egotist emerges in a later letter addressed to one of the assassins of Julius Caesar, Gaius Trebonius. On the fateful Ides of 44 BCE, in the year before this letter was written, Trebonius had pulled Antony to one side so that the conspirators could do their work undisturbed. Cicero suggests that now it is up to Cicero—and Cicero alone—metaphorically to finish off the patriotic undertaking they had merely started:

> How I wish that you had invited me to that most attractive feast on the Ides of March! We would have had no left-overs. But as things stand, the left-overs have caused such complications! That sacred service you rendered to the state is arousing some complaints. Indeed, since you, excellent man that you are, took that plague-ridden man aside and through your kindness he is still alive, this induces me from time to time to feel irritated with you (an attitude verging on impiety), for you have bequeathed to me more troubles than to all others.
>
> As soon as a meeting of the Senate could be held in freedom following Antony's most disgraceful departure, I restored that attitude of old which you, in company with your father, that most incisive citizen, always proclaimed and loved.
>
> (*Letters to Friends*, 10.28.1; tr. P. G. Walsh)

Other letters composed in the same period as the *Philippics* speak of Antony's disturbingly menacing tactics. They disclose Cicero's plans to escape overseas, or find him hesitating because he feels a sense of duty. Set alongside Cicero's murder and mutilation, such letters add a terrible poignancy and tragic splendour to Cicero's self-portrayal in the speeches as the defender of Rome's freedom against Antony's threats of enslavement:

> I defended this country when I was a young man: I shall not desert it now that I am old. I faced down the swords of Catiline: I shall not flinch before yours. Yes, and I would willingly offer my body, if the freedom of this country could at once be secured by my death, and

the suffering of the Roman people at last be delivered of that with which it has so long been pregnant. If nearly twenty years ago in this very temple I declared that death could not be untimely for a man who had reached the consulship, with how much more truth could I now say 'for an old man'? In fact, for me, conscript fathers, death is actually desirable now that I have discharged the responsibilities of the offices I attained and completed the tasks I undertook. Two things alone I long for: first, that when I die I may leave the Roman people free—the immortal gods could bestow on me no greater blessing; and, second, that each person's fate may reflect the way he has behaved towards his country.

(*Philippic* 2.118–19; tr. D. H. Berry)

Just over a year after writing these affecting, patriotic words, Cicero (we are told) faced death without flinching. The *Philippics* already contain an acknowledgement of that impending end. They already accept that political life at Rome has changed irrevocably—for Cicero and Antony never came face to face in senatorial debate in all the months after Julius Caesar's death. The issue is civil war; in that terrible predicament, failure to persuade will mean death. And the Republic itself is already dying; for power has shifted out of the senate house and onto the battlefield. Control of legions not votes now carries the day.

In these last months of Cicero's life, across his speeches, letters, and treatises, we have the privilege to observe him (as one critic so strikingly puts it) 'writing himself into courage'. *On Obligations* (also known as *On Duties*) is an ethical handbook addressed in particular to his son and directed more broadly to Rome's governing class. Its musings on honourable and beneficial courses of action would become hugely influential across the centuries. In it we also encounter Cicero depicting a man he has not yet (and may never quite) become: the very best kind of man—the ideal statesman.

The sober and courageous citizen who merits leadership of the state … will devote himself wholeheartedly to the state, will seek no resources or power for himself, and will protect the whole in such a way as to maintain the interests of the individual. He will not level false charges against any person and thus expose him to hatred or jealousy, and he will cleave so closely to justice and integrity that so long as he preserves them, he will endure any setback however daunting, and he will confront death rather than abandon those virtues which I mentioned.

(*On Obligations* 1.86; tr. P. G. Walsh)

It is not Cicero's political ineptitude, flaws and failings, then, that still catch our imagination and encourage political action. Rather it is this inspirational ethical lesson on how to be the best citizen delivered by a man who died trying to become one.

Cicero's life, his works, and his death have together taken on a powerful and long-lasting symbolic significance. He possesses 'the last voice of freedom' before tyranny takes hold. He lives and dies for the principle of 'the rule of law against the rule of force'. The mutilation of his tongue embodies 'the silencing of dissent to a new world order'. Might we succeed where he did not? From the Middle Ages through the Italian Renaissance, the English republican movement of the seventeenth century, and on into and beyond the American and the French revolutions of the eighteenth, many have wished to speak, write, and act as this *ideal* Cicero. A number of the American revolutionaries and Founding Fathers would have taken real pleasure in being labelled 'the American Cicero', excited by the prospect of renewing against British tyranny their ancient heroes' noble struggles for liberty. For example, John Adams, as lawyer, revolutionary, and second President of the United States, developed his own political identity and purpose from Cicero.

1545 - ROMA - Cicerone - Museo Capitolino - Anderson

FIGURE 7.2. Portrait bust of Cicero, mid first century CE.

He regularly read the Roman orator's speeches aloud. They offered, he remarked, the pleasure of their musicality, exercise for his lungs, and uplift for his spirits—in short, complete well-being. He drew on his readings of Cicero in debate and decision-making and tried to put into practice the difficult lesson of *On Obligations* 1.86: 'He will adhere closely to justice and equity, that, provided he can preserve these virtues, although he may give offence and create enemies by them, he will set death itself at defiance, rather than abandon his principles', in an older translation cited by Adams. During retirement, Adams continued to read, quote, and protect the reputation of his favoured Roman statesman. And just before his death in 1826, a portrait bust of Adams was sculpted in order to capture his wish to be memorialized materially and permanently as America's Cicero (Figures 7.2 and 7.3).

In the twenty-first century, Cicero continues to be part of political discourse about the United States. On the left, some commentators have described President Barack Obama as a new American Cicero for the stirring eloquence of his public speaking (*The Guardian*, 26 November 2008) or for his successful displacement of a purportedly dictatorial administration. On the right, Obama becomes the next American Caesar in need of a new Cicero to denounce him for acting above the law (*Washington Times*, 16 June 2011). But Cicero is also more than a potent name. For example, Scott Horton, the legal affairs and national security contributor to *Harper's Magazine*, regularly threads through his 'No Comment' blog quotations in both English and Latin from the works of Cicero. *On Obligations* made an appearance on 1 May 2010 to support his argument that American government officials must place their loyalty to the law and the Constitution above their loyalty to the President. Cicero's treatise is described as a modern manifesto for 'the preservation of the Republic in the face of an autocratic onslaught'. The desire to

0100969    JOHN ADAMS (1735-1826).
Credit: The Granger Collection, New York

FIGURE 7.3. Portrait bust of John Adams by John Browere (from a life mask), 1825.

speak and write and act as a modern Cicero does not cease. After all, for most of us it is indeed heartening to believe that civilian government can control military force, and that the word can be mightier than the sword.

MW

# VIII

# VIRGIL

Virgil's poetry invites its readers to associate the author with the landscape of Italy, both beautiful and demanding. Ancient biographies (often built out of inferences from the poems and expectations about how poets lived) place Virgil's birth near Mantua in northern Italy around 70 BCE. They depict him as rustic and shy, living a contemplative life on his small family farm until driven from it after 41 BCE, when properties were redistributed to veterans of the civil war as rewards. The story goes that the poet quickly regained his farm thanks to his Roman patrons (possibly even the future emperor Augustus himself) and incorporated his grati-tude into the verses of his first, pastoral, poem the *Eclogues*. His second work composed during the 30s, a poetic manual for farmers called the *Georgics*, takes agricultural labour as a metaphor for life—our hard efforts may bring fruit or failure. In his poetic career, Virgil steadily moved up the literary genres from pastoral, through didactic, to his epic the *Aeneid*. When Virgil died in 19 BCE, he left orders in his will to burn this already celebrated poem as unfinished. Yet it has been loved across the centuries for the perfection of its verse and its embrace of both darkness and light. Virgil was soon so revered that, in the Middle Ages, he was treated as a magician whose poetry could predict its reader's future.

The mezzo-soprano Sarah Connolly explains how best to sing the profoundly melancholic lament of the abandoned African queen Dido: let it come from deep within yourself; draw on your own most intimate experiences. The celebrated lament—for love's betrayal, life's fragility, and the sorrows that suicide brings to your family—is addressed by the queen to her sister at the close of Purcell's opera *Dido and Aeneas*:

> Thy hand, Belinda, darkness shades me,
> On thy bosom let me rest,
> More I would, but Death invades me;
> Death is now a welcome guest.
>
> When I am laid, am laid in earth, may my wrongs create
> No trouble, no trouble in thy breast;
> Remember me, remember me, but ah! forget my fate.
> Remember me, but ah! forget my fate.

In a performance at London's Royal Opera House in 2009, Connolly as the ancient queen holds out her arms at this point in a shocking display of both emotional and physical suffering. And soon her sister will herself lament over that wounded body (Figure 8.1). Along with Dido's sister, we cannot fail to remember both the woman *and* her fate—love for her princely guest Aeneas that has been shabbily betrayed, abandonment, anguish, and death.

FIGURE **8.1.** Dido's sister (Lucy Crowe) laments over the body of the queen (Sarah Connolly) in Purcell's *Dido and Aeneas*, performed at London's Royal Opera House in 2009.

Each time Purcell's seventeenth-century opera is performed on the modern stage, we are overwhelmed once again by that tragic voice: the voice of Woman who pays a terrible price for standing in the way of Man's epic quest.

Purcell's music showcases a woman's voice and the libretto accentuates her sorrow. While Aeneas is a trickster who scuttles silently off stage in order to fulfil his mission to reach Italy and to establish Rome and empire, Dido is honourable in her life and moving in her death, pleading to be remembered in the descending semitones of the ground bass. However, the queen is neither the beginning nor the end of the story in the opera's celebrated Latin source. In Virgil's epic poem the *Aeneid*, her grief is imprisoned in a grander narrative that holds all the fated travails of the exiled hero: his perilous escape from the burning city of Troy, his fugitive wanderings across the Mediterranean, his testing search for a mysterious new land in which to make his home, his battles fought against hostile inhabitants, and his relentless obstruction by the goddess Juno's careless anger. After all, how does the epic commence?—*arma uirumque cano* ('of weapons and a man I sing'). So whom should you care about the most? And whom do you care about the most? Woman or man? Dido and her love, or Aeneas and his war?

Composed towards the end of the first century before the Christian era (across the years 29 to 19 BCE), Virgil's twelve-book epic poem follows Homer in telling both the Odyssean journey of Aeneas and his Iliadic battles. Yet the poem's sophisticated play with time transcends the Greek epics. We experience only one year of the hero's harrowing life but are invited to look beyond its location in Greek myth far forward into Roman history: beyond Aeneas's arrival in Italy, the foundation of his city, the ultimate transfer of power to Rome, right up to the here-and-now of the 20s BCE and the military and political triumph of Rome's new (and sole) ruler Augustus. Yet, like Purcell, Virgil asks us to remember the agony of his poem's Dido. And were we to weep for her, we would join good company—Saint Augustine (shedding tears for her fate as a schoolboy in Africa in the fourth century) included.

In the first book of the *Aeneid*, the epic hero has been shipwrecked on North African shores and welcomed by Queen Dido into the new city of Carthage which she is building for her own displaced people. By the start of Book 4, he has completed for her his recollections of prior tribulations and fallen silent. Now the queen, who has been listening intently, experiences an erotic injury that burns. Through the imagery of fire and wounds, Dido's desire (*cura*) becomes almost a physical entity. Desire makes her ache. It runs through her veins. It eats her away from within. When the queen proceeds to pray for guidance at her city's shrines, Virgil again draws on the metaphor of love as fire and wound:

> Alas, what darkened minds have soothsayers!
> What good are shrines and vows to maddened lovers?
> The inward fire eats the soft marrow away,
> And the internal wound bleeds on in silence.
> Unlucky Dido, burning, in her madness
> Roamed through all the city, like a doe
> Hit by an arrow shot from far away
> By a shepherd hunting in the Cretan woods—
> Hit by surprise, nor could the hunter see
> His flying steel had fixed itself in her;
> But though she runs for life through copse and glade
> The fatal shaft clings to her side.
>
> (*Aen.* 4.65–73; tr. R. Fitzgerald)

The simile links the metaphorical wound of love to the literal wound made by an arrow. It also links woman with animal, love with the hunt, and man with the hunter. Through this traditional epic device, the poet interweaves a dense layer of interpretation into the action and invites our pity for the queen. The doe suggests innocence. The hunt violence. The wound suffering. The shepherd-hunter (even if he does not notice his hit) a purposeful expedition. The lethal shaft clinging to the deer's side as she runs for her life offers us a vivid image of Dido's condition: ensnared, injured, and bound to die.

Later in the fourth book, we fear for the Carthaginian queen's safety when we discover her literally out on a hunt with the Trojan prince (recall the doe fatally wounded by the hunter). Now the goddesses of love (Venus) and weddings (Juno) together orchestrate a thunderstorm that forces the mortal pair to take shelter in a cave. From Dido's perspective, the physical union which ensues consti-tutes a binding marriage. Aeneas, playing husband, lingers with her in Carthage until a divine messenger is sent to remind him of his destiny—to establish a new home for his Trojans in Italy, to create a new kingdom in the west for his son to inherit, to begin the grand history of Rome. The apparition amazes and shocks the hero. Instantly he burns not for the sweet life which has detained him but to be gone. His concern is how to tell the impassioned queen about his departure. Dido's emotional responses to this news, in her speeches and soliloquies of Book 4, range over disbelief, anguish, hate, and vengeful fury. Aeneas remains 'duty-bound' (*pius* is a recurring epithet for him throughout the poem), struggling physically with his feelings yet always obedient to the divinely ordered course. Virgil asks us to ponder the merits of a 'duty' (*pietas*) that involves self-abnega-tion of this magnitude. Should it be more important than desire?

The hero finally slashes his mooring-rope after the divine vision comes again to warn him against the dangers of womankind: 'Woman's a thing | Forever fitful and forever changing' (*uarium et mutabile semper | femina*, Aen. 4.569–70). Here the Latin contemptuously attaches neuter adjectives to 'woman'. Woman is a fitful and forever changing *thing*. Yet the remainder of the fourth book builds up an elaborate and moving picture of an extraordinarily tormented *person*—a Dido who is steadfastly resolved to die. All attention is given over to the desperate queen, not the departed hero. And her suicide retains an erotic colouring: frantic, with bloodshot eyes and quivering cheeks, pale with coming death, she bursts into the recesses of her palace, climbs the high pyre, and bares her beloved's sword. Her sister and companions draw us in to bear sorrowful witness to her bloodied hands, the steel blade, and the gash in her chest that hisses air. Now, finally, women cry out in their grief as Dido's wound ceases to be metaphor. Virgil encourages us to understand (remember again the simile of the hunter who wounds and kills the doe) that Aeneas inflicted this pain, and that Dido is pitifully innocent.

Even the epic narrator speaks to the queen empathetically, calls her pitiable and her death undeserved, cries out 'Unconscionable Love, | To what extremes will you not drive our hearts!' (*Aen.* 4.412). In front of epic scenery, performed by mythic queens and princely leaders, driven by divine machinery, we observe the tragedy of our human condition played out as elevated drama. In Virgil's epic, as in Purcell's opera, Dido articulates and projects on a majestic scale our own love betrayed, our shame, our loathing, our desire to die. Love, in truth, propels mortal hearts (*mortalia pectora*, Aen. 4.412) to bitter extremes. Throughout the centuries, again and again, artists (Henry Purcell and his librettist Nahum Tate included) have responded to Virgil's moving depiction of the suicide of the Carthaginian queen. Her suffering offers a secular counterpart to that of the Christian saints and martyrs and has left a strong impression in Western music, art, and literature. In the *Aeneid*, the anguish of Woman is set against Man's glorious fate. Yet, although Dido haunts us, the epic poem also calls upon us to remember and to rejoice at the Roman destiny of Aeneas. It is the triumphant 'Augustan' voice (as it is often called) that, in the twentieth century and beyond, many who have encountered the epic poem have wanted to challenge or refuse to hear.

We are using the metaphor of 'voices' in this book to suggest that even in modern times many classical texts can and do speak to us in ways that feel direct, intimate, even visceral. The texts speak (not always familiarly), we respond (not always comfortably). A dialogue emerges, sometimes of such intensity that it can have effects on the way we think or the way we live. The metaphor of 'voices' has also been employed regularly by classical scholars since the second half of the twentieth century to understand the complex tonality of the *Aeneid*. There is more than one voice for us to hear. Perhaps there are many. Within the heart-breaking cries of Dido, for example, there seems to resonate the fury of Euripides' murderous Medea. That literary echo renders Dido more violent and menacing. A premonition within the mythic time of the poem of the dangerous historical forces (the power of the Carthaginian empire in the Mediterranean, the seductions of Queen Cleopatra VII) that must be overcome for imperial Rome to rise and for Augustus to assume its command.

On 2 September 31 BCE, just a few years before Virgil began his epic poem, Augustus (then known as Gaius Julius Octavianus) defeated Mark Antony and Cleopatra at the sea battle of Actium. He emerged from civil war nominally as the Republic's 'first citizen' (*princeps*) but effectively became an autocrat ruling over Rome's world-empire. Despite contemporary declarations that the Republic would now be restored, the period of victory at Actium is conventionally marked by modern historians as ending Rome's republican system of government and opening the way to a new monarchical dynasty. It can therefore be disquieting to discover that the purpose of the *Aeneid* was bluntly described by a fourth-century commentator as being 'to imitate Homer and to praise Augustus through his ancestors'. The myth of Aeneas was not just the prerogative of poets. An official coin minted in Sicily during the years when Virgil was writing his poem captures a moment in the hero's story that had already become and would continue to be iconic (Figure 8.2). On one side of the coin Aeneas advances on his journey to Italy clutching a sacred statuette and carrying his father. His journey is

FIGURE 8.2. Sicilian coin minted *c.*27–21 BCE pairing Augustus on one side with Aeneas on the other.

overseen by Jupiter's eagle. The other side displays his journey's end—Augustus. The coupling on the coin proclaims the fitness of the *princeps* to govern: belonging to the family of Julius Caesar, which traced itself back to Aeneas (via his son variously known as Ascanius or Iulus); descendant of the goddess Venus and her son, Aeneas, the saviour-hero who had founded the Roman race.

Like the state coinage, the pivotal sixth book of the *Aeneid* also links Augustus to Aeneas as the hero's descendant and divinely ordained ruler of empire. Rome's foundation and history falls outside the primary, mythic time-frame of the poem, so it must enter the epic as a promise for the future. Aeneas has arrived on Italian shores and travelled down into the underworld in order to learn from the ghost of his father Anchises about what is to come. Anchises points out to his quizzical son a parade of souls who, made forgetful of their earlier lives, are waiting to be reborn. Deep among them is Augustus:

> 'Turn your two eyes
> This way and see this people, your own Romans.
> Here is Caesar, and all the line of Iulus,
> All who shall one day pass under the dome
> Of the great sky: this is the man, this one,
> Of whom so often you have heard the promise,
> Caesar Augustus, son of the deified,
> Who shall bring once again an Age of Gold
> To Latium, to the land where Saturn reigned
> In early times. He will extend his power
> Beyond the Garamants and Indians,
> Over far territories north and south
> Of the zodiacal stars, the solar way,
> Where Atlas, heaven-bearing, on his shoulder
> Turns the night-sphere, studded with burning stars.'
>
> (*Aen.* 6.788–97; tr. R. Fitzgerald)

Praise of Augustus rings out in the lofty tones of messianic prediction; he will bring a golden age at home in Italy as wonderful as that at the beginning of time, and abroad military power (*imperium*) that extends across the cosmos. Autocracy is Rome's goal. And empire is its cultural mission. For Anchises goes on later to proclaim:

> 'Roman, remember by your strength to rule
> Earth's peoples—for your arts are to be these:
> To pacify, to impose the rule of law,
> To spare the conquered, battle down the proud.'
>
> (*Aen.* 6.851–3; tr. R. Fitzgerald)

This triumphant 'Augustan' voice is at its most compelling here in Book 6, in Book 1 where providential Jupiter confirms that the wars fought by Aeneas will lead to Augustan peace, and in Book 8 where we learn that the shield Aeneas will carry into battle depicts an ordered world in which Augustus sits enthroned at its centre. But when absorbed and reproduced in isolation from the other voices that emanate from the epic poem as a whole, it has been distorted to extremely disturbing ends. You can saturate yourself in the trumpet blasts of just conquest, take pleasure in conceiving Virgil as a literary imperialist riding on the right hand of a military imperialist (as one critic has starkly put it), but you would be keeping company with Mussolini not Saint Augustine. Under the fascist regime, the Roman poet was claimed to live on in the souls of the Italian people, breathing into them love of country. A country vindicated by the poet's cultural authority as nationalist and imperialist, and under the blessed protection of a new dictatorial Augustus.

Roman identity is declared to be a matter of fathers and sons and imperialism. Women have no place in this proclamation. But the

*Aeneid* doesn't simply pit woman against man, or private against public (as the illustrations of feminine suffering and masculine genealogy juxtaposed in this chapter might at first imply). The voices of the *Aeneid* proliferate and in concert give the text a rich polyphony.

Early in the first book, Aeneas enters the city of Carthage and sees depicted on Juno's temple the terrible battles once fought at Troy, his own included. He finds comfort in understanding this art as compassionate remembrance: 'They weep here | For how the world goes, and our life that passes | Touches their hearts' (*Aen.* 1.462). In context, Aeneas may be very much mistaken. At Carthage, on Juno's temple, this is more likely art as hate-filled celebration of another civilization's fall. Yet *sunt lacrimae rerum* ('They weep here | For how the world goes', in Robert Fitzgerald's translation of the *Aeneid* which I have been using) also speaks to us as a profound reflection on the sadness of the human condition and art's capacity to weep for it (and with us). So Tennyson wrote, poet to poet, on the nineteenth centenary of Virgil's death: 'Thou majestic in thy sadness | at the doubtful doom of human kind' ('To Virgil', 1882). One of the greatest poems of empire thus gives emotional expression to its victims, among whom are included the agents of empire themselves. And those who, like Aeneas here, are warred-down or dispossessed are more likely to take notice of the epic's tears for suffering than its joy at foreign conquest.

On Augustan coinage, Aeneas advances into Roman history rescuing the burdens of his religion and his race. But the conventional iconography takes on a different shape in the words of *Aeneid* Book 2. In the company of Dido, we hear Aeneas remember his experience in burning Troy of utmost fear and blood-soaked flight after he had instructed his servants and advised his father on the details of escape:

'When I had said this, over my breadth of shoulder
And bent neck, I spread a lion skin
For tawny cloak and stooped to take his weight.
Then little Iulus put his hand in mine
And came with shorter steps beside his father.
My wife fell in behind. Through shadowed places
On we went, and I, lately unmoved
By any spears thrown, any squads of Greeks,
Felt terror now at every eddy of wind,
Alarm at every sound, alert and worried
Alike for my companion and my burden.'

(*Aen.* 2.721–9; tr. R. Fitzgerald)

Advance to Rome stamped upon Augustan coinage is, in the Latin poem, transformed into flight from Troy, confusion and loss—for the hero loses his city, his home, and (rather carelessly in the view of some readers) his wife Creusa. Within the epic also, the ending of Book 6 offers counterpoint to the triumphant inflections of the Augustan voice Aeneas's father has just been assuming in his underworld pronouncements. His son is required to depart back up into life through the gleaming ivory gate of false dreams, thus opening the possibility that all the hero has been told of his Roman future might be unreal, mere deception. Counterpoints like these have permitted the most diverse responses to Virgil's epic.

War on Italian soil begins in Book 7 of the *Aeneid*. And, for the American poet and scholar Robert Fitzgerald, the war books (7 to 12) offer an Iliadic second half to the epic but without the redemptive funeral rites for the dead with which the Homeric poem closes. Fitzgerald recalls that he first read through the entire poem in Latin in 1945, when he was stationed idly on an island in the west Pacific during the final months of the Second World War. There he was confronted by a seemingly civilized and imperial show: pressed khakis, gleaming caps, spacious huts, neat coral driveways, polite salutations between the officers, tennis by day, and, at least for this staff officer, Virgil by lamplight. In retrospect Fitzgerald understands Virgil to have written his epic poem in a century that, much like the twentieth, was torn apart by terror, massacre, and war, and that the divine fury of Virgil's Juno speaks to our human sense that malevolent forces must be at work in the modern world also. The second half of the poem, in his view, soon replaces 'martial magnificence' with 'essential war', that is war as combat and slaughter. For this soldier, reading in 1945 Virgil's descriptions of desperate battles, funeral pyres, and failed hopes of peace brought out the agony and abomination that was lying just beyond the Pacific island's civilized show—Japanese fighters smashing ships and their crew into flaming junk (as he puts it), American soldiers on shore using flamethrowers as weapons of choice to eradicate the enemy. If Fitzgerald concedes that the Latin epic tasks both Aeneas and Augustus with the waging of war to end war, for him it also suggests what that effort might cost, and how that effort might fail.

In our opening chapter, Christopher Pelling draws our attention to the moving ways in which some of the soldiers of the First World War constructed traumatic, sometimes therapeutic, interactions with Homer in their poetry. As a soldier of the Second World War, Robert Fitzgerald in turn interacted with Virgil in the translation of the *Aeneid* he published in 1983 (even though many years had now passed since he had seen military service). As a university academic after the war, Fitzgerald had already edited the celebrated and influential late seventeenth-century English translation of Virgil's poem by John Dryden. Dryden had provided a conspicuously 'Augustan' translation and a proudly imperial Aeneas, choosing not to reproduce directly the affecting aphorism *sunt lacrimae rerum*. Fitzgerald's *Aeneid*, in contrast, appears responsive to the critical movement that arose during the middle to late twentieth century in which the darkest aspects of the poem were accentuated because they seemed so eloquently to express modern distaste for nationalism, militarism, empire, and the abusive authority of states. As for Virgil, so for these moderns, war is 'brute insanity' (*scelerata insania*, 7.461).

Revulsion for war permeates the second half of the *Aeneid*. War destroys the natural order. Young men die before their time. Parents weep for the needless loss of their children. Again and again, Virgil stills the forward momentum of his narrative to dwell momentarily on some young man, the maiming of his body, the pathos of his demise:

> Euryalus
> In death went reeling down,
> And blood streamed on his handsome length, his neck
> Collapsing let his head fall on his shoulder—
> As a bright flower cut by a passing plow
> Will droop and wither slowly, or a poppy
> Bow its head upon its tired stalk
> When overborne by a passing rain.
>
> (*Aen.* 9.433–7; tr. R. Fitzgerald)

After this Trojan boy's delicate beauty has been so dispassionately destroyed, and the body of his devoted companion Nisus lies slaughtered on him, the epic narrator directly addresses the pair:

> Fortunate, both! If in the least my songs
> Avail, no future day will ever take you
> Out of the record of remembering Time.
>
> (*Aen.* 9.446–7; tr. R. Fitzgerald)

At this point, we may hear the voice of the American translator merging with that of the Latin poet as each through their poetic art memorializes war's dead. Taking on the voice of the ancients is not without some hazard, however. Opening its doors on 21 May 2014, the National September 11 Memorial Museum in New York displays for its visitors a translation of some of Virgil's words as a sixty-foot long, fifteen-inch high inscription: NO DAY SHALL ERASE YOU FROM THE MEMORY OF TIME. Some observers expressed concern that in his Augustan context Virgil is creating a poetic memorial to a loving pair of young Trojan warriors who have died undertaking a surprise night attack on the sleeping Greeks. But for the Museum, these solemn words are separable from their epic origins, to be read and felt differently. They speak movingly of the Museum's purpose to commemorate the men, women, and children who were killed on 11 September 2001: the events of that single day shall not remove the dead from the memory of those who loved them; the exhibitions in the Museum will testify to their lost lives for all time.

Endings of epic poems matter. So what tone emerges from the *Aeneid*'s close? The poem does not end in celebration of the promised time far beyond myth, that is the historical time of the poem's Augustan readers for whom Aeneas's father had predicted a golden age of domestic peace and foreign conquest. It ends instead even before the hero has founded a city on Italian soil, with single combat between 'duty-bound' Aeneas and Turnus, defender of the native Italian peoples. Turnus is wounded. He humbly begs for the restoration of his body to his poor father. Aeneas hesitates. But then he sees the belt Turnus is wearing, a trophy plundered from the corpse of the young warrior Pallas. Pallas, to whose fearful father Aeneas had offered assurances that he would protect his son on the battlefield.

> For when the sight came home to him
> Aeneas raged at the relic of his anguish
> Worn by this man as trophy. Blazing up
> And terrible in his anger, he called out:
> 'You in your plunder, torn from one of mine,
> Shall I be robbed of you? This wound will come
> From Pallas: Pallas makes this offering
> And from your criminal blood exacts his due.'
> He sank his blade in fury in Turnus' chest.
> Then all the body slackened in death's chill,
> And with a groan for that indignity
> His spirit fled into the gloom below.
>
> (*Aen.* 12.944–52; tr. R. Fitzgerald)

What sort of closure is this? Is there virtue in this killing? Sophisticated literary allusion adds to the potential meanings of this final scene. We can hear echoes of the single combat in *Iliad* 22. Virgil's Aeneas has become a second Achilles taking revenge for the death of his beloved soldier-companion Patroclus; Turnus a second Hector defending his people against foreign invaders. But there is also a noticeable absence of parallel with the very end of the Homeric epic, *Iliad* 24, where a humane Achilles agrees to return the corpse of his defeated opponent in order that the proper funeral rites might be administered to it by Hector's grief-stricken father and his fellow Trojans. Virgil's ending calls for debate—debate that draws us into questions about the ethics of war. Is rage and revenge justifiable on the battlefield? Is this killing a necessary sacrifice to remove military opposition, to fulfil prior obligation (here to the bereft father of Pallas)? Or is this a merciless and frenzied sword thrust?

A demonstration of how humanity can fail in war, how violent passion can override grand purpose? Should we look on hopefully to the ends of war (the supposedly civilized outcomes of victory) or linger sadly over the means (the sufferings and indignity meted out to the vanquished along the way)?

The ending of Virgil's *Aeneid* is satisfying (as one critic has neatly put it) only in so far as it presents in concentrated and amplified form the conflict that has occurred throughout the poem between its different voices. And among the Olympian councils, the thunderbolts of Jupiter, the delicate threads of Fate, the apparitions of Venus, and the rebirth of the dead, the Latin poem also offers us (through the ethereal exposition of father Anchises in the underworld) striking metaphysical explanation for the anguish of existence, 'for how the world goes, and our life that passes'. All creatures—man, beast, bird, and fish—nurture seeds of heavenly energy:

> But they are deadened and dimmed by the sinful bodies they live in—
> The flesh that is laden with death, the anatomy of clay:
> Whence these souls of ours feel fear, desire, grief, joy,
> But encased in their blind, dark prison discern not the heaven-light above.
>
> (*Aen.* 6.731–4; tr. C. Day Lewis)

Are we creatures such as these? Then, so long as we are confined in flesh, all achievement will be counterpoised by failure, and all joy will be steeped in grief.

Virgil's epic suggests no alleviation for the hardships of the human condition, only moving exposition of its complexity. But we as its readers have often sought in it a balance between the claims of empire and its victims, of duty and passion, of women and men, of good and evil. It is still worth conducting these debates about what the *Aeneid* means because it engages with such fundamental conflicts and because it has resonated throughout European culture, in sculpture, painting, theatre, and opera, as well as in literature. The whole poem, not just Dido, calls for remembrance.

Virgil provides escape from the disquiets of life neither in the *Aeneid* nor in his earlier works (the *Georgics* and, his earliest, the *Eclogues*). In all three, nature works both to mitigate and to exacerbate human suffering. The river Tiber rises wondrously from his deep stream, attired in sea-green linen and crowned with shady reeds, to assure troubled Aeneas that he has arrived at last at his home (in *Aeneid* 8), yet at the poem's opening the hero is blown off course by a storm of such violence that day turns into night, the sky flashes fire, and the sea gapes open. In the *Georgics*, nature may confer her fruits on farmers each year, but she can also ravage their crops and destroy their flocks. While, in the first of the pastoral *Eclogues*, we may find ourselves either lingering with the herdsman Tityrus (who is at liberty to recline in the shadows of a cool beech tree composing love songs) or departing with dispossessed Meliboeus (who has been forced into exile far from his sweet fields).

Few of us now are as intimately familiar with agricultural life as the ancients were. Its technologies have long been radically transformed. And in the modern world even its symbolism operates differently, for our struggle is no longer to dominate but to sustain our natural environment. Perhaps that is one reason why I am more attracted to Virgil's artful depictions of empathetic nature in the *Eclogues* than to his instructions in the farmer's calendar of hard exertion against nature in the *Georgics*. In the second *Eclogue*, a shepherd describes to a beloved boy how the nymphs are gathering flowers to give him as a gift (a fantastical blend of violets, poppy-heads, narcissus, fennel flower, cassia and other herbs, hyacinths, and marigold). In just one line of the Latin (*mollia luteola pingit uaccinia calta*, 2.50), the poet composes his words like a verbal bouquet. The verb *pingit* ('blends' or 'paints') is in the centre enveloped by a pattern of decorative adjectives to the left ('soft' and 'golden') and nouns to the right ('hyacinths' and 'marigold'). The line is simultaneously a beautiful arrangement of shapes, textures, colours, perfumes, and sounds. I take pleasure in the sensorial language of the *Eclogues*, even if I forget exactly what narcissus and cassia look like. But I harbour hopes that, in turn, my daughter will be enchanted both by the poetry of nature and the beauty of such poetry as this.

MW

# IX

# HORACE

Horace creates a biography for himself across his corpus of poems. What matters for him, as a Roman poet, is his origins as an outsider. He came from Venusia, a farm town in a once rebellious part of southern Italy. His father was a former slave. He fought on the side of Julius Caesar's assassins and against his heirs at the battle of Philippi in 42 BCE where, he says, he ignominiously dropped his little shield and ran away. Poverty then drove him to the composition of poetry. Across Horace's works, readers can then plot the poet's gradual movement from the margins of the Roman state to its centre of power. He becomes dependent on the new regime for his living in the city as a civil servant and for his new life in the country, at rest on his beloved Sabine farm. He takes on the role of a poet laureate, celebrating the victories of Augustus, lauding the prospect of an age of peace under the new order. Yet Horace's poetry and his persona glint with a kaleidoscopic variety: exuberant and humble, realistic and fanciful, ironic and prophetic, congenial and troubling. By the time Horace died in 8 BCE, his poetry had embraced all the seasons of human life including its descent into chill winter.

Horace talks about himself more than any other poet of antiquity. He writes himself into all his poetry (particularly his first and last works). His voice is compellingly personal, direct and characterful, rich in intimate self-revelation and detail incidental to it. In response, across the centuries, many readers of quite diverse cultures and societies have felt that they have come to know Horace through his poems—and to like him. We saw earlier in this book that every generation has found their own Sappho. In the case of Horace, the person readers have most often discovered in his poems has been a friend comfortably in their own image. Out of the Latin text emerges a virtual companion with whom you may converse amiably, and drink away the pleasures of good living and the pain of the seasons that must inexorably pass. As a teenager studying Latin years ago, however, I could find little to love in the poetry of Horace. Its author seemed to my tastes too middle-aged, too restrained, too smugly self-satisfied, too much an English gentleman—because that's how my outdated school books had instructed me to imagine him.

The Victorian male elite took possession of Horace. In public, grammar, and religious schools, his poems (after careful selection) were targeted at an ideal readership of 'well-bred' boys and taught as a secular catechism for mature, well-mannered living. This Horace could bestow the authority of classical antiquity on the Victorian values of moderation, gentility, patriotism, and empire. And, beyond school, exhibiting knowledge of this Horace in momentary acts of quotation or in more sustained literary efforts at translation, imitation, or parody provided confirmation of membership of (or authorization of entry into) the esteemed club of the cultured gentleman. Yet much manipulation of Horace's text needs to be undertaken in order to make him a congenial companion of that kind and to keep him that way.

If we really listen, we can also hear what is *different* in the voice of Horace, what sounds not familiar but decidedly alien. Horace's poetry resonates with the place, the period, and the language in which he composed. His poems emerge out of, and they tell us about, the death of a republic and the rise of an emperor. They describe gladiators, slavery, animal and even human sacrifice, or the social stratification that operated at dinner parties (brutal hierarchies of food, drink, and seating arrangements for patrons and their clients). They speak to us from a pre-Christian world, and engage with moral and sexual codes quite distinct from those of today. Love originates in the liver; women belong at the margins of political life and are fair game to be abused violently. Poetry holds a place in the centre of society, not just as entertainment, but as an important instrument of education and commemoration. Nowadays we are more willing to appreciate and find value in the pastness, the otherness, even the darkness of classical literature. And when we do, we find—refreshingly—that Horace is no gentleman and that his poetry is more torch than mirror, casting light on distant reaches of ourselves we may not have explored before.

Quintus Horatius Flaccus was born into violent times: wars on Italian soil, rebellions, conspiracies, and yet more civil wars, the failure of the republic, and the rise of the dictator Julius Caesar. Horace arrived in Rome doubly marked as an outsider, because his father originated from a quiet farm-town in a rebellious part of south-eastern Italy and because (even more significantly) his father had once been a slave. The poet was therefore vulnerable socially, and writes of himself as the frequent object of insult for his subsequent public promotion. But Horace was also vulnerable politically. After the assassination of Caesar, he had fought on the side of the Liberators Brutus and Cassius against Caesar's heirs, Antony and Augustus (known then as Octavian). When the struggle to restore the Republic was lost at the battle of Philippi in 42 BCE, and the republican generals had committed suicide in the field, Horace suffered the confiscation of his family's small estate. With his 'wings clipped' and 'no longer a flyer' (Horace recalls in *Epistle*

2.2.49–51), 'Lady Poverty' drove him to turn out verses. Although the poet gradually moved from the periphery to the centre of the Roman state (becoming ultimately a kind of poet laureate for the new order), he never achieved high social standing nor complete economic and political autonomy. This historical context gives a more subtle texture and extra vitality to the poetry we now read some 2,000 years later. And Horace becomes for us not just a satisfying companion for a lazy summer afternoon's contemplative drinking, but also an astute adversary for those long troubling nights.

Autobiography drives one of Horace's early poetic projects—the first of two books of satires published in 35 BCE. Both genre and style are deliberately grounded in the author's status as lowly outsider. When defending his choices in *Satire* 1.4, the poet displaces as stimulus for this work his celebrated precursor Lucilius, who in copious verses had held up members of the Roman elite to savage public ridicule for their alleged folly and vice. In Lucilius' place Horace puts his freedman father. This 'best of fathers' had discreetly pointed out the foibles of much humbler targets in order to inculcate in his growing son the lesson of moderation in all things if you wish to live virtuously:

> Yet if I'm a little outspoken or perhaps
> too fond of a joke, I hope you'll grant me that privilege.
> My good father gave me the habit; to warn me off
> he used to point out various vices by citing examples.
> When urging me to practise thrift and economy, and to be content
> with what he himself had managed to save, he used to say:
> 'Notice what a miserable life young Albius leads and how Baius
> is down and out—a salutary warning not to squander
> the family's money.' Steering me away from a squalid attachment
> to a whore, he would say: 'Don't be like Scetanus!' To stop me
> chasing another man's wife when legitimate sex was available:

'It isn't nice to get a name like that of Trebonius—he
was caught in the act.' He would add: 'A philosopher will give you reasons
why this is desirable, and that is better avoided. For me
it's enough to preserve the ways which our forefathers handed down,
to look after your physical safety and keep your name untarnished
while you need a guardian. When time has toughened your body and mind,
you'll be able to swim without a float.' And so he would talk
my young character into shape.

(*Satire* 1.4.103–21; tr. N. Rudd)

Horace describes vividly the practical education he received from his father in the streets of Rome, inserting fine realistic detail such as the cork used by Romans for water wings. Yet this is a trap that entertains readers not caught by it. The outraged country father who cautions his wayward son against city vices also figures in Roman comedy, but as an inept teacher and a butt of ridicule. This isn't the only place where Horace constructs elaborate tales about himself. In his lyrics (Ode 3.4), for example, he tells us that once as a worn-out little boy he fell asleep in his native countryside but to protect him from the vipers and the bears—miraculously— 'doves of fable' wove him a blanket of bay and myrtle leaves. He concludes there that he was a spirited child touched by the gods (and evidently preserved by them to compose poetry). Here, in his satires, the poet provides us with enjoyment of the comic theatricality of life, the literariness of childhood memory, the ironic fancy of autobiographic confession.

The Latin word *satura* (etymologically often linked to 'an assorted dish' or *satura lanx* piled so high it bloats those who consume it) gave the name 'satire' to a genre of literature that stood opposed to elevated poetry. Roman verse satire utilized the same hexameter metre as epic poems about heroes yet was much smaller in scale. An urban art, it focused on the everyday problems of city life and was conducted mainly as if it were a very personal monologue set at street level (in contrast to the god's eye view of epic). Horace tells the story about his moralizing father better to characterize the son's reformation of the genre. Although we have come to know the poet's project in terms of its genre as the 'Satires', he always calls these poems *Sermones*, or 'conversations' in verse. In the same metre as epic, Horace offers a corrective to that genre's grandeur and virile heroism—a platter of humanity's fears, ambitions, and flaws in all their messy imperfection. Yet this earthy dish is served with an aesthetic refinement and gentle humour that is novel. The speaker of the genre thus reformed presents himself as a sincere preacher of moral restraint and the absence of ambition bred at his freedman father's knee. Yet, simultaneously, the collection dramatizes the delicate manoeuvres by which the poet was being drawn into the patronage of Maecenas (adviser to Octavian). Disowning the previous menace of satire, representing his satiric voice as inoffensive, Horace confronts his readers with his own compromised position: he joins the cultural camp of Octavian at a time of bitter rivalry in word and action between Caesar's heirs and composes satires in a rapidly changing society where republican freedoms of speech have already vanished.

On other occasions, Horatian poetry possesses explicit savagery and bite. The Latin word *carmina* is often used by Horace in its meaning of songs or poems, but the same word can mean incantations—magic spells that can ruin or even kill you. Violent abuse, aggressive obscenity, and incantation are all threaded through another early collection of poems which Horace published in the 30s BCE that we know as the *Epodes*. Horace called them 'iambics' because they are composed in incisive iambic or 'epodic' couplets, a metre previously associated in Greek literature with the expression of bitter, biased anger.

In Epode 8, the iambic speaker formulates an attack on an old woman from rotten mouth down to gaping arsehole that, from the perspective of a modern reader, exudes a disgusting fear of women's sexuality. Yet, in Epode 17, it is the male's turn to suffer sudden and extreme physical decay (yellow skin, bony emaciation, whitened hair, constricted chest). He is aflame. He has gone mad. Earlier in the collection, Horace reported that the snake-haired witch Canidia had kidnapped a small boy in order to cut out and dry his liver and marrow for use in a love potion. Now, in the last epode of the collection, he complains directly to the witch that she is punishing him for that disclosure with her spells. First he pleads for mercy. Then she refuses to grant it, foretelling that:

'You soon in weariness and anguish and despair,
Will wish to leap from some high tower,
To take an Alpine sword and open up your breast,
To tie a noose around your neck—to no avail.
Then shall I be the rider on your loathsome back
And all the world shall bow before my arrogance.
Or do you think that I, who can cause waxen images
To move, as you have found by prying, and pluck
The moon from heaven by my spells,
Who can arouse cremated corpses,
And blend the elixirs of lust—do you believe that I
Shall weep because my arts are powerless against you?'

(*Epode* 17.69–80; tr. D. West)

The dialogue form directly sets male against female *carmina*, the powerless poet against the potent witch. Yet Canidia, embodiment of perverted incantations and therefore Horace's malevolent alter ego, has been given these final words. At the disturbing close of the *Epodes*, Roman hierarchies have been turned upside down; man becomes beast and woman rides him.

Across his works, Horace presents us with a programme of poetry that is in turns earthy, hellish, or sublime. In his later collection of lyric poems (three books of *Odes* were published around 23 BCE, a fourth book ten years later), the poet represents his *carmina* on more than one occasion as inspired by the god Bacchus (the Roman manifestation of Dionysus, Greek god of wine and song, whom we have found at his wild work in our chapter on Euripides and will meet again in our discussion of Lucian). In Ode 2.19, Horace assures his future readers that he has been privileged to see for himself the god teaching a group of nymphs and satyrs his divine *carmina* (or 'songs' in this translation):

> I have seen Bacchus among the lonely crags,
> teaching songs—believe me, generations yet unborn—
> and Nymphs learning them, and goat-footed Satyrs
> pricking up their ears.
>
> Euhoe! My breast is full of Bacchus. My mind
> thrills with the terror I have seen, and wildly rejoices.
> Euhoe! Spare me, Liber, spare me,
> fearful with your irresistible thyrsus.
>
> It is no sin for me to sing of your wilful Thyiades,
> and your fountain of wine, of rich rivers
> of milk, and again and again of honey
> dripping from hollow tree trunks.
>
> (*Odes* 2.19.1–12; tr. D. West)

The everyday realism of the city of Rome has been left behind for the 'lonely crags' of extraordinary myth. In the second stanza, the poet twice utters the ritual exclamation of those whom the terrifying god has possessed (*euhoë!*). Overwhelmed by both trembling terror and mad joy, he thus participates in the experience of the Thyiades or Bacchants (the ecstatic female devotees of the god whom we have already encountered in our chapter on Euripides). The power of Bacchus is so great, the pleasure he brings so mixed with pain, that his compassion must be sought. Such an astonishing experience of the divine compels the lyricist toward grandiloquence and the elevated themes of tragic choral lyric—first miraculous signs of the god's presence on earth (fountains of wine, rivers of milk, trees dripping with honey), then in the rest of the poem the god's glorious deeds of deliverance and punishment. While leaving some comic traces (such as the ears of the satyrs pricked to listen attentively to their divine master), Horace here lays fervent claim to transcendent inspiration. He boldly validates irrational experience and performs poetic allegiance to the sublime.

The *Odes* are a collection of lyric poems of exceptional ambition, variety, and innovation. Horace called them his *Carmina* (with an emphasis here on musicality), because into Latin he now adapts Greek lyric poetry which had originally been sung for audiences to the accompaniment of pipes or the lyre. The poet thus composes a single opus across which he performs 'the entire light and shade of human experience' (to utilize another metaphor). Ode 1.13, for example, borrows from Sappho fragment 31 the powerfully intense physical symptoms of desire the lover experiences when she catches even a glimpse of her beloved—as we saw earlier in this book, Sappho contrasts herself (losing speech, sight, and hearing) with the man who can listen in close proximity and imperturbably to her beloved's sweet speech and lovely laugh. But, in borrowing from

Sappho and from the Roman poet Catullus, who also exploited this celebrated Sapphic theme before him, Horace accentuates an approach to erotic desire quite distinct from theirs. He subjects the monologue of the impassioned lover to ironic alteration:

> When you praise Telephus's
> rosy neck, Lydia, and Telephus's
>     waxen arms, oh how my liver
> boils and swells in indigestible bile.
>
>     At such a time neither mind nor colour
> stays in its fixed seat, and moisture trickles furtively
>     on to my cheeks making clear how slow
> are the fires macerating me through and through.
>
>     I burn if drunken brawling
> sullies your white shoulders,
>     or if that wild boy's teeth
> print their tell-tale mark upon your lips.
>
>     If only you would listen to me,
> you would not imagine that he would be for ever
>     barbarously bruising those sweet lips
> dipped by Venus in the quintessence of her nectar.
>
>     Three times blessed and more than three
> are those held in an unbroken bond, whose love
>     untorn by scolding or bad temper
> will not release them till their last day comes.
>
> (Odes 1.13; tr. D. West)

The speaker experiences a grotesquely visceral version of the Sapphic symptoms of desire—a bilious, sweaty jealousy that from within cooks him slowly to burning pulp. This lover doesn't lose all sensory functions; he can still see, hear, and speak directly to his adored Lydia, and echoes with evident irritation her repetitions of his lovely rival's name. In the last two stanzas of the poem, the speaker turns to offer Lydia the wisdom of experience: the violent affairs of youth pass; tranquil union until the day of death is the greater erotic bliss. Yet, as a whole, the poem stages an oblique renewal of attempts at seduction. The speaker is not impartial. He contrasts his rival Telephus as barbarous bruiser with himself as exquisite poet of those sweet lips that savour of Olympian beauty. So we reread the last stanza's sentimental picture of a love that lasts and understand it as part of a self-serving argument. Held up as if it were in the gift of this older lover, the beautifully serene vision evaporates in the heat of his opening anger. Horace exposes to gentle mockery the ageing lover, the pose of detachment, our perennial failure to embrace cool reason over the erotic passion that so deludes us.

As well as a life of love, friendship, and conviviality, Horace's lyric poems depict some of the greatest political events of antiquity in subtle and surprisingly ambiguous ways. And to match his move into a higher genre (and his position closer to the centre of the new regime), Horace sometimes adopts the solemn, sacred voice of a priest or prophet pronouncing to the whole community on matters of state. Ode 1.37, opening with the famous motto *nunc est bibendum* ('now we must drink'), celebrates the momentous victory of Caesar Augustus at the naval battle of Actium in 31 BCE, the battle in which his Roman rival and enemy Mark Antony had been supported by the ships of Cleopatra, Queen of Egypt. Horace takes on the guise of a master of ceremonies announcing the news in Rome, insistent that drinking, dancing, and feasting should commence because at last the queen is dead. The first four stanzas sound like a patriotic adaptation into frenzied lyric verse of contemporary Augustan propaganda—in which the civil war had been reshaped into a struggle for survival of the West against the East, Man against Woman, liberty against enslavement. No mention here of Antony, of Roman fighting Roman. There is only a barbarian queen, mad, debauched, and drunk, whose plots to invade and destroy Rome have been thwarted.

> Now we must drink, now we must
> beat the earth with unfettered feet, now,
>     my friends, is the time to load the couches
>         of the gods with Salian feasts.
>
> Before this it was a sin to take the Caecuban
> down from its ancient racks, while the mad queen
>     with her contaminated flock of men
>         diseased by vice, was preparing
>
> the ruin of the Capitol and the destruction
> of our power, crazed with hope
>     unlimited and drunk
>         with sweet fortune. But her madness
>
> decreased when scarce a ship escaped the flames
> and her mind, which had been deranged by Mareotic wine,
>     was made to face real fears
>         as she flew from Italy...

> (*Odes* 1.37.1–16; tr. D. West)

At the halfway point in this poem, like a hawk after doves or a hunter after a hare, Caesar Augustus chases the queen across the seas back to the Nile; to him, 'she' is a damnable monster (for Cleopatra is never granted her name in this poem). Yet, at the same time as the double simile of hawk/doves and hunter/hare suggests the determination of the victor and the cowardice of the vanquished, so it also accentuates the cruel ferocity of the pursuer and the pathetic vulnerability of its prey:

> ... and Caesar
> pressed on the oars (like a hawk
> after gentle doves or a swift hunter

after a hare on the snowy plains
of Thrace) to put in chains

this monster sent by fate. But she looked
for a nobler death and did not have a woman's fear
of the sword, nor did she make
for secret shores with her swift fleet.

Daring to gaze with face serene upon her ruined palace,
and brave enough to take deadly serpents
in her hand, and let her body
drink their black poison,

fiercer she was in the death she chose, as though
she did not wish to cease to be a queen, taken to Rome
on the galleys of savage Liburnians
to be a humble woman in a proud triumph.

(*Odes* 1.37.16–32; tr. D. West)

With breathtaking precision, Horace pins the tonal turning point of the poem to the middle of line 21 (in Latin, *fatale monstrum quae generosius*). It sits in the gap between the dehumanized monster seen from Caesar's perspective in hot pursuit (in Latin *monstrum* is neuter in gender, it is a 'thing') and the queen's flight in search of a nobler death (introduced in the Latin by the feminine relative pronoun *quae*, and thus the monster 'who', not the monster 'which', holds death as a goal). In this English translation a full stop and 'But' marks the gap between pursued monster and fleeing heroine.

Cleopatra ends the poem not mad or cowardly but serene and fiercely courageous, prepared to commit suicide by snake bite rather than be paraded a captive in a Roman triumph. Some readers interpret the conclusion of Ode 1.37 as yet more toadying reproduction of Augustan propaganda; Horace lifts a deranged Egyptian woman up to become a conquest worthier of the great Roman who has captured her. Others find that the poet has deliberately orchestrated a damaging collision between two irreconcilable machineries of that propaganda. Horace has, after all, foreshortened the time between battle and suicide from almost a year to an instant. How can the crazy, emasculating, exotic queen change so *abruptly* into a sober, orthodox matron who welcomes death in order to preserve her dignity? Yet what stays with me (and others too) is the subversive potential of that conclusion. We never return to masculine Rome but linger in feminine Egypt. There, at the very end, Cleopatra evades the triumph of Augustus not by *transcending* her gender (earlier she demonstrates no 'woman's fear') but by *being* a woman who refuses to be humble. The arrangement of the final words in Latin is *superbo | non humilis mulier triumpho*. In terms of the word order of these final two verses, a woman (*mulier*) who is not humble is contained by a grand (*superbo*) parade (*triumpho*), but the driving force of the poem as a whole works to resist such linguistic containment. Perhaps this is not the only place and the only way in which Horace treats the ideology of the Augustan regime to a little scepticism.

Latin is an inflected language where endings rather than order indicate to readers the grammatical relationship between words. It is this characteristic of the language that Horace regularly exploits to shape the syntactical intricacy and compressed miniaturism for which his lyric poetry has been so admired across the centuries. In *Twilight of the Idols* (1888), Friedrich Nietzsche aptly pictured Horace's style as 'this mosaic of words, in which every unit spreads its power to the left and to the right over the whole, by its sound, by its placement in the sentence, and by its meaning, this *minimum* in the compass and number of the signs, that *maximum* of energy in the signs which is thereby achieved'. Together Horatian form and feeling have stimulated a profusion of translations, imitations, and original works in most of the languages of Europe and, in particular, the voice of Horace emerges through a great deal of literature written in English. The profoundly melancholic Ode 4.7 (*diffugere nives*) was described by the poet-classicist A. E. Housman as the most beautiful poem of all classical literature. It begins with the earth's changes of appearance that occur on the departure of winter and the arrival of spring, and invests their description with the delight such changes arouse. The ornaments of nature (the nymphs) join with the ornaments of man (the Graces) to dance in joyous celebration of nature's renewal. Here is the opening of the poem translated by the eminent English writer and critic Samuel Johnson. Published posthumously in 1787, Johnson's translation utilizes a fixed syllabic count per line and rhyming couplets to capture the neatly patterned, intricate metrical schemata of Horatian lyric:

> The snow dissolved no more is seen,
> The fields, and woods, behold, are green.
> The changing year renews the plain,
> The rivers know their banks again,
> The spritely nymph and naked Grace
> The mazy dance together trace.

> (*Odes* 4.7.1–6; tr. Samuel Johnson)

The exuberant mood swiftly changes as Horace suddenly proclaims the arrival of spring to be a warning of our mortality. We are as ephemeral as it. The poet now carries us swiftly through the cycle of the seasons, emphasizing the violence with which one usurps another, until we are back where we began, enveloped in cold winter (and the imminence of death). For, unlike the mutable seasons, we cannot be renewed:

The changing year's successive plan
Proclaims mortality to man.
Rough winter's blasts to spring give way,
Spring yields to summer's sovereign ray,
Then summer sinks in autumn's reign,
And winter chills the world again.
Her losses soon the moon supplies,
But wretched man, when once he lies
Where Priam and his sons are laid,
Is naught but ashes and a shade.
Who knows if Jove, who counts our score,
Will toss us in a morning more?

(*Odes* 4.7.13–18; tr. Samuel Johnson)

Horace invites us, given our fragile mortal condition, to live our lives to the full. (The sentiment has been distilled and widely disseminated in the form of the Horatian tag *carpe diem* found at Ode 1.11.8. Although in its original context *carpe diem* means 'harvest' or 'pluck' the day as if life were a vineyard and our present pleasures all the grapes that should be carefully savoured, it has been commonly mistranslated as 'seize the day'. In that more vigorous sense, it is beloved of tattoo parlours everywhere.) In Ode 4.7, in affective imitation of the brevity of our existence, Horace quickly passes over our life's companionable pleasures to return in the last part of the poem to the theme of ineluctable death. However highborn, eloquent, or dutiful we may be, once we die, we leave this earth never to return. Even the closest of friendships cannot break the chains that bind the deceased down. Johnson composed this translation—his last poem—in the month before he died. Translation provided him with an opportunity to face his own mortality (despite his commitment as a Christian to the belief that there is life after death), and to seek consolation in his own voicing of 'our friend Horace'.

Poets have found confidence as well as consolation in Horace. The last poem of his three-book collection of lyrics opens with a resounding proclamation of poetic deathlessness. And here I use the twenty-first-century translation by the American scholar and poet John Hollander:

> More enduring than bronze now is this monument
> I have made, one to reach over the Pyramids'
> regal heaps, one that no greedy devouring rain,
> that no blustering north wind nor the run of long
> years unnumbered nor ages' flight can ruin. I'll not
> die entirely, some principal part of me
> yet evading the great Goddess of Burials.

> (*Odes* 3.30.1–7; tr. J. Hollander)

Great poetry is an eternal monument to its author. It is immaterial and therefore cannot be worn away. It is a timeless epitaph for its poet who, through it, does not die. But you don't have to be a poet to be moved by these words. My own mother (a psychologist) has always taken considerable interest in my Latin studies and found the Horatian aphorism *non omnis moriar* ('I'll not die entirely') a perfect condensation of our family's somewhat humbler triad of aspirations which might leave some small legacy: plant a tree, write a book, have a child. *Non omnis moriar* appeals to her, and to me for her.

Horace returns to hexameter poetry (the metre of satire and of epic) later in his career, but now it is in the form of verse 'letters' or *Epistles* rather than conversations. The pretence of a letter places emphasis on both its author and its addressee. So the *Epistles* take up friendship, poetic composition, and philosophical reflection as key themes, and each poem develops them as the supposed circumstance of a letter requires. Horace presents himself, in these his later writings, as an old gladiator or a weary racehorse, retiring to the country from the competitiveness of city life, giving up his earlier forms of poetry to enquire into what might be the right way to live. We can see why this more sombre Horace and his 'geriatric intimations' might appeal most to readers when they are themselves in relative old age. Yet Horace does not supply systematic answers to the question of how to achieve the good life. The *Epistles* engage us because we see in them a correspondent who is still uncertain, dissatisfied, avowedly inconsistent, perplexed by (and not above posturing about) life's turns. In one epistle, a pretentiously contented Horace protests to the unhappy manager of his Sabine farm that although currently in Rome he much prefers the simple life of his country retreat: a modest meal, a siesta by the riverbank. In the next, a restless Horace complains to a wealthy friend that he is compelled to take a pleasure-seeking winter holiday because of poor health—and he will be sure to bring his own supply of the very best wine. Read in sequence as a poetry book, the *Epistles* entertain us with such ethical lapses. They make their irrational narrator appear not pompous but humane. It is also worth remembering when we hear that we should live the quiet life (savouring simple food, excellent wine, and very good friends; being content with little and restrained in all things) that this ex-slave's son was writing at a time and in a society where peace and contentment were very hard to come by.

At Ode 3.2.13, Horace famously pronounced *dulce et decorum est pro patria mori* ('it is sweet and fitting to die for one's country').

Sweet and fitting perhaps when in un-
spoken contrast to bitter death in civil
war. The motto has long been cherished
as a comfort by bereaved families of
the military. We see it on the campus
of the University of Alabama engraved
into a corner of a stained-glass window
designed in 1925 (Figure 9.1). A memorial
to the university students who lost
their lives in the American civil war

FIGURE **9.1.** Detail of a stained-glass
window on the campus of the University of Alabama. Designed in 1925 by
Tiffany Studios (NY).

fighting for the South, a memorial that through Horace roman-
ticizes 'the Lost Cause' as an act of patriotic sacrifice. For very
different ends, it also appears on an Italian stamp issued in 1935.
The stamp artfully celebrates the bimillennium of the Roman
poet's birth while simultaneously legitimating the aggressively
imperialist ambitions of the fascist regime. In contrast, at the
Gardening World Cup held in Japan in 2012, an award-winning
entry by the French designer John Basson displayed a peaceful,
fragmented outdoor space inspired by an apartment in Gaza that
had been torn apart by a missile. Inscribed repeatedly across its
screens was the partial phrase *dulce et decorum est* (Figure 9.2).
The Latin words are here mediated by their prior use as the title
of the celebrated poem Wilfred Owen composed in the trenches
of the First World War, a poem in which he exposes the motto as
'the old Lie' corrupted by the brutal ugliness of dying in a gas
attack. For Basson, the garden demonstrates how nature can
reclaim and make beautiful once again (*dulce et decorum*) what
humans have destroyed. These verbal images display just some of
the many and diverse responses to the poetry of Horace that

Figure **9.2.** James Basson's garden 'dulce et decorum est' at the Gardening World Cup, Japan, 2012.

have emerged in the twentieth and twenty-first centuries. They also remind us graphically of how much the beauty of Horace's poetry—his mosaic of words—still has the power to comfort, to incite, to renew.

MW

# X

# TACITUS

A fundamental paradox confronts readers of Tacitus. He writes from the heart of Rome's monarchic system of government yet analyses, from the perspective of a republican and a senator, that system's corruption. Under a series of emperors (Vespasian, Titus, Domitian, Nerva, and Trajan), across more than thirty years from the 80s to the middle of the 110s CE, he advanced up the traditional career ladder of a Roman aristocrat. He experienced military service and a series of magistracies both in the city and abroad (even becoming consul and the governor of a province). He may still have been alive at the accession of Hadrian in 117 CE. Yet as historian of the years from the death of Augustus to the death of Domitian (14 to 96 CE), Tacitus was all too aware of the paradox that he was composing critiques of imperial government after being involved in some of its worst manifestations. He describes movingly his sense of complicity in the enslavement of the Roman people during Domitian's reign of terror. Surviving that is a partial death of self. Writing history is then a means of recovery for both the author and his readers. Yet the cure Tacitus offers is challenging. For what certainties, he asks, are there when we interpret the past? What exactly does it teach us for a better future?

Florence 1967: a student poster protesting against American aerial bombardments of North Vietnam displays a grimacing skull over which flaps the flag of the United States. In large type, the accompanying Italian caption declares (when translated into English) 'they have made a desert and called it peace' and carries the Italianate name 'Tacito' as a stamp of ancient authority for this critical judgement (Figure 10.1). In the history of modern political

FIGURE 10.1. An Italian poster from 1967 protesting against American military intervention in Vietnam.

protest and debate, variations on the quotation have been deployed with considerable frequency, ingenuity, and rhetorical force—most recently, for example, in the context of the euro crisis, climate change denial, and the repressions of the Syrian regime. It originates from within an extraordinary speech that the Roman historian Cornelius Tacitus attributes to the Caledonian chieftain Calgacus in one of his earliest works, the *Agricola*. The rebel leader delivers it to a united force of more than 30,000 Britons who have mustered at Mount Graupius in the far north of Scotland to make a stand for their freedom and that of the whole of Britain against the inexorable legions of Rome:

> 'To us who dwell on the uttermost confines of the earth and of freedom, this remote sanctuary of Britain's glory has up to this time been a defence. Now, however, the furthest limits of Britain are thrown open, and the unknown always passes for the marvellous. But there are no tribes beyond us, nothing indeed but waves and rocks, and the yet more terrible Romans, from whose oppression escape is vainly sought by obedience and submission. Robbers of the world, having by their universal plunder exhausted the land, they rifle the deep. If the enemy be rich, they are rapacious; if he be poor, they lust for dominion; neither the east nor the west has been able to satisfy them. Alone among men they covet with equal eagerness poverty and riches. To robbery, slaughter, plunder, they give the lying name of empire; they make a desert and call it peace.'

> (*Agricola*, 30; tr. Church and Brodribb)

The speech in its entirety has justly been celebrated as a searing indictment of imperialism, and as a rousing appeal to fight for national independence or for liberty more broadly. It is—paradoxically—a very finely crafted piece of Roman oratory, full of balanced clauses, poetic imagery, disturbing metaphor, and pithy sentiment, rising to this grand climax where the imperialists are revealed as 'robbers of the world' ('rapists' even, if the erotic connotations of the Latin vocabulary are brought to the surface), and their placatory cant of 'empire' and 'peace' decoded as butchery and desolation.

But Tacitus, who puts such moving words into the mouth of a Caledonian rebel, is writing from a Roman perspective. His work, published around 98 CE (some fifteen years after the battle took place in Scotland), is a curious mix of history, ethnography, biography, and funeral oration. The writer explains at the outset that his purpose is to record the life and deeds of his late father-in-law Agricola and to foster in Roman readers the memory of his excellence. So, in Tacitus' battle narrative, Calgacus does not have the last word. For, just at the moment when the barbaric British troops are singing and yelling and advancing all across the battle-line in enthusiastic response to their leader's call, Agricola as governor of Britain rouses his soldiers to courageous retaliation. The Roman general, in the speech which Tacitus assigns him in turn, eloquently transforms those 'who dwell on the uttermost confines of the earth and of freedom' into 'the most confirmed runaways', and reduces the rebel Britons to the level of timid and feeble animals scared away by the sound of the Romans' approach. It is this second Tacitean speech that wins the day at Mount Graupius. The Caledonians are crushed. Silence and fire fill the land. Britain is completely conquered. And Tacitus has commemorated for his readers the excellence that Romans have always valued the most—victory in wars abroad.

Yet Tacitus' voice continues to amplify modern cries of political dissent, such as those of the Florentine anti-Vietnam demonstrators. For, although the historian seems to treat empire as a system that is capable of holding back chaos, across all his works there emerges a strong, stirring critique of the autocratic government at Rome (the 'principate') that sustains it. At the centre of empire lodges a corruption so profound that its contagion spreads out even to empire's outermost edges. Tacitus publishes the *Agricola* just a few brief years after the death of the emperor Domitian (officially entitled not emperor but *princeps*, implying 'first citizen' and thus yet another Roman name that lies). At a time when the most avidly consumed biographies were about the victims of the Caesars, about the senators who had given up their lives in opposition to bloody tyranny, Tacitus explores instead the terrible problem of how to survive and even achieve excellence in such circumstances. Towards the end of his biography, he declares 'that there may be great men even under bad emperors, and that obedience and submission, when joined to activity and vigour, may attain a glory which most men reach only by a perilous career, utterly useless to the state, and closed by an ostentatious death' (*Agricola*, 42.3–4). The writer constantly presents Agricola (firm administrator, victorious general, loyal subject) as just such a great man: a benefactor of his country, who retired quietly into civil life when his jealous and fearful emperor ordered his return from Britain and did not permit him further military command.

Tacitus frames his account of the career of Agricola with a passionate denunciation of the emperor who curtailed it. Domitian turned the freedom which Rome had once known under the Republic into slavery. A parallel begins to emerge between his brutal rule over Rome (the corrupted 'principate') and of Rome over its subject peoples (the plundering empire). In both cases, the removal of liberty softens and disables those from whom it is taken. They forget their duty and what they are due. Now we can understand the attractiveness of the Caledonian rebel to the Roman historian who gave him so compelling a voice. The Roman world has become so diseased under tyranny, that only at the remotest edge of empire can its best values still be realized. For Calgacus embodies and expresses the Roman values of old: freedom, courage, family loyalty, dedication to one's ancestors, duty to one's descendants. The British chieftain is what his Roman enemy should have been. So, although Tacitus attempts to vindicate his father-in-law's pragmatic qualities as the best form of service to your country, he also invites us to consider whether such qualities really constitute true excellence. Are 'obedience' and 'submission' the actions that should be memorialized after a period of terror and repression? Or does Agricola put on display the best one can achieve under a tyrant and just how slight that best is? After all, Tacitus tells us that 'empire' is just another name for butchery and 'peace' for desolation. We might then reasonably be driven to ask what are the true names for 'obedience' and 'submission'? Complicity perhaps or, worse still, fawning?

Agricola died before the worst crimes of Domitian's regime took place, whereas Tacitus was witness to them. The Roman historian provides a painful and absorbing account of his sense of the complicity of senators like himself who received considerable political advancement during that reign of terror. *We* senators, he says emphatically, led the emperor's opponents to prison. *We* watched their suffering in shame. *We* stained ourselves with their innocent blood (*Agricola*, 45). Even those who outlived such tyranny have suffered a kind of death. In a remarkably suggestive Tacitean turn of phrase, the complicit are described as survivors of *ourselves*

(*Agricola*, 3.2). Yet, in the face of that traumatic loss of self, something can be salvaged. For fifteen years, as highly successful statesman, Tacitus silently acquiesced. Books were thrown onto bonfires, and senators exiled or executed, so that the emperor might crush the voice of the Roman people and the freedom of the Senate. But now, at last, the author says he can speak out about the slavery Romans once suffered and the blessings they presently enjoy. To remember, to speak, to write is to begin recuperation.

Tacitus never did go on to write about the present blessings he may have enjoyed in the subsequent reigns of the emperors Nerva, Trajan, and Hadrian—perhaps outright fawning was just a step too far beyond complicity. The *Agricola* is a taster for his later histories of Rome, where, in dark, angry narratives, he focuses instead on memorializing its past slavery to tyrants and the diseases of the principate (despotism, excessive militarism, moral collapse, subservience, distrust, treason trials, and death). Consequently, his works have been taken up in many later periods as political treatises and as calls for the restoration of political freedoms when they have been endangered by tyranny. Yet this Roman writer's voice is extraordinarily subtle and complex, as well as compelling. In the modern world, it has been understood to issue from a liberal or left-wing Tacitus (critic of monarchy, defender of liberty, republican, revolutionary), a conservative or right-wing Tacitus (imperialist, pragmatist, guide for absolutists), or even—and most dangerously—a Nazi Tacitus (anti-Semite, champion of Aryanism, ideologue of the German Volk and nation).

The latter, deeply disturbing figure was assembled largely out of the *Germania* (an ethnographic treatise Tacitus published around the same time as the *Agricola*). There the Germani are categorized as a diverse and factious assortment of northern tribes drawn together by geography (above the Alps and east of the river Rhine). In the first half of the work, they are described as if a single entity:

> For my own part I agree with those who think that the tribes of Germany are free from all taint of intermarriages with foreign nations, and that they appear as a distinct unmixed race, like none but themselves. Hence, too, the same physical peculiarities through-out so vast a population. All have fierce blue eyes, red hair, huge frames, fit only for a sudden exertion. They are less able to bear laborious work. Heat and thirst they cannot in the least endure; to cold and hunger their climate and their soil inure them.
>
> (*Germania*, 4; tr. Church and Brodribb)

The Germanic tribes (as Tacitus describes them) also frequently exhibit the characteristics of ideal primitives. They exist without money, greed, duplicity, or luxury. They are faithful and fecund within their homes; out in their communities, they are devoted to liberty and remain loyal to their leaders even in the face of death. On that basis, from around the sixteenth century, the *Germania* was annexed by nationalists as an authoritative and unequivocal cele-bration of an ancient German nation and its spirited Volk. With the rise to power of the Nazi party from the late 1920s, Tacitus' work was utilized institutionally to shape and endorse the ideologies of National Socialism. On the orders of the leader of the SS, Heinrich Himmler, an unsuccessful attempt was even made in 1943 to steal from Italy the fifteenth-century manuscript in which the *Germania* had been preserved—so sacred had the text become.

What kind of voice narrates this ethnography? And what does the text tell us about how we might choose to write of peoples unlike ourselves? Scrutiny of Tacitus' text since the latter part of the twentieth century has revealed it to be literary, in that it reproduces standard topics and stereotypical characteristics drawn from earlier ethnographies of other peoples (both the Egyptians and the Scythians had been described as pure and distinctive races). It is morally instructive, in that the exaggerated depiction of admirable practices by Germanic tribes across the frontier of empire constitutes an implicit condemnation of the Roman national character at the degraded centre. It is imperialist, in that the text also analyses why the Germani have been able to resist or overthrow Roman conquest (shockingly they give war absolute priority over farming or civilian life) and probes how they are vulnerable (they are idle, reckless, and lack self-control). After emperor Domitian's ineffectual campaigning in Germany and his sham triumph back in Rome, the *Germania* offers its readers pleasingly proper textual conquest. Tacitus enacts a form of mastery over the land of 'Germania' through his survey of its territories and peoples, and points the way for the new emperor Trajan. Finally the text is also entertaining, for the further you move away from Rome the more fantastical and inauthentic the tribes become—possessing, for example, the faces and expressions of men, but the bodies and limbs of wild beasts (*Germania*, 46). Literary, moralistic, imperialist, and entertaining, the *Germania* is neither a celebration of an ancient German nation nor even reportage (Tacitus, critics generally agree, probably never stepped across the Rhine). After the classicist Christopher Krebs published a book in 2011 that summarized and expanded this post-war understanding of the *Germania* and distanced it from the ideologies of National Socialism, he was swiftly and nastily attacked in the online magazine of the extreme movement 'the

American New Right'. Historical scholarship also can be an act of recuperation.

It is in his later historical writing, however, that Tacitus engages most notably and most acerbically with the troubling consequences of autocratic power (for its possessors and for their senatorial prey). Why does ancient historiography, and especially *this* kind of historiography, transfix us so? It can appear less cogent and more suspect than the modern writing of history because it is less concerned with data and documents, material culture, economics, slavery, old age, women, children, outsiders (the list could be very much longer). Yet it can also appear more cogent, because it is so committed and involving. Certainly it constitutes 'great men' historiography, but written by a very successful senior statesman, in a manner that is parts dissenting, poetic, ironic, sceptical, and on occasion deliberately suspect, for an elite and alert readership that still expected to obtain and exercise executive power (however constrained by the household of the emperor). Tacitus writes from the centre of imperial government in order to preserve the memory of past excellence and evil, and provide a moral investigation of power. He does so because writing history in this way is understood to offer lessons that will improve the health of the nation and the political morality of its leaders. His focus is therefore on exemplary characters and their actions, beginning in his *Histories* with an analysis of Rome's collapse (69 to 96 CE) and then moving further back in time in his *Annals* to an analysis of Rome's decline (14 to 68 CE). Neither work has reached us intact, but enough survives of each to demonstrate Tacitus' extraordinary narrative style and purpose, the vividness of his psychological portraits, the acuteness of his historical sensitivity, and his constant invitation to readers to exercise your own critical judgement. What certainties are there about the past or the future? What counts as the truth?

Published most probably around 109 CE, the *Histories* look back to relatively recent calamities, savage battles, civil strife, and seemingly unending violence. The third of the text that survives focuses on the civil wars that broke out after the emperor Nero committed suicide and brought the Julio-Claudian dynasty to an ignominious end. The year 69 embraced four emperors; Galba, Otho, and Vitellius each in turn seized and held power with the support of their soldiery only to lose it swiftly, until Vespasian initiated a new dynasty of Flavian emperors. Many of the battles took place in Italy and some—a nadir in Roman history—even in the streets of the imperial capital itself:

> The populace stood by and watched the combatants; and, as though it had been a mimic conflict, encouraged first one party and then the other by their shouts and plaudits. Whenever either side gave way, they cried out that those who concealed themselves in the shops, or took refuge in any private house, should be dragged out and butchered, and they secured the larger share of the booty; for, while the soldiers were busy with bloodshed and massacre, the spoils fell to the crowd. It was a terrible and hideous sight that presented itself throughout the city. Here raged battle and death; there the bath and the tavern were crowded. In one spot were pools of blood and heaps of corpses, and close by prostitutes and men of character as infamous; there were all the debaucheries of luxurious peace, all the horrors of a city most cruelly sacked, till one was ready to believe the Country to be mad at once with rage and lust. It was not indeed the first time that armed troops had fought within the city [ ... ] but now there was an unnatural recklessness, and men's pleasures were not interrupted even for a moment. As if it were a new delight added to their holidays, they exulted in and enjoyed the scene, indifferent to parties, and rejoicing over the sufferings of the Commonwealth.
>
> (*Histories*, 3.83; tr. Church and Brodribb)

Tacitus employs a Latin prose style peculiarly challenging for the reader (and even more challenging for its translators into English); the diseases of the principate do not submit to easy diagnosis. We are forced to probe beneath the surface narrative, thanks in particular to the author's extreme brevity (such as omission of verbs or connectives, and use of epigrammatic phrasing), variation (of diction, imagery, metaphor, sentence structure, tonal register, topic, literary genre; and of attributed source or motive), and imbalance (within a sentence emphasis is often shifted from a main statement of action to subordinate suggestions of cause or motive, or descriptions of reaction; a final element of irony often distils or undermines the surface sense of what has gone before).

Here, in this passage, Tacitus paints an extraordinarily vivid and disturbing picture of the legions of Vitellius and Vespasian fighting in the heart of Rome. Incongruous juxtapositions mark out the scene as a horrifying breakdown of the neat topographic separations that occur in traditional Roman historiography. In Republican histories, political debate and decision occurs in Rome, military campaigns are fought and won abroad (against barbarians). Now history has to be written differently (differently too from the accounts of foreign war that we have seen in Julius Caesar on Gallia or Tacitus himself on Britannia and Germania), for Rome of the principate accommodates simultaneously within its walls battle and death, bath and tavern, prostitutes and rent boys, blood and corpses. The populace deploys better tactics than its soldiers, distracting each army with the attractions of butchery so that they meanwhile can go about pillaging their own city. Tacitus frames this grotesque battle narrative with a vision of it, from the point of view of Rome's citizens, as the pleasurable performance of a conflict and an innovative entertainment to pass the holidays. The citizenry watch perversely as if civil war were a mere show of gladiators. The imagery of ludic spectacle highlights their stunningly cruel detachment. They shift their allegiance. They cheer and applaud. They are indifferent to the political outcome.

In epic poetry, the principal causes of war are divine anger or human madness. The inclusion here of epic poetry's themes ('a city most cruelly sacked') and emotive vocabulary (*furere* or 'to be mad with rage') gives all the more credibility and drama to the historical account. We (the meta-audience who stand outside and above the arena of this disgusting spectacle and its debased spectators) are invited on this occasion to share unequivocally in the narrator's indignation. The Roman historian exposes and commemorates the collective degradation of soldiers *and* civilians in this appalling civil war. The subordinate clause with which the passage closes is made up of just three brief words (in the Latin *malis publicis laeti* or, literally, 'delighted at the misfortunes of *their* state'). Together the words distil into a bitter paradox the unnatural depths to which Romans of the principate have finally sunk. Tacitus' description of the battle in the imperial city memorably demonstrates how civil war strips us (soldiers and civilians alike) of our humanity.

Both Tacitus' *Histories* and his subsequent work, the *Annals*, make approximate use of a year-by-year structuring device familiar from histories of the Republic, in which major sections of narrative would begin with the names of the two consuls who had entered office at the start of the year and whose political authority would be exerted over the action of that year's course. In writing of the new order, Tacitus ensures that such yearly political time-keeping is manifestly challenged and superseded by the length of the emperor's reign. The *princeps* is now at the centre of history and its driving force. Thus the original title of the *Annals* was 'from the death of the divine Augustus'. Published around 114 CE, its estimated eighteen books subjected to biting analysis a period of about fifty-four years and the reigns of four Julio-Claudian emperors—Tiberius, Caligula, Claudius, and Nero. It has been described as a superb 'archaeology of tyranny', excavating down to the initial foundations of the principate better to understand its subsequent collapse into the destructive civil wars Tacitus has already described.

In the *Annals*, character takes on a crucial explanatory function (the character of emperors, senators, governors, kings, henchmen, minions, mothers, and wives). It was through the assessment of character that historians could best fulfil their moral duty of exemplarity and provide pragmatic lessons for a political life. So Tacitus neatly divides the reign of Tiberius across the first six books of the *Annals* into better and worse manifestations of his character and of those surrounding him. At the start of Book 4, he claims that the emperor suddenly turned savage under the intimate influence of the commander of his guard, Sejanus. The historian therefore pauses at this critical turning-point to supply a psychological portrait of Sejanus that clarifies how he was able to grasp at supreme power with disastrous consequences for Rome:

> Soon afterwards he won the heart of Tiberius so effectually by various artifices that the emperor, ever dark and mysterious towards others, was with Sejanus alone careless and free-spoken. It was not through his craft, for it was by this very weapon that he was overthrown; it was rather from heaven's wrath against Rome, to whose welfare his elevation and his fall were alike disastrous. He had a body which could endure hardships, and a daring spirit. He was one who screened himself, while he was attacking others; he was as cringing

as he was imperious; before the world he affected humility; in his heart he lusted after supremacy, for the sake of which he was sometimes lavish and luxurious, but oftener energetic and watchful, qualities quite as mischievous when hypocritically assumed for the attainment of sovereignty.

(*Annals*, 4.1.2-3; tr. Church and Brodribb)

This depiction of a person who conceals himself while attacking others shadows (and gives greater density to) that of Tiberius; the distinction between what was done 'before the world' and 'in his heart' is one made increasingly after this in relation to the secretiveness and dissimulation of the emperor. Moral qualities are set in conflict with each other: mysterious/free-spoken; cringing/imperious; humility/ambition. Or the virtues of an ideal general (enduring hardships, energetic, watchful) are assumed for unworthy ends, namely an aspiration to unconstitutional power. Epic causation (the wrath of heaven) again intensifies our sense that the state is in danger, as does a sustained echo of the depiction of the notorious Republican revolutionary Catiline which had appeared in the work of the historian Sallust. The final word *finguntur* ('are hypocritically assumed' or 'are contrived') concludes this profile of Sejanus emphatically in terms of the pretence of virtue.

When Tacitus produces an obituary of Tiberius at the end of Book 6, the development of the emperor's reign is assessed in more complex terms. The historian no longer utilizes the rise of Sejanus as he had in Book 4 to mark a turning point at which Tiberius experienced moral disintegration. Instead the emperor is assessed as having progressively indulged innate perversities; as each restraint on his true character is removed, so his initially concealed monstrosity becomes exposed. Concealment, deceit, and pretence are presented as features of power in the early principate. But they are also represented as problems for the writing of its history. Despite the confidence with which the historian imputes phoney virtues, conflicting behaviours, and concealed feelings to Sejanus and Tiberius, he also invites the readers of his work to understand that, if individuals mask their true natures, indicators of their character are all potentially unreliable and interpretation of them can never be conclusive nor ultimately completed.

One of the ways I was first drawn to the ancient world's bright glow was through the pair of novels *I, Claudius* and *Claudius the God*, which Robert Graves published in the 1930s. These I read at break times in school between the covers of a *Lives of the Saints* and found the pagan sinners a great deal more interesting (my father, a confirmed atheist, was suitably impressed by this subterfuge). By the time I was heading to university, the BBC had just won considerable acclaim for a memorable television adaptation of the two books. I was curious to compare the novels' disillusioned Claudius and his murderous wives Messalina and Agrippina with the characters in the Roman sources (the narrative of Tacitus and the biography of Suetonius), and to reflect upon the role of women in masculine literature and the way that the political is so often made to intersect with the sexual.

The books of the *Annals* which deal with the first part of Claudius' reign have not survived. Nonetheless, it is clear that—in stark contrast to Graves—Tacitus accepts the hostile tradition in which the reluctant emperor is a fool and a puppet whose strings are pulled entirely by his scheming wives and the freedmen of the imperial household. The Roman author sustains a decidedly sensational and melodramatic narrative of the downfall of Messalina across thirteen chapters of *Annals* Book 11. The empress was executed for adultery and treason in 48 CE after, we learn, having comported herself like a whore in the imperial palace (we will meet the satirist Juvenal dwelling on the filthy details in the next chapter). Finally, bored with the mechanics of mere adultery, Messalina (we are told) lusted after the even greater treason of bigamy:

> I am well aware that it will seem a fable that any persons in the world could have been so obtuse in a city which knows everything and hides nothing, much more, that these persons should have been a consul-elect and the emperor's wife; that, on an appointed day, before witnesses duly summoned, they should have come together as if for the purpose of legitimate marriage; that she should have listened to the words of the bridegroom's friends, should have sacrificed to the gods, have taken her place among a company of guests, have lavished her kisses and caresses, and passed the night in the freedom which marriage permits. But this is no story to excite wonder; I do but relate what I have heard and what our fathers have recorded.
>
> The emperor's court indeed shuddered, its powerful personages especially, the men who had much to fear from a revolution. From secret whisperings they passed to loud complaints. 'When an actor', they said, 'impudently thrust himself into the imperial chamber, it certainly brought scandal to the State, but we were a long way from ruin. Now, a young noble of stately beauty, of vigorous intellect, with the near prospect of the consulship, is preparing himself for a loftier ambition. There can be no secret about what is to follow such a marriage.' Doubtless there was a thrill of alarm when they thought of the apathy of Claudius, of his devotion to his wife and of the many murders perpetrated at Messalina's bidding. On the other hand, the very good nature of the emperor inspired confident hope that if they could overpower him by the enormity of the charge, she might be condemned and crushed before she was accused. The critical point was this, that he should not hear her defence, and that his ears should be shut even against her confession.

> (*Annals*, 11.27–8; tr. Church and Brodribb)

At the outset, Tacitus invites us to weigh up the truth-value of his extraordinary tale. It is authenticated by oral and written report, yet it seems 'a fable' (*fabulosus*, that is 'dramatic', 'of the theatre') and resonates as a tragi-comedy starring a duped old man, an adulterous young wife, and a gang of clever slaves. Undoubtedly, however, the event it details puts the principate in extreme danger. The 'bride' is an emperor's wife, the clever 'groom' is about to enter high office and plans through this union to ascend right up to the imperial throne. The coupling exhibits a disturbing pseudo-legality, mimics the formal rituals of a Roman marriage, includes sacrilege, is publicly witnessed, and concludes with consummation (at which point Tacitus produces a marvellous paradox in the Latin; the lovers indulge in *licentia coniugali* or 'the permissiveness of marriage'). The scene now shifts to the imperial palace, where the drama intensifies: Claudius' freedmen whisper, complain, and plot to prevent Messalina from throwing herself on the mercy of her malleable husband and to achieve her execution without trial. So how did they succeed? The narrative is rich in suspense.

Claudius displays an extreme passivity as his wife and his freedmen fight over control of what he sees and hears. Book 11 ends with the death of Messalina (not the end of an administrative year) and the next book opens with an important new development in imperial government—the inauguration of a new wife. The emperor has been pushed to the margins of his own history. Within the rhetorical structures of Roman historiography, dominating women and scheming slaves demonstrate colourfully the extreme degree to which the principate has eroded senatorial government. Power has been transferred from the masculine, civil space of the Senate into the murky, domestic corners of the imperial palace. Now, in the reign of Claudius, politics is perversely sexualized (suggestively, a usurper is thrusting himself into 'the imperial chamber') and even the emperor has been emasculated. Government has become both unconstitutional and unnatural (at least as the Romans conceived the nature of gender relations). Later, with Nero, it will become a dark art.

On occasion, Tacitus seems simultaneously to write history and to reflect conspicuously on the process of writing and reading it:

> Germanicus upon this was seized with an eager longing to pay the last honour to those soldiers and their general, while the whole army present was moved to compassion by the thought of their kinsfolk and friends, and, indeed, of the calamities of wars and the lot of mankind. Having sent on Caecina in advance to reconnoitre the obscure forest-passes and to raise bridges and causeways over watery swamps and treacherous plains, they visited the mournful scenes, with their horrible sights and associations. Varus's first camp with its wide circumference and the measurements of its central space clearly indicated the handiwork of the three legions. Further on, the partially fallen rampart and the shallow fosse suggested the inference that it was a shattered remnant of the army which had there taken up a position. In the centre of the field were the whitening bones of men, as they had fled, or stood their ground, strewn everywhere or piled in heaps. Near, lay fragments of weapons and limbs of horses, and also human heads, prominently nailed to trunks of trees. In the adjacent groves were the barbarous altars, on which they had immolated tribunes and first-rank centurions. Some survivors of the disaster who had escaped from the battle or from captivity, described how this was the spot where the officers fell, how yonder the eagles were captured, where Varus was pierced by his first wound, where too by the stroke of his own ill-starred hand he found for himself death. They pointed out too the raised ground from which Arminius had harangued his army, the number of gibbets for the captives, the pits for the living, and how in his exultation he insulted the standards and eagles.

> And so the Roman army now on the spot, six years after the disaster, in grief and anger, began to bury the bones of the three legions, not a soldier knowing whether he was interring the relics of a relative or a stranger, but looking on all as kinsfolk and of their own blood, while their wrath rose higher than ever against the foe. In raising the barrow Caesar laid the first sod, rendering thus a most welcome honour to the dead, and sharing also in the sorrow of those present. This Tiberius did not approve, either interpreting unfavourably every act of Germanicus, or because he thought that the spectacle of the slain and unburied made the army slow to fight and more afraid of the enemy...
>
> (*Annals* 1.61–2; tr. Church and Brodribb)

The man called 'Caesar' is Germanicus, the nephew and adopted son of the emperor Tiberius. Germanicus here visits the profoundly distressing site in the Teutoburg forest where six years earlier, in 9 CE, the Germanic chieftain Arminius had ambushed, tortured, and slaughtered the legions of the Roman general Varus, and then left their corpses to rot. The scene of present confrontation with a terrifying past is vividly captured in a late nineteenth-century history painting by the French artist Lionel Royer (Figure 10.2), where even the Roman commander's horse is recoiling in fear from the equine skeleton lying nearby. Like a writer of history, the general desires to revisit the past and pay homage to its horrors. While his army, like good readers, finds the past emotionally involving, and experiences individual grief over dead family and friends but also collective pity for the calamities of war and our wretched human condition. Historical narration of a battle past is made to emerge out of fragmentary material remains and human traces imprinted on the landscape. Whitened bones are brought gruesomely back to life as they become the subjects of verbs of motion ('as they [the bones] had fled or stood their ground'). And it is the survivors of the

Figure 10.2. *Germanicus before the remains of the legions of Varus*, c.1896, by Lionel Royer.

horror who are given the most powerful stories to tell (represented in the painting by the centrally framed, gesticulating soldier)—of slaughter, suicide, torture, and insult.

So is writing and reading about the past help or hindrance? In the context of this Tacitean narrative, most immediately history is a hindrance. As the emperor Tiberius anticipates, memory of the past does indeed become a burden that slows down the grieving soldiers and puts their mission of vengeance in jeopardy. By the end of *Annals* Book 2, however, the anger which their encounter with the past has stimulated spurs them to fight and triumph (at least momentarily) over their vicious German enemies. Yet looking even further, beyond Book 2, we see that Germanicus has been operating as a somewhat flawed and out-of-date republican hero who is not going to survive the cruelties and deceits of the principate.

The nineteenth-century French painting also captures some of these Tacitean ambiguities about history. There the encounter with a recent disaster offers a longer-term lesson for Roman imperialists about their inevitable decline and fall: the living horse's protective garment looks ominously like the ribcage of the dead horse; the Roman general's billowing red cloak is a match in colour with the autumnal leaves falling from the tree directly above him. Tacitus, the sceptical historian, understands all too well the complexities of our relationship to the past. But when we read his works, we also understand the importance of writing history. Interpreting the past is a necessary step toward mastery of our future.

MW

# XI

# JUVENAL

Juvenal's satire is an urban art, mainly presented as a monologue delivered loudly on Rome's street corners about the revulsions of city life. In contrast to the disgusting creatures the speaker sees all around him, he (so he protests) is a man of old-fashioned Roman decency. Scarcely any evidence survives, however, that can help us map the life of the author Juvenal onto the monstrous metropolis he depicts. His ancient biographies are very late in date, contradict each other, and deduce personal data from his poems. His sixteen satires come to us collected into five different books and were composed roughly between 110 and 130 CE—during the reigns of the emperors Trajan and Hadrian. Yet they contain no contemporary political targets. Juvenal begins with the declaration that he is unable to exercise the freedom of speech enjoyed by poets in the bygone Republic. His scorn is directed at notorious members of the imperial court from the previous century or present-day nobodies. The satirist picks out with extreme bigotry an outlandish parade of scheming Greeks, pretentious ex-slaves, effeminate and over-privileged aristocrats, and women (the whole lot of them). Although Juvenal's satires invite readers to treat with suspicion the outraged voices from which they issue, their sharp indignation and their graphic power exerted a hold over later Christian moralists and gave shape to the modern genre of satire.

W hen Samuel Johnson wanted to launch his literary career in 1738, he adopted the acerbic voice of the Roman poet Juvenal. Johnson's verse satire *London*, written in close imitation of Juvenal's third satire on the ancient capital of empire, Rome, was an instant success. *London* conjured up a nostalgic vision of an ideal past of fierce national independence (when English kings like the fourteenth-century Edward III had led their rough warriors to victory against the French and the Spanish). That patriotic ideal was pointedly set against the insidious corruption of the present, in which London has now turned into an unbearable French metropolis, its once hardy soldier-citizens reduced to soft beaux who ape fancy foreign manners, and the criminal dregs of Paris are welcomed into the houses of the great or wheedle their way into even the most menial of our jobs:

> The cheated nation's happy fav'rites, see!
> Mark whom the great caress, who frown on me!
> London! the needy villain's general home,
> The common shore of Paris and of Rome:
> With eager thirst, by folly or by fate,
> Sucks in the dregs of each corrupted state.
> Forgive my transports on a theme like this,
> I cannot bear a French metropolis.
>
> Illustrious Edward! from the realms of day,
> The land of heroes and of saints survey;
> Nor hope the British lineaments to trace,
> The rustic grandeur, or the surly grace,
> But lost in thoughtless ease, and empty show,
> Behold the warrior dwindled to a beau;
> Sense, freedom, piety, refined away,
> Of France the mimic, and of Spain the prey.
>
> All that at home no more can beg or steal,
> Or like a gibbet better than a wheel;
> Hissed from the stage, or hooted from the court,
> Their air, their dress, their Politics import;
> Obsequious, artful, voluble and gay,
> On Britain's fond credulity they prey.
> No gainful trade their industry can' scape,

They sing, they dance, clean shoes, or cure a clap;
All sciences a fasting Monsieur knows,
And bid him go to hell, to hell he goes.

(Samuel Johnson, *London*, lines 91–116)

In the same year, and in similar satiric vein, William Hogarth published *The Four Times of the Day* as a series of engravings—a progressive walking tour through the chaotic streets of London captured with Juvenal's eye for vivid and provocative microscopic detail. Gazing upon the second London scene, entitled *Noon* and set in Soho (Figure 11.1), viewers are invited to observe a world divided between the English and the French, between low and high class, coarse corporeality and cultural artifice. On our left, in front of a tavern and a cook-house, the vulgar yet passionate English 'family': a footman fondling a servant-girl who thus inadvertently tips the juice of her pie over a little boy wailing beneath her. On our right, in front of and obscuring an older generation of French Protestant refugees coldly exiting their church, the foppish French (or mock-French) family: the strutting, fashion-conscious couple, and the boy dressed up in absurd imitation of his father. The dead cat lying by the fop's foot symbolizes the dire consequences of such self-absorbed affectations.

The word *satura* (as we saw with Horace) originally meant a 'mishmash' or 'farrago', so that the literary genre has been understood as a form of Roman dish crammed with all kinds of foodstuffs. What then is the secret to the recipe for the sixteen satires which Decimus Iunius Iuvenalis published in five different books between 110 and 130 CE, a recipe so successful that Johnson adapted it to a different city, for a very different consumer, many centuries later? Juvenal's principal ingredient, which was to flavour so many later satires, was anger or moral outrage (*indignatio*)—not understating

Figure 11.1. William Hogarth, *Noon* (engraving and etching), 1738.

irony, or calm reflection, or reasoned argument, but virulent, ranting, hot anger. Anger determines the character of the satirist who
speaks in Juvenal's poetry, as well as the content and the style of
what he says. He claims to be a decent man, forced to speak out
*right now* about the corruption that has infected his city and made
him suffer. He stands at the crossroads surveying all around him,

scribbling in his notebooks what people get up to: 'their hopes and fears and anger, | their pleasures, joys, and toing and froing–is my volume's hotch-potch. | Was there, at any time, a richer harvest of evil?' (*Satire* 1.85–8, tr. N. Rudd). Rome becomes a monstrous metropolis grown fat with vice: a place where men and women swap roles, as do the upper and lower classes; where power is constantly abused; where a deluge of foreigners sweeps away the livelihoods of honest Romans. In such a topsy-turvy world, loyalty goes unrewarded and virtue brings disgrace. This repulsive spectacle is displayed before us exuberantly, expansively, exaggeratedly. Grotesque vignettes of urban degeneracy are brought to life through a disturbing mixture of elevated diction and coarse colloquialism. Such jarring contrasts make the satirist's voice sound even angrier and more savage. This is Juvenal's distinctive technique that shaped the genre of satire when it grew to importance in eighteenth-century Britain, and influenced many of its subsequent manifestations.

In the original satire of Juvenal that Johnson imitated, the angry attack on life in the city is not spoken by the figure of the author but by his old friend Umbricius. The satirist remembers how poor Umbricius stood with him at the gates of Rome, all his possessions piled high on a cart, poised to abandon the place in which he was born and bred. His friend complains bitterly that men like him have been displaced by shameless liars, cheats, and criminals. He lists the sordid skills that he cannot muster, but which are now essential for success in Rome (mendacity, fortune-telling, go-betweening, thievery, extortion, criminal complicity):

> What can I do in Rome? I can't tell lies; if a book
> is bad I cannot praise it and beg for a copy; the stars
> in their courses mean nothing to me; I'm neither willing nor able

to promise a father's death; I've never studied the innards
of frogs; I leave it to others to carry instructions and presents
to a young bride from her lover; none will get help from me
in a theft; that's why I never appear on a governor's staff;
you'd think I was crippled—a useless trunk with a paralysed hand.

(*Satire* 3.41–8; tr. N. Rudd)

By means of a variety of negatives (in this translation, 'can't',
'cannot', 'nothing', 'neither', 'nor', 'never', 'none') and words for
disability ('crippled', 'useless', 'paralysed'), Umbricius stakes his claim
to being a simple, honourable man. Too conventionally Roman for
his own good, he is a failure and about to become an outcast.

While Johnson attacked an influx of French immigrants into
eighteenth-century London, Juvenal's third satire voices a wildly
extravagant, and much fouler, assault on Greeks and Semites arriving from the East who are supposed to be polluting the centre of
empire with their filthy, affected, and wheedling foreign ways:

I now proceed to speak of the nation specially favoured
by our wealthy compatriots, one that I shun above all others.
I shan't mince words. My fellow Romans, I cannot put up with
a city of Greeks; yet how much of the dregs is truly Achaean?
The Syrian Orontes has long been discharging into the Tiber,
carrying with it its languages and morals and slanting strings,
complete with piper, not to speak of its native timbrels
and the girls who are told by their owners to ply their trade at the race-track.
(That's the place for a foreign whore with a coloured bonnet.)
Romulus, look—your bumpkin is donning his *Grecian* slippers,
hanging *Grecian* medals on a neck with a *Grecian* smudge.
*He's* from far-off Ámydon, *he's* from Sícyon's heights,
*these* are from Andros and Samos and Tralles, or else Alabanda.
They make for the Esquiline, or the willows' hill, intent on becoming
the vital organs and eventual masters of our leading houses.
Nimble wits, a reckless nerve, and a ready tongue,
More glib than Isaeus'. Tell me, what do you think he *is*?

He has brought us, in his own person, every type you can think of;
teacher of grammar and speaking, geometer, painter, masseur,
prophet and tightrope-walker, doctor, wizard—your hungry
Greekling knows the lot; he'll climb to the sky if you ask him.

(*Satire* 3.58–78; tr. N. Rudd)

Juvenal constantly pilfers the language and the plotlines of heroic epic to decorate his lowbrow tales of decadence (while Johnson exhibits a more even tenor). In the course of Satire 3, Umbricius constructs a grand epic fancy—a parody of Rome's most sacred myth—in which he plays the poor man's dutiful Aeneas. He too is a refugee from a war (against corruption), setting off to find a new home, after he has bravely fought and lost against a massive army of wicked Greeks that is now devastating his city, just as it had once toppled King Priam's Troy. Yet Aeneas is on a quest to find Rome, whilst Umbricius is constrained to leave it. He here forgets that he is just chatting to a friend and, carried away with outrageous chauvinism, launches into a grandiloquent speech addressed directly to the imperial city's native inhabitants and its original founder Romulus ('my fellow Romans', he proclaims). Strongly characterized in this way, the speaker also parades a whole series of rhetorical special effects to jab home his bigoted points. He piles up irate questions and exclamations in punchy sentences, adds sweeping generalizations and graphic illustrations (like the foreign whore with the coloured bonnet working the race track), and litters his tirade with Grecisms to reinforce in words what he thinks is happening in society (the slanting strings and the oriental timbrels provide an appropriate prelude to the exotic sounds of all those far-flung places in the Greek-speaking East). A mock-epic catalogue of mundane professions is then topped by the pejorative diminutive *Graeculus*

('Greekling'): those multi-talented, sycophantic little migrants will do anything to ensure they get some supper.

While Samuel Johnson engaged satirically with notions of Britishness (conjuring up a long-lost past of national strength, sufficiency, audacity, and control of the seas), Juvenal before him played about with the qualities of Romanness (*romanitas*) and masculine virtue. The speakers of Juvenal's satires are always attacking Rome's citizens for no longer being sufficiently Roman. Umbricius takes his name from the Latin word *umbra*. He is the shadow or ghost of good old Roman values. Despite being born a free man, he has lost all substance because of the upward social mobility of all those cunning, foreign ex-slaves (he protests furiously). Across the satires, vicious abuse is flung at those who flout Rome's traditional hierarchies and social stratifications, and who thus threaten the security of the elite Roman male—predominantly Greeks, ex-slaves, women, and effeminate men. Thus the vivid details of how Umbricius, as the demeaned client of the privileged rich, was forced to walk home in terror through the city's dark streets clutching his guttering candle strikes a distinctively Roman and political note. The only 'freedom' this poor citizen has left is to implore a drunken, violent thug to be allowed to go home with a few teeth still left in his head (*Satire* 3.299–301). True freedom (*libertas* in the Latin) has long since vanished along with republican government.

For Romans of the Republic, one vital aspect of *libertas* (as we have seen with Cicero) had been the freedom to speak without compromise, yet Juvenal tells us in his first satire that he cannot speak freely. Writing under the emperors Trajan and Hadrian, the satirist concedes that after all he should only target living nonentities or the infamous dead. While Johnson's satire hits out explicitly at contemporary political targets—the corruption of the current British government, the court, and its foreign king—Juvenal's is stuck in a political graveyard (as one critic has neatly put it), whipping the corpses of first-century imperial tyrants, their thuggish favourites, and their terrified underlings. Yet the Roman poet does invite his readers to speculate on how past vice might be relevant to the appalling conditions of the present day.

In Satire 4, a fisherman from distant Picenum catches a gigantic turbot and comes all the way to court to present it to the emperor Domitian. The fish is as monstrous as the emperor is gluttonous:

> The senators, still shut out, beheld the morsel's admission.
> Ushered into Atreides' presence, the Picene spoke:
> 'Accept a gift too great for a commoner's oven; let this
> be a holiday: come, expand your tummy with excellent feed,
> and eat a turbot preserved to adorn your glorious epoch.
> He *wished* to be caught!' Could anything have been more blatant? No matter;
> his comb began to rise. When power which is equal
> to that of the gods is flattered, there's nothing it can't believe.
> However, no dish of the requisite size could be found for the turbot.
> So the privy council was summoned. He hated them all, and their faces
> carried the pallor that goes with a great and sickening friendship.
>
> (*Satire* 4.64–74; tr. N. Rudd)

The entire story of the capture, presentation, and discussion of the fish is told as epic parody. The satirist first calls loftily upon the Muses to recount the tale of the turbot. At the start of this passage, Rome's once powerful senators are shut out, whilst a fishy titbit is granted entry into the imperial presence. The satirist bestows upon the Roman emperor the mock-heroic title 'Atreides', that is son of Atreus (Agamemnon), leader of the Greek armies at Troy and crucial protagonist in Homer's *Iliad*. The directives of the fisherman to this 'hero' initially take on suitably splendid ceremonial tones but swiftly collapse into the common vernacular, as the prosaic 'tummy' and 'feed' of this translation suggest. In epic, advisers are most often summoned to debate the initiation or the strategies of war, not to opine on how best to dish up a fish. The contrast in purpose is exacerbated by the deployment of burlesque—the catalogue detailing the hasty arrival and culinary advice of Domitian's privy council mimics those epic catalogues that recount the quantity, origins, and courage of warriors mustering for battle. The stylistic admixture of epic and the everyday spices up the dish of Rome's political degradation, a dish now served up for the delectation of one single, insatiable diner.

Juvenal's satiric speaker bursts out in furious indignation at the crude flattery pronounced by the fisherman. The emperor is presented as bestial in his behaviour (he enjoys a feed; he puffs up his cock's comb) yet, perversely, he is divine in the authority he can command. His tyranny is magnified by the triviality of the incident over which he exercises supreme control. Summoned to debate a recipe, Domitian's ministers are pale with fear. None seem to decline the invitation. They all rush to the call of the master who hates them. Those who speak do not do so freely, instead they engage competitively in abject sycophancy designed for their own preservation or advancement. No one retains integrity. The poem thus constructs 'a moral hierarchy' of how you should address those in power, where flattery (*adulatio*) appears to be the worst and satire like this the best. Yet this, we are not meant to forget, is a satire that attacks the dead (Domitian had been assassinated twenty or so years earlier, in 96 CE). So where does that place such a satirist?

His stance appears feeble by comparison with that of 'the workers' who (we are told pointedly at the end of Satire 4) found the courage to do what no elite Roman had managed and strike the emperor dead.

The irate speaker of Juvenal's satires despises the gambler, the mentally ill, the wretched elderly, and the corpulent glutton who boozes and belches his way through the day and can eat an entire dinner-party all on his own. He poses not just as a guardian of free speech and political morality but also as a spy on the private— assailing through his peephole the vices of greed, cruelty, impotence, adultery, rape, and effeminacy (all those noble togate men who secretly cross-dress, wear make-up, shave themselves smooth, and enjoy being penetrated like a woman). For Romans, private blended into public space. To breach the boundaries of class, gender, or sexuality (even in the seeming seclusion of your own home) was to launch an attack on the integrity of the elite Roman male and to confound his claim to political and social mastery. Nonetheless, many of these rants seem capable of translation all too easily to later works of satire set in other times and other cities, whether those rants are brutally xenophobic, racist, misogynist, homophobic, or merely snobbish.

Satire 6 is especially infamous for its rampant, frenzied misogyny. An enormous poem on an epic scale, it fills the whole of Juvenal's second book of satires with an unrelenting catalogue of the perversity of wives. To select just a few outrageous faults from the speaker's extensive list: wives are self-indulgent, cruel, arrogant, gluttonous, intoxicated busybodies (thoughtlessly humiliating their husbands with superior knowledge, vomiting all over the dinner plates); they are vain, superstitious, sacrilegious, uncontrolled nymphomaniacs

(obsessing indiscriminately over soft actors, foreign musicians, and
the weapons of hideous gladiators; pissing and copulating all over
the street-side statues of the goddess Chastity). Messalina, wife of
the emperor Claudius in the 40s CE, provides one extraordinary
example of such perversity; she is no ordinary adulteress, but an
insatiable whore *and* an emperor's wife combined:

> Look at our quasi-divinities; think of what Claudius had to
> endure. As soon as the wife perceived her husband was sleeping,
> she would steal away from him, taking with her a single maid,
> and actually bear to prefer a mat to her bed in the palace.
> The imperial harlot did not blush to don a hooded cloak at the dead of
>      night.
> No, with a yellow wig concealing her raven locks,
> she made for a brothel warm with the stench of a much-used bedspread,
> and entered an empty cell (her own). Undressing, she stood there
> with gilded nipples under the bogus sign of 'The She-wolf',
> displaying the womb which gave the lordly Britannicus birth.
> She smilingly greeted all who entered, and asked for her 'present'.
> Then, when the brothel's owner allowed the girls to go home,
> she lingered as long as she could before closing her cell
> and sadly leaving, still on fire, with clitoris rigid.
> At last she returned, exhausted, but not fulfilled, by her men;
> and with greasy grimy cheeks, and foul from the smoke of the lamp,
> she carried back to the emperor's couch the smell of the whorehouse.
>
> (*Satire* 6.115–32; tr. N. Rudd)

Extreme disgust is manufactured from startling juxtapositions of
detail. The bed in the palace high on Rome's Palatine hill is set
against the mat (and later the worn-out bedspread) in the backstreet
brothel. At the close of the lurid vignette, the imperial couch has
been stained by the stink of the whorehouse. In between, Messalina's sterile, commercial, secretive copulations are contrasted with
the official reproduction required of an empress to ensure smooth

succession to supreme power. The whole disturbing picture is captured and concentrated into that caustic title 'imperial harlot' (*meretrix Augusta*). The body of the imperial whore is fragmented into parts (and subjected to fetishistic scrutiny). On offer to all entrants: a pair of gilded nipples, a used womb, and a rigid clitoris. The clitoris even becomes a sensate entity independent of Messalina's control; it burns with its own unquenchable lust. Through sight, smell, and touch, the satire depicts how a wife's base corporeality can befoul even the absolute political power of a husband. We have already learned from Tacitus, in the previous chapter, of the punishment such behaviour was thought to deserve.

The vicious harangue bursting out of Satire 6 is notionally addressed by the speaker to his friend 'Postumus' to dissuade him from getting married. The name in this context is suggestive of a man born too late to find a wife that's any good. For the poem opens with the elaborate evocation of a primordial age when Chastity lived on earth, when home was a cave, and a 'mountain wife' spent her time breast-feeding her sturdy babies. Yet the detail arouses our suspicion: the cave is freezing; the home tiny, gloomy, and packed with livestock; the bed is put together uncomfortably from leaves, straw, and animal skins; the wife is ugly and coarser even than her acorn-belching husband. The voice of the satiric speaker is both irrational and extremist in his hostility to women. How seriously can you take his propositions that it would be better to kill yourself than marry? That actually a decent wife would be insufferably condescending? That Rome is now a city crammed wall-to-wall with modern Clytemnestras and Medeas, all busy slaughtering their husbands and poisoning their children? This is the frenetic yelling of a bigot gone mad.

Our suspicions are further aroused by the outpourings of another aggrieved Roman citizen in the third book of Juvenal's satires. There in Satire 9, it is a character called Naevolus who, in conversation with the satiric speaker, is incited to disclose why his physical condition has deteriorated so markedly. Naevolus proceeds furiously to deplore the meanness of his patron Virro:

> 'Many have made a profit from this kind of life, but I
> have had no return for my efforts. Now and again I am given
> a greasy cloak to protect my toga (rough and coarse,
> and loose in texture, thanks to the comb of a Gallic weaver),
> or a piece of brittle silver from an inferior vein.
> Men are governed by fate, including those parts which are hidden
> beneath their clothes. For if the stars are not in your favour,
> the unheard of length of your dangling tool will count for nothing,
> even though, when you're stripped, Virro stares at you drooling
> and sends you a continuous stream of coaxing billets-doux.'

(Satire 9.27–36; tr. N. Rudd)

We listen to a tirade in which the Roman social status of a client has deteriorated into prostitution. Once a sophisticated man-about-town, Naevolus has been reduced to playing 'husband' to an effeminate aristocrat. His pretensions to moral indignation, when issuing clearly from such a moneygrubber, expose him to ridicule. Naevolus rails with vivid specificity against the miserly gifts of greasy cloaks, bristly togas, and cheap silver plate he occasionally receives in return for his 'efforts'—although they turn out to consist of the penetration of his patron (and his patron's wife) in secret. He incongruously applies an abstracted conception of astrological determinism to the workings of the penis (described first in a coy periphrasis as 'those parts which are hidden | beneath their clothes', and then in crudely sexual terms as 'your dangling tool'). If the stars are out of alignment, you will wilt and your patron will cruelly reject you. Like the mixture of epic and the everyday, the conjunction of the philosophical with the blatantly sexual punctures any moral conceit. The male prostitute scornfully deploys the vocabulary of love poetry to picture his patron's prior lust and attempts at seduction, while 'drooling' conjures up a distasteful image of Virro anticipating fellation. Later in the poem, Naevolus further exposes his greed as he sets the just reward for his services much higher than simple self-sufficiency. This absurdly indignant moralist, however, is not unlike the speakers of Juvenal's earlier satires who couldn't make an honest living in present-day Rome. He is just much more compromised. Jealous, greedy, pathetically self-pitying and without scruple, he yearns not to cleanse the city but to excel in the disorders of vice.

The loud, irate voice of the satiric speaker seems to quieten and calm down across the satires of Juvenal's third and fourth books. On occasion, it even takes on more contemplative and optimistic timbres, as in Satire 10 which ends, after consideration of our folly in praying for the wrong things, with a declaration that the gods know best and a digest of more appropriate prayers:

> They care more for man than he cares for himself; for we
> are driven by the force of emotion, a blind overmastering impulse,
> when we yearn for marriage and a wife who will give us children; the gods,
> however, foresee what the wife and children are going to be like.
> Still, that you may have something to ask for—some reason to offer
> the holy sausages and innards of a little white pig in a chapel—
> you ought to pray for a healthy mind in a healthy body.
> Ask for a valiant heart which has banished the fear of death,
> which looks upon length of days as one of the least of nature's
> gifts; which is able to suffer every kind of hardship,
> is proof against anger, craves for nothing, and reckons the trials

and gruelling labours of Hercules as more desirable blessings
than the amorous ease and the banquets and cushions of Sardanapállus.
The things that I recommend you can grant to yourself; it is certain
that the tranquil life can only be reached by the path of goodness.
Lady Luck, if the truth were known, you possess no power;
it is we who make you a goddess and give you a place in heaven.

(*Satire* 10.354–66; tr. N. Rudd)

The satire's benign appraisal of what we should actually wish for in order to bear the human condition (health, courage, endurance, dispassion, diligence, and simple living) has met with much sympathy from readers across the centuries. At the same time as *mens sana in corpore sano* ('a healthy mind in a healthy body', 10.356) has become Juvenal's most celebrated and widely quoted aphorism, the poem as a whole has undergone many translations and imitations. Samuel Johnson entitled his celebrated version 'The Vanity of Human Wishes' and transformed Juvenal's ending into a mediation on the consoling value of prayer to God (for a healthful mind, obedient passions, a will resigned, love, patience, and Christian faith). Yet, in the original, the sentiments are expressed with at least a touch of irony. Mocking diminutives and prosaic terminology are arrayed to describe offerings made to the gods as 'predictive little sausages' from 'a pretty little piglet', while at the close we discover that none of this religiosity may even be necessary since (although the gods do care about us) it is *we* who make our own luck.

These concluding lines even include a prayer for the absence of anger, thus contributing to our sense that we are now in converse with a satiric speaker quite unlike that of the earlier poems. Yet this semblance of melancholic detachment from life's vicissitudes cracks open and the old satiric rage breaks out all over Satire 10, as the speaker excitedly catalogues a host of examples of men who foolishly prayed for things which only brought them ruin (namely power, eloquence, military glory, a long life, and good looks). The first of these illustrations, which refers to the fall of Sejanus (commander of the imperial guard and a quasi-regent during the reign of the emperor Tiberius, as we saw in the previous chapter), is perhaps the most vicious and memorable. The satirist describes the vicarious pleasure with which, after the execution of Sejanus in 31 CE, the Roman people mutilated the statues of him as a triumphant general riding in a four-horse chariot:

> Some are sent hurtling down by the virulent envy to which
> their power exposes them. Their long and impressive list of achievements
> ruins them. Down come their statues, obeying the pull of the rope.
> Thereupon, axe-blows rain on the very wheels of their chariots,
> smashing them up; and the legs of the innocent horses are broken.
> Now the flames are hissing; bellows and furnace are bringing
> a glow to the head revered by the people. The mighty Sejanus
> is crackling. Then, from the face regarded as number two
> in the whole of the world, come pitchers, basins, saucepans, and piss-pots.
> Frame your door with laurels; drag a magnificent bull,
> whitened with chalk, to the Capitol. They're dragging Sejanus along
> by a hook for all to see. Everyone's jubilant...
>
> (*Satire* 10.56–67; tr. N. Rudd)

This dramatic picture, full of vengeful delight, brings to mind all that modern documentary footage of tyrants and their monumental effigies toppled. The swift downfall of those who once wielded supreme power is conveyed by the rapid movement of the verse (there are few 'ands' in the Latin), the radical transformation of the metal into pots for eating, drinking, and pissing, the celebration of a holy day while the despot's body is dragged along for tossing into the river Tiber. Then the satirist turns his livid abuse on the spectators who proceed to kick the corpse because they want to be seen to have hated Sejanus, even though they are hypocrites who would have lauded him had he outlasted the emperor. In fact, worse than hypocrites, because nowadays the people of Rome are politically apathetic and too easily satisfied with just the bread dole and the races (or *panem et circenses*, 'bread and circuses', in Juvenal's other most famous maxim, 10.81). But isn't the speaker making a whole career out of kicking corpses? We might wonder how the satirist can evade his own derision.

Juvenal's sixteen satires are a complex, chaotic dish. The satirist stands at the junction of a city street. He records what he sees. He responds instantly and with rage at the nightmare of corruption which passes him by, and describes it with extraordinary vividness and immediacy. Yet, politically these poems describe a Rome of the past, and socially they describe an imaginary metropolis populated by outlandish caricatures stolen from history and from other literature. The outraged speakers of Juvenal's satires are as bogus as the city life they abhor. Contradicting each other, they often betray a disturbing lack of moral authority or seriousness. How do they know that noble Romans are busy behind closed doors primping in front of mirrors, applying eyeliner, adjusting golden hairnets, and swirling transparent gowns of yellow and sky blue? Why do they relish telling us about it in quite such lurid detail? The fictitious Umbricius who pours out his anger in Satire 3 clearly speaks from a position of self-interest just like the others. He turns out to be not so much the honourable ghost of Rome but its ignoble Mr Shady—jealous of Greeks and rich upstarts only because they have succeeded where

FIGURE 11.2. 'Juvenal scourging Woman', frontispiece for *The Sixth Satire of Juvenal*, 1896, by Aubrey Beardsley.

he has failed miserably. Both the bigotry and the volume of the satiric speakers' voices undermine their moral judgements. This intensity of style and content draws our attention to satire as a show, a performance in which 'righteous' anger is comically ventriloquized. But, if this is Juvenal's recipe, how does it retain any satiric bite?

The answer lies with YOU, the consumer of this dish. Take a look at this late nineteenth-century engraving designed by Aubrey Beardsley to illustrate Juvenal's sixth satire and entitled 'Juvenal scourging Woman' (Figure 11.2). Do you take pleasure in the sensuality and the suffering of the satiric target? Are you amused by the exposure of the brutality of the satirist? Or are you disturbed by both? Juvenal's satires tempt you with their repulsive images expressed so vividly, so exquisitely, so wittily, so ferociously. Whether they titillate, amuse, disgust, or disturb you, they draw you into the satiric performance and force you to make your own judgements, to face up to your own values. What's your opinion on aristocrats or the *nouveaux riches*, immigrants, transvestites, prostitutes, or uppity women? How much violent abuse against them are *you* prepared to tolerate? The victims of Juvenal's satires are its readers—invited to savour the pigswill of a bloated capital city (whether it is imperial Rome or London) and to decide what you make of it.

MW

# XII

# LUCIAN

Five centuries have now passed after Euripides and Thucydides, and we are in the second century CE. The Greek world by now is a very different one, for now it is Greece under Rome. Lucian himself was born around 120 and lived till about 180. He was not a Greek but a Syrian from Samosata, a busy city on the Euphrates: when he refers to himself in his works he almost always does so obliquely, and it is sometimes just as 'the Syrian'. His native language may well have been Aramaic, but he would have begun learning Greek when he was very small. We have almost eighty of his essays, mostly written in a Greek style that carefully mimicked the diction and mannerism of the Athenian writers of the classical age. The works range widely in topic and form—many are in dialogue, and one, *Gout*, is in iambic trimeters—and they doubtless vary in seriousness too, but most are notable for their satiric edge. He clearly travelled widely, getting as far as Italy and Gaul; he also spent time in Athens, which is the setting for many of his works, and he seems to have been an eye-witness of the spectacular self-incineration of the cynic Peregrinus at the Olympic Games of 165. In old age he held an administrative post in Egypt; it is doubtful whether this was really burdensome.

Sometimes the Greek gods put on a rather different face.

*Scene: A Street in heaven. Hermes is strolling along, looking very elegant, when he is stopped by a stranger whose appearance is positively sub-human.*

STRANGER: Morning, Dad.

HERMES [COLDLY]: Good morning to you, sir. But why did you call me that?

STRANGER: Well, you're Hermes of Cyllene, aren't you?

HERMES: Of course I am, but how does that make me your father?

STRANGER [CHUCKLING]: I'm a little love-child, all your own work!

HERMES: All the work of a couple of goats having a naughty, I should think! You can hardly be anything to do with me, with those horns on your head—and a nose that shape—and a great shaggy beard—and cloven hooves—and a tail dangling over your backside!

STRANGER: You can jeer at me as much as you like, Dad, but you're only fouling your own nest. It's not my fault that I'm like this—if it's anyone's fault, it's yours.

HERMES: Then who was your mother, may I ask? Have I inadvertently had an affair with a she-goat?

STRANGER: No, not exactly—but have you forgotten that young lady you raped in Arcadia? Oh, do stop biting your nails and pretending not to remember! You know perfectly well whom I mean—Penelope, the daughter of Icarius.

HERMES: In that case, why do you look like a goat? Why don't you take after me?

STRANGER: Well, I can only tell you what she told me, when she packed me off to Arcadia. 'My child', she said, 'it's time you knew who your parents are. My name's Penelope, and I come from Sparta, but your father's a god called Hermes, the son of Zeus and Maia. So even if you have got horns and rather peculiar legs, don't let it worry you. The fact is, your father disguised himself as a goat to preserve his incognito, and that's why you've turned out like this.'

HERMES: Good Lord, I seem to remember doing something of the kind. Well, it's a fine situation, I must say. I've always prided myself on my looks, and to all appearances I'm still a beardless youth—but as soon as it gets about that I'm your father, everyone will laugh at me for producing such a handsome son!

STRANGER: But really, Dad, I'm nothing to be ashamed of. I've got quite a good ear for music, and I can make a tremendous noise on my shepherd's pipe. Dionysus says he can't get on without me—in fact I do most of his choreography. And you've no idea what beautiful sheep I've got round Tegea and Parthenius. And only the other day I fought with the Athenians at Marathon, and put up

such a good show that they voted me a special cave. If you ever go
to Athens, you'll find that Pan is a very important person there.

HERMES: But tell me, Pan—for I gather that's your name—are you
married yet?

STRANGER: No fear, Dad! I'm far too highly sexed to be satisfied with
just one wife.

HERMES: Then I take it that you confine your attentions to the she-
goats?

STRANGER: There you go again, making fun of me! But I've been to
bed with Echo, and Pitys, and every single girl in Dionysus's
chorus—and they all think I'm terrific.

HERMES: Well, my boy, do you know the first favour that I want to
ask you?

STRANGER: No, Dad. What is it?

HERMES [*LOOKING ROUND ANXIOUSLY*]: Let's keep all this to ourselves,
shall we? Come and give me a kiss, but—don't call me Dad when
there's anyone listening!

(Lucian, *Dialogues of the Gods* 2: tr. P. Turner, adapted)

I owe my own discovery of Lucian to a fellow 16-year-old at our
Welsh grammar school, who brought that Penguin translation
of Paul Turner into class. 'Look at this,' he said: 'this stuff is really
good.' He was right. That translation put paid to any lingering
suspicion in our minds that the classics might be a crusty and
dusty discipline. Not, to be fair, that we had much of that impression anyway, as the first Greek drama we were given to read was
Euripides' *Cyclops*, itself a rumbustious story of drunken satyrs
behaving very badly; a year later we were also reading Lucian's
own *True History*—anything but 'true' in fact, a proto-science-fiction
story including a journey into space—and Aristophanes' *Frogs*, on
which more in a moment. But Lucian's jokiness did seem a little
different from Aristophanes', and much more modern. These were
the 1960s, and Lucian's subversive sense of humour was in tune

with the times, with a new surge in satire—*Beyond the Fringe, Private Eye, That Was The Week That Was*—appealing to a generation that was less programmed than earlier ones to be deferential. Anyone used to Vicky's *Supermac* version of prime minister Harold Macmillan (Figure 12.1) could tune in without much difficulty to Lucian's gods: that cartoon was initially derisory, but the image and the nickname stuck, and after a few years it captured a mockability

**FIGURE 12.1.** Vicky: *Supermac*. Cartoon in the *Evening Standard*, 6 November 1958.

that was not without sympathy, even a tinge of affectionate familiarity, though it always carried a real edge as well.

That embarrassed Hermes captures the tone of those *Dialogues*
well enough. A lot of the humour comes from the domestication of
the gods, picturing the very human-like way they might have
responded if the myths and legends were really true: it's a mix of
the ordinariness of the characters and the extraordinariness of the
situation. There is, for instance, Zeus complaining that he has a
terrible headache: can Hephaestus please strike Zeus' head open to
let Athena be born and jump fully-armed into the world? Then we
have Poseidon and Hermes impressed by the way that Zeus can
even give birth from his thigh: 'What a thing! It looks as if the whole
lot of him can be pregnant, anywhere on his body!' This time it is
Dionysus, snatched from Semele's womb when she has asked Zeus
to come before her in full thunder-and-lightning mode. That was
unwise: her house has burnt down. Or there is Ganymede wondering naïvely, or false-naïvely, whether Zeus will really like sharing a
bed, as 'my father never likes it when I wriggle and whisper and
keep him awake'; I think I'd rather like that, says Zeus, lewdly.
There are Apollo and Hermes in locker-room chat, wondering how
it can be that grimy and smelly Hephaestus has not just one
beautiful goddess to sleep with but two, both Aphrodite and Charis;
Apollo never seems to have much luck himself with anyone he
fancies, with their frustrating tendency to turn into trees (Daphne)
or get killed by mistake (Hyacinthus). Whatever else all this may
be—and perhaps it isn't much else, and doesn't need to be—it is
certainly fun.

This sort of humour is not altogether new. True, Homer would
not have had Zeus complaining of his obstetric headache or licking

his lips at Ganymede's wriggling, but he already has something of that mix of extraordinary situation and all too ordinary, human-like characters. At the banquet at the end of *Iliad* 1 Zeus and Hera have a full-scale marital tiff because Hera rightly suspects that he's been going behind her back yet again; at the beginning of Book 4, Zeus decides to try teasing his irate wife in a way that goes familiarly awry, even if their making-up involves the exchange of cities to destroy rather than apologetic chocolates or flowers. Nor is there anything new in having gods that can be laughed at. In that same banquet the tension is broken with Hephaestus limping around to serve the drinks (*Iliad* 1.595–600), much to the amusement of the other gods and presumably of Homer's audience too, however chilling the contrast of that bonhomie with what is happening on earth. There is similarly boisterous divine comedy in the *Odyssey* too, when Ares and Aphrodite are trapped in bed together by a super-net crafted by her husband Hephaestus, who promptly calls all the other gods to have a look, a leer, and a laugh (*Odyssey* 8.266–366, where this is the subject of a song sung by the bard Demodocus). Apollo is already in locker-room mode there, agreeing with Hermes that the super-net might be worth it to have sex with Aphrodite. The laddishness is not so very different in Lucian's own version of the story (*Dialogues of the Gods* 21), even if he does linger a little on the naked details: and 'lucky old Ares, not just to have sex with the most beautiful goddess but also to be chained up with her . . . '. Maybe that touch of lubricious kinkiness, too, wasn't so out of keeping with the swinging sixties, as a wave of celebrity sex scandals hit the press.

All this may still seem a long way away from the daunting grimness of Euripides' gods, but even there it was important to remember the joy-giving aspects of Dionysus as well—'most dread, but most gentle to mortals', as we saw (Chapter V). In the same year as the first performance of the *Bacchae* itself (405), the Athenian theatre audience had seen a very different Dionysus in Aristophanes' *Frogs* a few months earlier, with the god so terrified by a doorkeeper in the underworld that he soils himself, then later gets a beating on stage. It seems a long way from the Dionysus who toys so coolly with his victim Pentheus. Admittedly, it may be a particular feature of Dionysus' divine personality to bring together so many diverse and even contradictory aspects, but it is not just Dionysus; the half-divine Heracles too is fairly comical in Euripides' *Alcestis*, striking a very different note from his tragic version in Sophocles' *Women of Trachis* or Euripides' own *Heracles*.

This divine duality may seem odd to us. We are too used to contemporary religions where God is not mocked, where joking at divine expense can be taken as 'blasphemy' and excite responses ranging from a disapproving glare to a death threat. Yet these Greek gods don't seem to mind, any more than Harold Macmillan much minded those satire shows. (When the cabinet minister in charge of the BBC said he was going to take action about *That Was The Week That Was*, Macmillan told him to do no such thing.) The gods do care about what mortals say about them, but when they take offence it is usually a matter of human negligence or dishonour: presuming to contend with the Muses in song, omitting a sacrifice, preening oneself on having more children than a god who, a mortal should have remembered, can take instant and brutal vengeance. It is their honour that matters, but to smile, even to laugh, is not necessarily to dishonour.

Lucian's age, the second century CE, was one when *Paideia*–both 'Culture' and 'Education'–was very important to the way members of the elite thought of themselves in Greece and Asia Minor. It helped them to keep a level of self-respect despite the knowledge that ultimate power rested with the Romans ('those above', as Plutarch had tellingly described them a generation or so earlier, in language more normally used of the gods). The two worlds were not wholly separate: Roman grandees too sometimes prided themselves on their Hellenism, and two of the emperors of Lucian's lifetime, Hadrian and Marcus Aurelius, were particularly enthusiastic for (rather different brands of) Greek culture and philosophy. Easterners could themselves get to positions of authority, as Lucian himself did late in life, holding some sort of administrative position in Egypt.

Still, cultural life was often the more important badge; indeed, one thing that Lucian's works show is how, once you had got used to Roman power, you could spend most of your time not thinking, or at least not talking, about it at all. Rhetorical virtuosity could be a path to celebrity, and the stars could travel extensively, preceded by their fame. Lucian himself travelled the world, and he gives the impression that he was something of a star. He could also bite the hand that had brought the stardom. In *Twice on Trial* he has Rhetoric herself denouncing 'that Syrian word-merchant'–clearly himself–for abandoning her after what had started as so happy a marriage. She'd made him her favourite when he was young, they'd travelled the world together, and now he'd deserted her for this new lover-boy 'Dialogue'. Lucian retorts that it is Rhetoric's own fault for becoming so shallow and flirty, giving far too much encouragement to those overblown young drunks who've been serenading her: anyway, he's over 40 now, and getting too old for all her nonsense; and Dialogue just happened to be lodging in a neighbour's house ... True, Lucian's trials are not then over: Dialogue himself protests at how Lucian has dragged him down from the heights reached in all those philosophical conversations of Socrates that Plato described. Too many laughs, thinks Dialogue; far too many laughs. But Rhetoric is the one who comes off worse.

That is one of the times when Lucian gives a glimpse of his own career. It would be unwise to believe that tongue-in-cheek 'conversion narrative' literally, even if it may give some distant version of what really happened in his life. In *The Dream*, too, he is doubtless giving us an embroidered version of, this time, the moment in his youth when his family had to choose his future career. His maternal uncle was a sculptor; that at least may be true, though the memory of that other figure who trained as a sculptor, Socrates, may not be far away. Lucian, too, had himself always shown some talent with his hands, happy once school had finished to play with a lump of wax and fashion an ox or a horse or a human being. So he was sent off to his uncle as an apprentice. The first day was a disaster. Given a block of marble to prepare, he managed to ruin it. His uncle gave him a good beating, earning his own tongue-lashing for it later that day from his angry sister, Lucian's mother: one can picture the Mediterranean family scene well enough. Lucian fled home in tears.

That night he had a dream in which he was confronted by two women: Craft (*Techne*), dirty, unkempt, with calloused hands and a masculine expression; and Culture (*Paideia*), good-looking, nicely turned out, and altogether more attractive and alluring. The two tussled over him and his future. Craft does not conceal the hard work ahead if he chooses her; Culture promises a quick path to fame, wealth, a fine life, and acclaim wherever he travels. Not a difficult choice, then, for the boy Lucian, and Culture duly rewards him with a chariot-ride across the heavens in lovely clothes, watching the adoring multitudes below. The work ends with Lucian priding himself on the way the dream has come true: let me be an example to all you young men to 'turn to the better and embrace culture', and not shy away because you may be poor...

Smug smug smug, one thinks. Yet the work becomes more enigmatic if one places it in a literary context that Lucian's audience would know very well. There are many other examples of such 'choices', often as here featuring two women offering alternative rewards. The ultimate model is the choice facing 'Heracles at the crossroads', developed by the fifth-century BCE sophist Prodicus and related to us by Xenophon. That was a choice between Virtue and Vice, and most of the other 'choices' we have are versions of that one. The odd thing here is that Craft—hard-working, dirty, tough—echoes a lot of what is often said about Virtue: the road is hard, but it's worth it, and ultimately more rewarding. Vice herself is usually the alluring one, as she was for Heracles: often more tartily alluring than Culture is here, certainly, but still marked by nice clothes, a sexy smile, and a promise of easy success. What Culture has to offer is often too flip for comfort:

> I will make you an expert in virtually everything: I shall give your soul, your most important part, adornment after adornment—good sense, justice, piety, mildness, reasonableness, intelligence, courage, love of the beautiful, an ambition for the highest and grandest...
>
> (*The Dream* 10)

Great stuff—but this is very much what Plato's Socrates (who was also hot on the soul as 'your most important part') had complained about in his *Gorgias* five hundred years before, the way that orators trampled on all sorts of difficult ground that was not their own, and made over-simple judgements that befuddled an audience. True, this is 'Culture' as a whole making the claim, not just Rhetoric; but it is a very rhetorically slick sort of Culture, one who can claim that it will all happen so *quickly*.

> After a short time you will be an object of envy and jealousy for all; you'll get honour and praise and high respect, turning the heads of the rich and noble: you'll be dressed like this (and she pointed to the fine things she was wearing herself), and you'll get power and the best seats; if you go abroad, they'll have heard of you and your glory even there; I'll make you so recognizable that everyone who sees you will nudge his neighbour and point and say 'That's him!'
>
> (*The Dream* 11)

This is all reminiscent of that rhetorical celebrity culture of the day, a world of fancily dressed intellectual showmen going the rounds, travelling the world, loving the adulation of their audiences. One feature of this particular showman is that he can make fun of that showmanship and of himself. In another work (*Professor of Oratory*) he has a further twist on the Choice set-piece, contrasting two ways to learn Rhetoric, one shallow and slick and the other hard and disciplined. What Lucian chooses in *The Dream* is clearly the superficial, Culture-lite version. 'Let me be an inspiration to you all...'— well, perhaps, but only with a healthy dose of irony. If the young really look up to him with those blandly adoring eyes, they may be being just as naïve as Lucian himself was all those years ago, and they may come to know that there's less to that sort of life than meets the eye.

This celebrity culture has often been known as that of 'The Second Sophistic'. That term is, probably rightly, falling out of fashion, as it fails to capture so much of a complex and very varied literary production; but it does capture the way that it looked back to many features of the first 'Sophistic', the burst of intellectual and rhetorical experimentation that characterized the fifth and fourth centuries BCE and formed the background for Socrates and Plato, in many ways the greatest 'sophists' of them all. That was true linguistically, with an almost superstitious fear of using any word that lacked the authority of use by one of the classical Athenian greats: we hear of pursed lips and vocal disapproval from an audience when they thought a speaker had used an uncanonical word. 'Dioskoroi is more correct than Dioskouroi' when you're talking about Castor and Pollux, recommends the grammarian Phrynichus, Lucian's contemporary: 'then you can laugh at people who pronounce it with a "u"' (*Ecl.* 205). Some of Lucian's essays too recall exercises where his classical predecessors paraded their ingenuity. Not all are to modern tastes. His *Encomium on a Fly* belongs in a line that goes back to works like *In Praise of Salt* or *In Praise of Mice* by the fourth-century sophist Polycrates: there is plenty of inventiveness there, but it is too clever-clever for most of us—wit rather than humour. His two defence speeches for Phalaris, whom everyone thought one of the most villainous of tyrants in history, are again ingenious, and do sometimes touch the spot: when a worried citizen of Delphi argues that they should not nitpick about accepting Phalaris' offering in case this puts off future donors, those who have served on university ethics committees will recognize the moves.

Another favourite literary game of this period was to describe a work of art, real or imagined. Lucian has a whole essay (*Pictures*) discussing the practice, but a particularly impressive example comes in another essay, *Don't believe Slander!* He is there describing a work of the great painter Apelles, the *Calumny*:

> On the right sits a man with immensely big ears, almost like those of Midas, and he is stretching his hand out some way to greet Calumny while she is still approaching. Two women are standing on either side of him, presumably Ignorance and Prejudice. Calumny is coming up from the other direction: she is an extraordinarily beautiful woman, hot and excited, as if she is conveying her frenzy and rage; in her left hand she is carrying a flaming torch, in the other she is dragging a young man by the hair as he holds out his hands to heaven and calls upon the gods to witness his innocence. A pale, misshapen man is leading the way, with a piercing expression and looking as if he has been wasting away through a long illness. This is presumably Envy. There are two other female figures too in attendance, urging on Calumny and attending to her dress and her adornment. The guide explained to me that these two were Plotting and Deception. Behind followed a woman in full mourning, wearing black and with torn flesh. This was said, I think, to be Remorse, and certainly she was turning to look behind her with tears in her eyes, and was glancing in a stealthy and very shamefaced way at the approaching Truth.

(Lucian, Don't Believe Slander 5)

This description was well-known in the Renaissance, and many painters produced their own versions of Apelles' original. We have pieces by Mantegna, Dürer, Brueghel, Rembrandt, one after Raphael, and—best-known of all—Sandro Botticelli's version of 1494–5 (Figure 12.2). His version is very exact, but the elaborations are interesting: Calumny less beautiful and more astute than excited, for instance, leaving the comeliness to Truth; Truth herself pointing heavenwards, and portrayed as naked in contrast to the heavy garb of everyone else except the victim. 'The naked truth' was not yet a cliché, and this in fact set a fashion for later portrayals of Truth.

FIGURE 12.2. Sandro Botticelli, *The Calumny of Apelles*, c.1495.

Botticelli has perhaps drawn the idea from a phrase of Horace, *nuda Veritas* (*Odes* 1.24); if so, it is not the only parading of classical knowledge. The centaurs relief at the foot of the throne is based on another description given by Lucian himself, this time of a painting of Zeuxis, while the sumptuous architectural setting recalls some passages in his essay on *Halls*. That lavish background, with its mix of classical and biblical figures, may also convey the lasting nature of the moral: it was true then, it is true still.

This description, then, was regarded as an exercise for the painter who tried to imitate it; another exercise is one for the viewer, or originally for Lucian's reader. There must be a story behind this, one thinks. Why did Apelles paint this scene, or Botticelli, or anyone else? Lucian mentions the 'guide' that showed him the picture, and no guide, surely, could resist finding an answer. Lucian duly gives us the story that was told about Apelles. One of his jealous rivals had denounced him to King Ptolemy IV of Egypt, claiming that he had been part of a treacherous conspiracy in Tyre, though in fact Apelles had never even seen the place. Apelles' head was only saved by a last-minute intervention from one of the real conspirators, then under arrest and willing to tell the truth. When Ptolemy realized how close he had come to an appalling injustice, he was so mortified that he rewarded Apelles with a huge sum of money and enslaved his rival: hence the prominence of Remorse in the picture. In fact, this cannot be true: Apelles had been dead for the best part of a hundred years by the time of that revolt. But it was the sort of tale that would inevitably be told. People have wondered in similar fashion about Botticelli too. He was certainly no stranger to controversy, as is still visible in the unfriendly touches in Vasari's biography half a century later, and we know that a few years after the *Calumny* he was denounced by a jealous rival for sodomy: was such talk already in the air? Or might the painting be a response to the rule of Piero de' Medici ('Piero the Unfortunate'), who since his accession in 1492 had been talked into dismissing two of his senior counsellors? Or might it be about some other victim of slander, perhaps the dominating city figure of Savonarola himself or one of his associates? Or Botticelli's friend the banker Antonio Segni, to whom Vasari says he gave the painting? All those suggestions have been made. The interesting thing is the way we are drawn in to ask, and to speculate.

And what of Lucian himself? Why write such an essay in the first place? Had he similarly been traduced? Some have wondered. As with Botticelli, there is no way that we can know; but it does again bring out the teasing quality of his writings, and the temptation for us to fill in more about the author than he actually tells us.

Lucian smiles a lot. But how sharp is the knife that this smiler wields? Does he really hate both gods and men, as the solemn and unsympathetic have sometimes claimed? Or is the denunciation itself felt as posturing, with the shrillness making the speaker part of the target? In the previous chapter we saw the same question raised with the satires of Juvenal a generation or so earlier, and some of Lucian's vignettes have a distinctly Juvenalian flavour. In *Philosophers for Hire*, for instance, he paints the miserable life of the Greek philosopher worming his way into the entourage of a rich Roman who likes to have a bearded intellectual on show. The philosopher suffers indignity after indignity, from the embarrassment of the first dinner where he has to keep an eye on his neighbour to know what to eat first, through the hardship of all those early rises to pay his respects, to finally a glorious picture of a real task at last—but what a task! The mistress just entrusts him with her pet bitch to take care of on a journey, and the animal nestles in his lap, licking his beard, pissing down his front, and finally giving birth to her litter under his cloak.

Or take *Nigrinus*, where a young man falls in love with philosophy—this is one of those passages we noted in Chapter II which borrow Sappho's description of erotic passion—and has his eyes opened to all the shallowness of the Roman city. How different from Athens, where philosophy is treated with reverence and vulgar luxury earns a stylish put-down (*Nigrinus* 12–14)! Yet elsewhere Lucian does not spare Athens either, and the criticisms of Roman materialism and high living are ones that were made of Athens too; the butt in *Nigrinus* may be as much the over-exuberance of the convert, especially in view of Lucian's acid opinion of contemporary philosopher-phoneys elsewhere. But still that work has a dedicatory letter to Nigrinus himself, the man whose inspiring philosophy converted the young student, and that sort of dedication should guarantee that the work is a compliment—always assuming that 'Nigrinus' really existed at all. So is the teacher fine, and it is just the pupil whose response is over the top? Possibly: but again the voice is elusive, and Lucian's reader, just like Juvenal's, can take it several ways.

What, finally, of those gods, knockabout as they often are? Many have thought the tone too disrespectful to go with serious belief in the gods at all. 'When you say things like that, it sounds to me as if you don't believe the gods exist at all', is the indignant expostulation when a certain Tychiades (Fortune's Child, doubtless another thinly disguised version of Lucian himself) expresses a rather mild scepticism about divine healing charms (*Compulsive Liar* 10). He is not left without a reply, as we will see.

Certainly, atheism is available on the religious menu of Lucian's thoughtworld. Even his gods are uneasily aware of it. *Zeus Rants* takes us back to Olympus. Something has driven Zeus into a furious rage, and he boils over into tragic metre—

> O what is fearful, what is dread to say,
> What passion, or what dire and tragic fate,
> That ten iambics cannot now o'erbeat?
>
> (*Zeus Rants* 1)

And Hermes and Athena reply in kind, though they soon run out of metrical steam. What is it all about? Hera is wearily sanguine: oh, it will just be sex again—Zeus and yet another mortal girl. But no, it is more serious. There has been a debate down below on the gods and Providence. Timocles the Stoic had spoken up in their defence; Damis the Epicurean had claimed 'that the gods do not exist at all, far less notice or direct events' (4), and had had much the better of the argument before the close of play. It will all be resumed tomorrow. What should the gods do? A divine assembly is called, and as they arrive there is much wrangling over precedence. What pulls more rank, the workmanship of one's statues or the preciousness of their metal? What about foreign gods—surely they can't push in ahead of Greeks? And what about the Colossus of Rhodes? If he sits down, he'll occupy the whole Assembly area. Oh, do get on with it, cries Zeus. Everything does settle down, but Zeus is still at a loss for words. He tries some Homer, then borrows from the beginning of Demosthenes' *First Olynthiac*, which began 'Men of Athens':

> O men . . . of Godland, I think you would pay lots of good money to be clear about what it is that has brought you here today. Now that you have come, please listen to me attentively. The present crisis, gods, almost cries aloud to demand that you get a firm grip, but we give the impression of being altogether too casual . . .
>
> (*Zeus Rants* 15)

And this is where Demosthenes gives out, and Zeus is left on his own. He does indeed rant, and there is not much there except bluster: but the crisis is a real one, for if Damis wins the temples will be deserted, people will stop sacrificing, there will be no meat to savour, and the gods will go hungry and homeless. One grumpy voice is raised, that of Momus ('Blame'): we've only ourselves to blame, we've been neglectful, and look at all those bad stories they tell about us. The mortal debate resumes the next day, and Damis continues to have the better of it. The godly Timocles produces a portentous comparison of the gods with the pilot of a boat, but Damis points out crushingly that in that case we might expect the steering to be rather better. In the end Timocles has to resort to chasing out Damis with physical threats: so even violence, ruled out earlier by Zeus on the grounds that divine freedom of action is constrained by Fate, is managed better by the mortal. Zeus' last line, echoing a passage in Herodotus, is that he would prefer to have Damis on his side than 10,000 Babylons.

So: do we infer that Lucian is altogether on Damis' side? Maybe; but we just cannot tell. It is notable that that last line does not have Zeus coming to doubt his own existence, though Lucian could easily have fashioned a joke along those lines: that really would be existential *Angst*. It is just that Zeus would have liked a better spokesman. In *Compulsive Liar* 'Fortune's Child' did have an answer to the charge of atheism: 'don't say that, sir: nothing precludes the possibility that gods may exist but things like that may be false' (*Compulsive Liar* 10). 'Things like that' are in this context the claims of healing charms and magic, and Fortune's Child prefers to believe that Asclepius healed people with drugs and ointments rather than anything supernatural; but that essay has already made play with all the lying myths that people say about the gods as well. If Lucian had really intended a serious attack on any sort of religious thinking, there were other targets in his own day that might have figured more prominently: followers of Isis or of Mithras, for instance, or even Christians, who get only a brief reference in his *Peregrinus*. He treats Christians as gullible rather than wicked, but doesn't seem to care very much. It is interesting, too, to note that Lucian's heyday in later European culture came in the fifteenth (as we have already seen with Botticelli) and sixteenth

FIGURE 12.3. Folly steps down from the pulpit after finishing her harangue. Hans Holbein the younger, illustration of final page of Erasmus' *In Praise of Folly*, 1515.

centuries. That is partly to do with the spread of printing, but it is also no coincidence that this was the time of the religious controversies that led to and surrounded the Reformation, with Lucian providing believers with a useful model for satires on different forms of Christianity and—especially—on the hypocritical behaviour of their adherents. True, Lucian caused offence too (partly because of that Christian reference), first to Luther, who loathed him, and then to the Vatican, which banned him. But those like Erasmus and More who exploited Lucian's model were certainly not atheists. For them it was what other people said about God that could be doubted, not the divine existence itself.

Still, as with Juvenal, it is eventually up to you, the reader, what to make of it all. The younger Holbein illustrated an early edition of Erasmus' very Lucianic *In Praise of Folly*, and his final page has Folly descending from the pulpit, her arm stiff from ranting gestures, and an audience looking rather bemused (Figure 12.3)—though the cap and bells worn by several suggest that they had come for the laughs. Lucian's audiences, then and now, might not be so very different.

One last thought about those gods. They may or may not be believable, but they are, somehow, thoroughly likeable. They remind us too of how flexible Greek religion could be, how many aspects there are to the Greek gods and how many perspectives they allowed and invited. I have no religion myself, but if I had, that sort would have its attractions. After all, many followers of the Hebrew Bible no longer believe in the literal truth of all those stories either, and still find that they convey something meaningful about the world. Of course, you don't necessarily choose your religion; the religion, many would say, chooses you. Going for a religion you like the look of does not increase its chances of being true, either. But if one does need or want a religion, and if, like Lucian's Damis, one finds it hard to see any single coherent steering in the world; if one is looking for a god or gods that help make sense of the conflicting multiplicities of human life, experience, and thought; if one wants gods that might do something to explain the presence of both evil and good, both immense suffering and immense fun—maybe polytheism, Greek polytheism or some other, might have some mileage in it after all.

CP

# TRANSLATIONS
# AND FURTHER READING

## I Homer

Translations from Homer have mainly been taken from the Penguin translations of the *Iliad* by Martin Hammond (Harmondsworth, 1987) and of the *Odyssey* by E. V. Rieu (revised version, Harmondsworth 1991). The Cavafy poem is quoted in the translation of Evangelos Sachperoglou (Oxford World's Classics, 2007).

'When I was one, in Shillingstone...' is quoted and briefly discussed by R. M. Ogilvie, *Latin and Greek* (London, 1964), 171, attributing it only to 'a young man'. His older brother James fought in France, Flanders, and Germany in 1944–5 before being invalided home with a serious wound; his father had himself been seriously wounded in Flanders in the First World War, losing an arm. The poem, dated 24 April 1945, is included in a collection of James Ogilvie's letters, privately published after his death in a climbing accident in 1948. (I am most grateful to Jennifer Ogilvie and Isobel Pinder for their advice here.) The resonance of Homer in First World War poetry is now explored in Elizabeth Vandiver's *Stand in the Trench, Achilles* (Oxford, 2010); she treats Shaw-Stewart's 'I saw a man this morning' at pp. 270–7, Sorley's 'When you see millions of the mouthless dead...' at pp. 292–7, and Owen's *Strange Meeting* at pp. 303–9. The Great War is only one of the contexts in which twentieth-century writers have responded to and moulded Homeric ideas in their own idiom: a sketch of that landscape is given by Barbara Graziosi and Emily Greenwood (eds.), *Homer in the Twentieth Century* (Oxford, 2007), and that is one of several perspectives taken in Edith Hall, *The Return of Ulysses* (London and New York, 2008) and Robert Fowler (ed.), *The Cambridge Companion to Homer* (Cambridge, 2004). Walcott's treatment of the hanging of the slave-girl Melantho is discussed by Lorna Hardwick in Fowler, pp. 354–5, and Graziosi–Greenwood, pp. 62–6; Cavafy's *Ithaka* is explored by Hall at pp. 161–3 and Tennyson's *Ulysses* at pp. 211–12.

Besides Fowler's *Companion*, I. Morris and B. Powell (eds.) *A New Companion to Homer* (Leiden, 1997), is also very helpful, and R. B. Rutherford's *Homer* is one of the best in the series of *Greece & Rome: New Surveys in the Classics* (2nd edn., 2012). A watershed in twentieth-century Homeric English-speaking scholarship was the demonstration by Milman Parry that the epics' formulaic language, in particular their use of recurrent epithets such as 'swift-footed Achilles' or 'much-enduring Odysseus', had been developed in so thoroughgoing and systematic a way that it must be the work of a continuous oral tradition over many generations; Parry's most important work was collected by his son Adam Parry and published as *The Making of Homeric Verse* (Oxford, 1971). He, like Albert Lord in *The Singer of Tales* (Cambridge, Mass., 1960), drew illuminating parallels with Yugoslav oral tradition. The implications of this for literary criticism are still being worked through, with ideas like that of 'traditional referentiality' (J. M. Foley, *Homer's Traditional Art*, Pennsylvania, 1999) and 'epic resonance' (B. Graziosi and J. Haubold, *The Resonance of Epic*, London, 2005) exploring the ways in which an audience's awareness of such a tradition may affect their understanding of the poems. B. Graziosi, *Inventing Homer* (Cambridge, 2002) gives an insightful discussion of the early biographical tradition, and brings out how such 'invented' biography can be used to illuminate the poems' early reception.

Good brief introductions to the literary qualities of the poems are given by M. Silk (*Iliad*) and J. Griffin (*Odyssey*) in the Cambridge Landmarks of World Literature series (both 1987). Griffin's *Homer on Life and Death* (Oxford, 1980) is also outstanding. Influential modern articles are usefully collected in *Oxford Readings in the Iliad*, ed. D. L. Cairns (2001) and *Oxford Readings in the Odyssey*, ed. L. E. Doherty (2009): the latter includes a perceptive article by R. B. Rutherford on 'The Philosophy of the *Odyssey*' that suggests the view taken here of the Laertes scene.

## II Sappho

Most of the translations are taken, with small adaptations, from M. L. West's *Greek Lyric Poetry* (Oxford World's Classics, 2008). The translation of the 'brothers poem' is my own, and was first published in the *Times Literary Supplement*, 7 February 2014. Anne Carson's 'free space of imaginal adventure' is quoted from the introduction to her own translation under the title *If not, Winter: Fragments of Sappho* (New York, 2002).

Wilamowitz-Moellendorf's picture of Sappho is presented in his *Sappho und Simonides* (Berlin, 1913). 'Tweedy games-mistresses' figure in George

Devereux's unfortunate and unpersuasive 'The nature of Sappho's seizure in fr. 31 LP as evidence of her inversion', *Classical Quarterly* n.s. 20 (1970), 17–31. 'Sappho taught them just what to do': thus Anne Pippin Burnett, *Three Archaic Poets: Archilochus, Alcaeus, Sappho* (Cambridge, Mass., 1983). 'Essentially plausible' is the verdict of Emmet Robbins in the German encyclopaedia *Der Neue Pauly* (2001; English translation 2008), and Franco Ferrari, *Sappho's Gift: The Poet and her Community* (tr. B. Acosta-Hughes and L. Prauscello, Michigan, 2010) still believes in 'Sappho's school', the title of his chapter 3. But Holt Parker's trenchant rejection of the idea of 'Sappho schoolmistress' has been rightly influential (*Transactions of the American Philological Association* 123 (1993), 309–51); some good points are also made by André Lardinois in his reply in the same journal (124 (1994), 57–84). Jane McIntosh Snyder's *Lesbian Desire in the Lyrics of Sappho* was published in 1997 (New York). The way that scholarly assumptions about 'Sappho's circle' have developed can be seen by comparing Reinhold Merkelbach, 'Sappho und ihr Kreis', *Philologus* 101 (1957), 1–29, with 'Sappho's group: an initiation into womanhood', a chapter in Claude Calame's *Choruses of Young Women in Ancient Greece*, tr. J. Orion and D. Collins (1994; repr. in Ellen Greene's *Reading Sappho*, mentioned below), and with 'Sappho's circle', a chapter in Eva Stehle's *Performance and Gender in Ancient Greece* (Princeton, 1997).

The new, fuller version of the poem on the dance was first published in 2004 by M. Gronewald and R. Daniel (*Zeitschrift für Papyrologie und Epigraphik* 147, 1–8 and 149, 1–4); the collection of E. Greene and M. Skinner, *The New Sappho on Old Age: Textual and Philosophical Issues* (*Classics@4*, Center for Hellenic Studies, 2011, on-line at http://chs.harvard.edu/wa/pageR?tn= ArticleWrapper&bdc=12&mn=3534) is devoted to it, and Deborah Boedeker and Gregory Nagy there suggest that the shorter and longer versions might both be authentic and suited to different performance contexts. Dover's comment on Lesbian women's sexual inventiveness is in the note on Aristophanes, *Frogs* 1308 in his Oxford commentary (1993). The new 'brothers poem' is published by Dirk Obbink in *Zeitschrift für Papyrologie und Epigraphik* 189 (2014).

Margaret Williamson's *Sappho's Immortal Daughters* (Harvard, 1995) is particularly accessible and perceptive. Ellen Greene's *Reading Sappho* and *Rereading Sappho* (Berkeley and London, 1996 and 1997) are useful anthologies: the second, like Margaret Reynolds' *The Sappho Companion* (London, 2000) and Joan DeJean's *Fictions of Sappho 1546–1937* (Chicago and London, 1989), concentrates on the poet's reception. Douglas E. Gerber (ed.), *A Companion to the Greek Lyric Poets* (Leiden, 1997) and Felix Budelmann (ed.), *The Cambridge Companion to Greek Lyric* (2009), are useful for setting Sappho against a wider background.

## III Herodotus

Translations are taken, with small adaptations, from Robin Waterfield's Oxford World's Classics version (1998), a volume to which Carolyn Dewald contributed an outstanding introduction and notes.

*Forgotten Empire* was on display at the British Museum from September 2005 to January 2006, and subsequently travelled to Chicago; the book of the exhibition by J. E. Curtis and Nigel Tallis appeared under the same title. Jonathan Jones's review, concluding that 'The Persian empire visible in its surviving artefacts turns out to be as grandiose, luxurious and remotely despotic as Herodotus said it was', appeared in the *Guardian* of 8 September (http://www.guardian.co.uk/artanddesign/2005/sep/08/architecture). The response to Jones can be traced at http://culturalchenarestan.blogspot. co.uk/; the letter taking a different view of Herodotus came from me. The Cyrus Cylinder was subsequently loaned to Teheran in 2010. This is not the place to discuss the fierce and continuing debate stimulated by Edward Saïd's *Orientalism* (originally published in 1978; further editions in 1995 and 2003, including an 'Afterword'). Athenian responses to Persia in fifth-century art are traced and illustrated by Margaret C. Miller, *Athens and Persia in the Fifth Century BC* (Cambridge 1997): they too went well beyond simple triumphalism. Plutarch brands Herodotus as 'barbarian-lover' at *Malice of Herodotus* 857a.

Valuable Companion volumes to Herodotus are *Brill's Companion to Herodotus*, ed. E. Bakker, I. de Jong, and H. van Wees (Leiden, 2002) and the *Cambridge Companion to Herodotus*, ed. C. Dewald and J. Marincola (Cambridge, 2006). John Marincola's *Greek Historians* (*Greece & Rome: New Surveys in the Classics* 31 (2001)) gives a good overview of Herodotus. R. Munson's *Oxford Readings in Herodotus* (two volumes, 2013) collects recent articles, including one of my own in which I argued that East–West distinctions are not as simple as they might seem (C. Pelling, 'East is East and West is West—or are they? National stereotypes in Herodotus', first published in *Histos* 1997). Other valuable collections are *The Historian's Craft in the Age of Herodotus*, ed. N. Luraghi (Oxford, 2001), *Herodotus and his World*, ed. P. Derow and R. Parker (Oxford, 2003), and the detailed studies of Book 5 gathered in *Reading Herodotus*, ed. E. Irwin and E. Greenwood (Cambridge, 2007). F. Hartog's *The Mirror of Herodotus*, tr. J. Lloyd (Berkeley, Los Angeles, and London, 1988; French original 1980, second edn. 1991) has been influential on Herodotus' reading of Greek and foreign cultures. Outstanding book-length studies of different sorts have been J. Gould, *Herodotus* (London, 1999), R. Thomas, *Herodotus in Context* (Cambridge, 2000), R. Munson, *Telling Wonders* (Michigan, 2001), and E. Baragwanath, *Motivation and Narrative in Herodotus* (Oxford, 2008). There is still much of value in H. R. Immerwahr, *Form and Thought in Herodotus* (Cleveland, Ohio, 1966). For the view that Herodotus was writing for an audience that would include those who, unlike himself, knew how the Peloponnesian War would end, see C. Dewald, 'Wanton kings, pickled heroes, and gnomic founding fathers: strategies of meaning at the end of Herodotus's *Histories*', in *Classical Closure*, ed. D. Roberts, F. Dunn, and D. Fowler (Princeton 1997), 62–82.

The Cambridge green-and-yellow series will include commentaries on each book of Herodotus, and the introductions of these are usually accessible to the non-Greek reader. Already published are the commentaries on Books 5 (S. Hornblower), 8 (A. Bowie), and 9 (M. Flower and J. Marincola); those on Book 1 (C. Dewald and R. Munson), 2, 3 (A. Griffiths), 4 (S. West), 6 (S. Hornblower and C. Pelling), and 7 (C. Carey) will follow.

## IV Thucydides

Translations are taken, with some very slight adaptations, from Martin Hammond's Oxford World's Classics version (2009), which also includes an introduction by P. J. Rhodes. *The Landmark Thucydides* version, edited by Robert Strassler (New York, etc., 1996), should also be mentioned: the nineteenth-century version it uses (that of Richard Crawley, 1874) inevitably sounds dated, but it is particularly lavish in its use of maps, and that is very valuable for those wanting to trace out the campaigning on the ground.

*Brill's Companion to Thucydides*, ed. A. Rengakos and A. Tsakmakis (Leiden and Boston, 2006) is useful; so is Jeffrey Rusten's collection of influential articles in his Oxford Readings in Classical Studies volume on Thucydides (Oxford, 2009). A further recent collection on *Thucydides and Herodotus*, ed. E. Foster and D. Lateiner (Oxford, 2012) explores the connections and contrasts between the two historians from various angles.

Particularly useful general books are W. R. Connor, *Thucydides* (Princeton, 1984) and Simon Hornblower, *Thucydides* (London, 1987); Connor takes the reader through the text book-by-book, with many perceptive remarks, while Hornblower treats the author thematically, with a particularly strong chapter on his 'intellectual affinities'. Tim Rood's *Thucydides: Narrative and Explanation* (Oxford, 1998) makes effective use of modern narratology in analysing Thucydides' technique. Emily Greenwood's *Thucydides and the Shaping of History* (London, 2006) is succinct and very thought-provoking.

Lisa Kallet's two books on Thucydides—*Money, Expense, and Naval Power in Thucydides' History 1–5.24* (as Lisa Kallet-Marx, Berkeley, etc., 1993) and *Money and the Corrosion of Power in Thucydides: The Sicilian Expedition and its Aftermath* (Berkeley, etc., 2001)—are both very rewarding: the second is particularly good on literary aspects, bringing out how important it is for the historian to be alert to these. That was also the theme of several Thucydidean chapters in my own *Literary Texts and the Greek Historian* (London, 2000). A more traditional approach to Thucydides' material was followed by Donald Kagan in his various volumes on the Peloponnesian War, all of them still valuable: *The Outbreak of the Peloponnesian War*, *The Archidamian War*, *The Peace of Nicias and the Sicilian Expedition*, and *The Fall of the Athenian Empire* (Cornell, 1969–87).

There have been two monumental commentaries on Thucydides over the last seventy years, first the five-volume *Historical Commentary on Thucydides* begun by A. W. Gomme and completed by K. J. Dover and A. Andrewes (Oxford, 1944–81) and then Simon Hornblower's three-volume *Commentary on Thucydides* (Oxford, 1993–2008). Hornblower also collected some of his separate articles on Thucydides in *Thucydidean Themes* (Oxford, 2011). Many of these are specialist, but still the general reader will find plenty of value, and his *Commentary* is now the natural first stop for anyone pursuing a particular point or problem.

Thucydides' modern reception is treated in Neville Morley's forthcoming Wiley-Blackwell *Handbook to the Reception of Thucydides* (2014), including a chapter by Elizabeth Sawyer on his treatment by International Relations theorists. I am grateful to Jennie Kiesling for the phrasing of the US Naval College syllabus. David A. Welch wrote on 'Why International Relations Theorists should stop reading Thucydides' in *Review of International Studies* 29.3 (2003), 301–19, insisting that this title should not be taken literally: simply '[w]e should stop trying to bend him to our will by making him speak to debates about which he would understand little and care even less', and regard him as providing 'a rich treasure-trove of evidence', no more.

## V Euripides

Translations used in this chapter are my own. Versions of all the extant plays were included in Richmond Lattimore and David Grene's *Complete Greek Tragedies* (2nd edn., Chicago, 1992) and in David Kovacs' Loeb Classical Library edition (Cambridge, Mass., 1994–2002). The new Penguin versions are by J. Davie (tr.) and R. Rutherford (intr. and notes): *Electra and Other Plays* (*Suppliant Women, Andromache, Trojan Women, Hecuba*, 1999), *Heracles and Other Plays* (*Iphigeneia among the Taurians, Helen, Ion, Cyclops*, 2002), *Medea and Other Plays* (*Alcestis, Children of Heracles, Hippolytus*, 2003), and *The Bacchae and Other Plays* (*Phoenissae, Iphigeneia at Aulis, Orestes*, and the non-Euripidean *Rhesus*, 2006). There are verse translations by various authors in the University of Pennsylvania series edited by David R. Slavitt and Palmer Bovie (4 volumes, 1997–9).

Most of the plays now have good modern commentaries: for those treated in this chapter, see those by D. Mastronarde (Cambridge, 2002) and J. Mossman (Warminster, 2010) on *Medea*; W. S. Barrett (very detailed, Oxford, 1963) and M. Halleran (Warminster, 1995) on *Hippolytus*; K. H. Lee (London, 1976) and S. Barlow (Warminster, 1986) on *Trojan Women*; E. R. Dodds (2nd edn., Oxford 1960) and R. Seaford (Warminster, 2006) on *Bacchae*. There are also recent Duckworth Companions to these plays by W. Allan (*Medea*, 2002), S. Mills (*Hippolytus*, 2002 and *Bacchae*, 2006), and B. Goff (*Trojan Women*, 2008), and a book-length study of *Trojan Women* by N. Croally (*Euripidean Polemic*, Cambridge, 1994). The chapter on Euripidean drama in Edith Hall's *Greek Tragedy: Suffering under the Sun* (Oxford, 2010) illuminatingly discusses the plays one by one.

Gilbert Murray's *Euripides and his Age* was first published in the Home University Library in 1913; a second edition appeared in 1948. Ancient biographical traditions about Euripides are treated by M. Lefkowitz in *The Lives of the Greek Poets* (2nd edn., Oxford, 2012). Influential articles are gathered by J. Mossman in *Oxford Readings in Euripides* (2003). Various aspects of Euripidean drama are handled by J. Gregory, *Euripides and the Instruction of the Athenians* (Michigan, 1991), C. Segal, *Euripides and the Poetics of Sorrow* (Durham and London, 1993), J. Mossman, *Wild Justice*

(Oxford, 1995), M. Wright, *Euripides' Escape-Tragedies* (Oxford, 2005), and D. Mastronarde, *The Art of Euripides* (Cambridge, 2010).

General works on Greek Tragedy naturally give much space to Euripides, e.g. S. Goldhill's *Reading Greek Tragedy* (Cambridge, 1986), M. Silk (ed.), *Tragedy and the Tragic* (Oxford, 1996), and C. Pelling (ed.), *Greek Tragedy and the Historian* (Oxford, 1997). An outstanding recent contribution is R. Rutherford, *Greek Tragic Style* (Oxford, 2012). *The Cambridge Companion to Greek Tragedy* edited by P. Easterling (1997) and the Wiley-Blackwell *Companion to Greek Tragedy* edited by J. Gregory (2005) cover many features, including modern reception. E. Hall and F. Macintosh, *Greek Tragedy and the British Theatre 1660–1914* (Oxford, 2005) is a magisterial treatment of British productions.

## VI Caesar

It is difficult to reproduce the purity of Caesar's Latin in English translation. Greater variation of expression tends to creep in, especially in the most recent translations. I have therefore used here, apart from some minor variations, the translations of *de bello Gallico* (*The Gallic War*) and *de bello civili* (*The Civil War*) by W. A. McDevitte and W. S. Bohn (New York, 1869). In the case of *The Gallic War*, their translation is conveniently available online at http://www.perseus.tufts.edu along with the Latin original and extensive notes. In the Oxford World's Classics series, Carolyn Hammond's *Caesar: The Gallic War* (1996) includes a useful introduction, notes, and the text of the supplementary eighth book written by Caesar's lieutenant Aulus Hirtius. Similarly, *Caesar: The Civil War* translated by John Carter (Oxford, 1997) includes the anonymous accounts of the Alexandrian, African, and Spanish wars that continue where Caesar's account of the Civil War breaks off.

Biographies of Julius Caesar can supply much of the cultural and historical context needed to understand his war commentaries and their purpose. The standard biography is still that of Matthias Gelzer, *Caesar: Politician and Statesman* (originally published in German in 1921, translated by P. Needham (Oxford, 1968) and multiply reprinted). Adrian Goldsworthy's *Caesar: The Life of a Colossus* (London, 2006) is a recent substantial study that pays particular attention to ancient warfare. There are also a number of shorter, readable introductions such as W. Jeffrey Tatum, *Always I am Caesar* (Oxford, 2008). Blackwell's *A Companion to Julius Caesar* edited by Miriam Griffin (Oxford, 2009) contains a range of helpful essays covering Caesar's career, his writings, his reputation in antiquity, and his influence from the Middle Ages to the twenty-first century, as well as plenty of suggestions for further reading in these categories. Christopher Pelling offers a detailed commentary on the text of Plutarch's *Caesar* (Oxford, 2011). A representative taste of the many approaches to Shakespeare's tragedy can be found in the collection edited by Horst Zander, *Julius Caesar: New Critical Essays* (New York, 2005). Surveys of Caesar's impact on Western culture and on American culture in particular can be found in, respectively, Maria Wyke's *Caesar: A Life in Western Culture* (London, 2007) and *Caesar in the USA* (Berkeley, 2012).

On *The Gallic War* and the literary strategies it forcefully deploys to present the character Caesar as an ideal Roman general, see the collection edited by Kathryn Welch and Anton Powell, *Julius Caesar as Artful Reporter: The War Commentaries as Political Instruments* (London, 1998). An especially accessible and thought-provoking analysis of Caesar's *Civil War* is that by William W. Batstone and Cynthia Damon (Oxford, 2006). Recent analysis of the authority Caesar's commentaries accrue from the use of the writer 'I-Caesar' to tell us about the activities of the general 'he-Caesar' can be found in C. Pelling, 'Xenophon's and Caesar's third-person narratives—or are they?', in *The Author's Voice in Classical and Late Antiquity*, ed. J. Hill and A. Marmodoro (Oxford, 2013), 39–73. Further discussion of the literary, political, and ideological significance of the war commentaries can be found in Andrew M. Riggsby, *Caesar in Gaul and Rome: War in Words* (Austin, Texas 2006) and Luca Grillo, *The Art of Caesar's* Bellum Civile: *Literature, Ideology, and Community* (Cambridge, 2012). Details of commentaries on individual books of *The Gallic War* and *The Civil War* can also be found in those works.

## VII Cicero

Translations used with only minor variations: *Against Verres*, D. H. Berry in the Oxford World's Classics series: *Cicero: Political Speeches* (2006); *On the Nature of the Gods*, J. M. Ross (London, 1972); *Philippics* 2, Berry (as above); *Philippics* 3 and 5, G. Manuwald in *Cicero, Philippics 3–9* Volume 1 (Berlin, 2007); *Letters to Friends* 14.4 and *Letters to Friends* 10.28, P. G. Walsh, *Cicero: Selected Letters* (Oxford, 2008); *On Obligations*, P. G. Walsh in *Cicero: On Obligations (De Officiis)* (Oxford, 2000).

While modern translators have found it difficult to reproduce the purity of Caesar's Latin in English translation, they are often reluctant to reproduce the exuberance, repetition, rhythm—the sheer 'rhetoric'—of Cicero's. The closest approximation to Cicero's style (but perhaps also the most alienating) is in the Loeb Classical Library editions of all his writings. To date Oxford World's Classics have produced six volumes of selected translations and Penguin Classics nine. They all contain introductions and suggestions for further reading. Many of Cicero's individual works have Latin editions with thorough commentaries (details are contained in many of the works below).

On Cicero broadly, see Elizabeth Rawson, *Cicero: A Portrait* (London, 1975; 2nd edn. Bristol, 1994) and Andrew Lintott, *Cicero as Evidence: A Historian's Companion* (Oxford, 2008). Cicero appears as a sensible conservative in the popular biography by Antony Everitt, *Cicero: The Life and Times of Rome's Greatest Politician* (London, 2001) and as a contemptible villain in Michael Parenti's *The Assassination of Julius Caesar, A People's History of Ancient Rome* (New York, 2003). See also Kathryn Tempest, *Cicero: Politics and Persuasion in Ancient Rome* (London, 2011).

Useful studies of Cicero's oratory and its relationship to the written word are C. Steel, *Reading Cicero: Genre and Performance in Late Republican Rome* (London, 2005) and Shane Butler, *The Hand of Cicero* (London, 2002). Cicero's 'conceptual inventiveness' in his speeches is explored by Ingo Gildenhard, *Creative Eloquence: The Construction of Reality in Cicero's Speeches* (Oxford, 2011). Collections of essays on his philosophy include *Cicero the Philosopher: Twelve Papers*, ed. J. G. F. Powell (Oxford, 1995) and *Cicero's Practical Philosophy*, ed. W. Nicgorski (Notre Dame, Ind., 2012). L. P. Wilkinson provides some brief discussion of the variety of Cicero's correspondence in *Letters of Cicero: A Selection in Translation* (London, 1966). G. O. Hutchinson concentrates interestingly on their literary rather than historical interest in *Cicero's Correspondence: A Literary Study* (Oxford, 1998). Peter White in *Cicero in Letters: Epistolary Relations of the Late Republic* (Oxford, 2010) supplies a sense of ancient letters as a form of social intercourse. See also J. M. May (ed.), *Brill's Companion to Cicero: Oratory and Rhetoric* (Leiden, 2002) and C. Steel (ed.), *The Cambridge Companion to Cicero* (Cambridge, 2013).

Cicero's importance to the American revolutionaries and Founding Fathers is traced in Carl J. Richard, *The Founding Fathers and the Classics: Greece, Rome, and the American Enlightenment* (Cambridge, Mass., 1994) and *Classical*

*Antiquity and the Politics of America: From George Washington to George W. Bush*, ed. M. Meckler (Waco, Texas, 2006). Finally, you can listen to some performed speeches of Cicero at http://www.utexas.edu/depts/classics/documents/Cic.html (by A. M. Riggsby), http://courses.missouristate.edu/josephhughes/cicero.htm (by J. Hughes) and http://cicero.humnet.ucla.edu/.

## VIII  Virgil

Robert Fitzgerald's translation of the *Aeneid* is used throughout this chapter (New York, 1983), except on one occasion as indicated where I draw on that of the Poet Laureate C. Day Lewis first published in 1952 and available in the Oxford World's Classics series (1986). Other easily accessible English translations of the *Aeneid* include one in prose by the scholar David West (London, 1990). Dryden's canonical translation of 1697 is frequently reprinted. In *Virgil in English* (London, 1996), K. W. Gransden offers an anthology of English translations and imitations from Chaucer to Seamus Heaney. Verse translations of both the *Eclogues* and *Georgics* by C. Day Lewis first published in 1963 and 1940 respectively are usefully contained in the Oxford World's Classics series, accompanied by an introduction from R. O. A. M. Lyne (1983). There are also readily available verse translations of the *Eclogues* by Guy Lee (London, 1984) and of the *Georgics* by L. P. Wilkinson (London, 1982).

There exists a vast sea of literature on Virgil's poetry, including multiple introductions, surveys, companions, and guides. Of note is the rich and broad-ranging survey of all three works by Philip Hardie, *Virgil* (*Greece & Rome: New Surveys in the Classics*, 28 (Oxford, 1998)). He covers clearly many of the central issues they raise about poetic traditions, allusion, politics, structure, and imagery. He also sets out succinctly the history of interpretation of Virgil's outlook on the human condition as it separated out into 'optimistic' or 'pessimistic' readings. There is an earlier but still useful introduction by Jasper Griffin, *Virgil* (Oxford, 1986) and, recently, one by R. Alden Smith, *Virgil* (Malden, Mass., 2011) that includes discussion of the survival and transmission of Virgil's text. The collection edited by Charles Martindale, *The Cambridge Companion to Virgil* (Cambridge, 1997), offers a range of essays with significant emphasis on responses to Virgil over the centuries including, as responses, translations and illustrations.

On the *Aeneid* in particular, see Oliver Lyne, *Further Voices in Vergil's Aeneid* (Oxford, 1987) for explicit use of the metaphor of 'voices'. Lyne argues that 'further voices' comment upon, question, or subvert an 'epic' voice. Two substantial essays by Alessandro Schiesaro suggest that literary allusion back to earlier works creates even greater tonal complexity in the poem, 'Furthest voices in Virgil's Dido', *Studi italiani di filologia classica* 100 (2008), 60–109 and 194–245. In *Virgil's Aeneid: Cosmos and Imperium* (Oxford, 1986), Philip Hardie demonstrates how the forces of order in nature (*cosmos*) are made to harmonize with the creation of the Roman state (*imperium*) in order to produce a profoundly panegyrical epic poem. A useful selection of important articles on the *Aeneid* from the 1930s to the 1980s are to be found in *Oxford Readings in Vergil's Aeneid*, ed. S. J. Harrison (1990), including an introduction that details movements to and fro in the history of twentieth-century scholarship on the epic. In *Virgil's Aeneid: A Reader's Guide* (Malden, Mass., 2007), David O. Ross provides an accessible and engaging entry point into the epic poem, placing strong emphasis on reading it in terms of the futility of heroism, and its cost in human terms. There is also a conveniently concise student guide to the historical context and literary significance of the epic in *Virgil: The Aeneid* by K. W. Gransden (Cambridge, 1990), published in a second edition in 2004 with an updated guide to further reading by S. J. Harrison. Gransden also takes up the challenge of explaining to the non-specialist how Virgil exploited the Latin language to produce textured, musical, and empathetic poetic meaning.

Richard F. Thomas, *Virgil and the Augustan Reception* (Cambridge, 2001) examines the ideological reception of Virgil over the last two millennia. Joseph Farrell and Michael C. J. Putnam have edited *A Companion to Vergil's Aeneid and its Tradition* (Malden, Mass., 2010) that includes a wide array of over thirty essays exploring the extraordinary diversity of its reception from antiquity to the twentieth century and the latter's separation into the opposing camps of imperial and anti-imperial interpretation.

Commentaries aimed at specialists are listed in many of the works cited above. The Vergil Project (http://vergil.classics.upenn.edu/) is a website based at the University of Pennsylvania that provides a range of linguistic resources for readers of Virgil's Latin including word-for-word translation and assistance with grammar and syntax.

## IX Horace

Translations used with only minor variation: *Satires* 1.4, Niall Rudd in *The Satires of Horace and Persius* (London, first published 1973, most recent reprint with revisions 2005); *Epodes* 17, *Odes* 2.19, *Odes* 1.13, and *Odes* 1.37, David West in *Horace: The Complete Odes and Epodes* (Oxford, 1997); *Odes* 4.7, Samuel Johnson in *Samuel Johnson: The Major Works* edited with an introduction and notes by D. Greene (Oxford, 2000); *Odes* 3.30, John Hollander in *Horace, The Odes: New Translations by Contemporary Poets*, ed. J. D. McClatchy (Princeton, 2003). In *How to Read a Latin Poem: If You Can't Read Latin Yet* (Oxford, 2013), William Fitzgerald gives an excellent sense of what it is like to read a Latin poem in the original (and why we might want to), and includes a whole chapter on the poetic techniques of Horace.

A variety of user-friendly Latin texts, accompanied by commentary and English translation, are available: Michael Brown, *Horace Satires I* (Oxford, 1993) and Emily Gowers, *Horace Satires I* (Cambridge, 2012); Francis Muecke, *Horace Satires II* (Oxford, 1993); David West, *Horace Odes 1: Carpe Diem* (Oxford, 1995), *Horace Odes II: Vatis Amici* (Oxford, 1998), and *Horace Odes III: Dulce Periculum* (Oxford, 2002); M. C. J. Putnam, *Artifices of Eternity: Horace's Fourth Book of Odes* (Cornell, 1986). A. G. Lee's *Horace: Odes and Carmen Saeculare* (Leeds, 1998) gives a flavour of Horace's original metres and the differences between them by producing 'metrical' translations. More elaborate commentaries include R. G. M. Nisbet and M. Hubbard, *Horace Odes 1* (Oxford, 1970) and *Horace Odes 2* (Oxford, 1978); R. G. M. Nisbet and N. Rudd, *Horace Odes 3* (Oxford, 2004); D. Mankin, *Horace Epodes* (Cambridge, 1995); L. C. Watson, *Horace Epodes* (Oxford, 2003); R. Mayer, *Horace Epistles 1* (Cambridge, 1994); N. Rudd, *Horace Epistles 2 and Ars Poetica* (Cambridge, 1989).

The secondary literature on Horace is copious. A recent useful introduction can be found in Philip Hills, *Horace* (Bristol, 2004). *A Companion to Horace*, ed. Gregson Davis (Oxford, 2010), contains essays covering historical context, genres, and reception. *The Cambridge Companion to Horace*, ed. Stephen Harrison (Cambridge, 2007), covers biography, political, and cultural context, Horatian genres, and issues ranging from ethics to erotic desire and reception. Other collections of essays that cover a wide array of themes include: *Traditions and Contexts in the Poetry of Horace*, ed. T. Woodman and D. Feeney (Cambridge, 2002); *Why Horace? A Collection of Interpretations*, ed. W. S. Anderson (Wauconda, 1999); *Homage to Horace* (Oxford, 1995), ed. S. J. Harrison; *Horace 2000: A Celebration. Essays for the Bimillennium*, ed. N. Rudd (Ann Arbor, 1993).

Some relatively recent monographs of interest: Ellen Oliensis, *Horace and the Rhetoric of Authority* (Cambridge, 1998) on how Horace develops his self-image in negotiation with the powerful and, similarly, Randall L. B. McNeill, *Horace: Image, Identity, and Audience* (Baltimore, 2001). Kirk Freudenberg, *Satires of Rome: Threatening Poses from Lucilius to Juvenal* (Cambridge, 2001) explores Horace's satires within a narrative of Rome's progressive loss of Republican liberty.

For collections of responses by poets to Horace, see *Horace in English*, ed. D. S. Carne-Ross and K. Haynes (London, 1996), which demonstrates the deep imprint of Horace on English literary culture from Ben Jonson to Ezra Pound, and *Horace, The Odes: New Translations by Contemporary Poets*, ed. J. D. McClatchy (Princeton, 2003). For assessments of Horace's literary influence, see *Horace Made New*, ed. C. Martindale and D. Hopkins (Cambridge, 1993), and *Perceptions of Horace: A Roman Poet and His Readers*, ed. L. Houghton and M. Wyke (Cambridge, 2009).

# X Tacitus

All translations here used, apart from minor variations, are those by Alfred John Church and William Jackson Brodribb, which were first published by Macmillan, London between 1864 and 1877. Their translations have also appeared in many subsequent reprints, most recently that of the Everyman's Library, *Tacitus: Annals, Histories, Agricola, Germania* (New York, 2009), which also includes a useful modern introduction by Robin Lane Fox, and revised notes by Eleanor Cowan. Church and Brodribb's translations have also been published on a variety of websites, including The Internet Classics Archive (at http://classics.mit.edu), the Perseus Digital Library (at http://www.perseus.tufts.edu) and the Forum Romanum (at http://www.forumromanum.org). Other useful translations of Tacitus' works are available from Penguin and in the Oxford World's Classics series. A. J. Woodman's translation of the *Annals* (Indianapolis, 2004) is interesting for its efforts to replicate the distinctive style of Tacitus in English.

C. S. Kraus and A. J. Woodman, *Latin Historians* (Oxford, 1997) positions Tacitus in relation to Roman traditions for writing history. Victoria E. Pagán (ed.), *A Companion To Tacitus* (Malden, Mass., 2012), contains essays that cover the transmission of the manuscripts of Tacitus and his early-modern rediscovery, the ancient genre of historiography, issues of the interrelation of his work with other literature, and theoretical concerns such as gender and postcolonialism. Alongside chapters on Tacitus, the collection edited by T. J. Luce and A. J. Woodman, *Tacitus and the Tacitean Tradition* (Princeton, 1993), contains discussion of how Tacitus was read and used from the sixteenth to the eighteenth centuries. R. Ash (ed.), *Oxford Readings in Classical Studies: Tacitus* (2012), reprints a representative selection of influential articles dating back to the 1950s and contains a helpful introduction on the history of that scholarship. A. J. Woodman (ed.), *The Cambridge Companion to Tacitus* (Cambridge, 2009), contains samples of contemporary scholarship and carries a strong focus on the reception of Tacitus. It includes a chapter which explores how Tacitus influenced the work of the great historian of imperial Rome Ronald Syme and how, in turn, Syme's exhaustive two-volume appraisal of the Roman historian in his social context–*Tacitus* (Oxford, 1958)–long shaped our understanding of Roman history in terms of a dark and destructive lust for power within the aristocracy. Rhiannon Ash, *Tacitus* (Bristol, 2006), is a conveniently short and clear introduction. An earlier but still useful assessment can be found in R. H. Martin, *Tacitus* (Berkeley, 1981 and revised 1994). Dylan Sailor, *Writing and Empire in Tacitus* (Cambridge, 2008), explores the complex relationship between the historian's literary works and his political career.

On the *Histories* in particular, see Rhiannon Ash, *Ordering Anarchy: Armies and Leaders in Tacitus' Histories* (London, 1999), where she analyses Tacitus' collective characterization of the civil war armies and the individual portraits of their leaders. On the *Annals*, Ellen O'Gorman, *Irony and Misreading in the Annals of Tacitus* (Cambridge, 2000), demonstrates how the historian comments obliquely on the perversion of Republican structures of government under the new principate. See also Ronald Mellor, *Tacitus' Annals* (Oxford, 2011) as a work especially designed for the general reader. On the *Germania* and its reception, see the elegant and captivating book of Christopher B. Krebs, *A Most Dangerous Book: Tacitus' Germania from the Roman Empire to the Third Reich* (New York, 2011).

# XI Juvenal

The whole of Johnson's satire *London* is available conveniently in *Samuel Johnson: The Major Works*, edited by D. Greene (Oxford, 2000). Translations of Juvenal used, with only minor variation, are all taken from Niall Rudd, *Juvenal: The Satires* (Oxford, 1991), with an introduction and notes by

William Barr. Other translations include that by Peter Green, *Juvenal: The Sixteen Satires* (London, 1967 and most recently reprinted in 2004).

A number of collections of essays or monographs explore Juvenal in relation to the other notable Roman verse satirists, Lucilius, Horace, and Persius. These works emphasize as an important theme in Juvenal his self-positioning as successor to the others in this genre. Susanna Braund and Josiah Osgood, *A Companion to Persius and Juvenal* (Malden, Mass., 2012) includes discussion of the debts to Persius and Juvenal of later 'successor-poets' and the history of their place in classical scholarship, of their translation, and their role in education. Frederick Jones, *Juvenal and the Satiric Genre* (London, 2007) emphasizes the fluidity of the satiric genre, Juvenal's embrace of earlier satire and other genres, and satire's performative dimension. Kirk Freudenburg (ed.), *The Cambridge Companion to Roman Satire* (2005), collates its essays in terms of Roman satire as a literary genre, as a form of social discourse, and in relation to later English (mainly Elizabethan) literary culture. Kirk Freudenburg, *Satires of Rome: Threatening Poses from Lucilius to Juvenal* (Cambridge, 2001) argues that the genre gradually changes from an open to a cryptic mode and, in so doing, stages Rome's loss of its republican identity and freedoms. See also the important work of Susanna H. Braund in *The Roman Satirists and their Masks* (Bristol, 1996) and *Roman Verse Satire, Greece and Rome: New Surveys in the Classics* 23 (Oxford, 1992), and the useful essays she edited in *Satire and Society in Ancient Rome* (Exeter, 1989). All these works lay emphasis on the importance of not taking satire at face value and on the concept of the satiric 'mask'.

Useful monographs on selected satires of Juvenal include John Henderson, *Figuring Out Roman Nobility: Juvenal's Eighth Satire* (Exeter, 1997), which demonstrates the poem's dazzling mauling of the Roman culture of aristocracy, and Susanna H. Braund, *Beyond Anger: A Study of Juvenal's Third Book of Satires* (Cambridge, 1988) which argues that irony replaces anger as the dominant mode in the third book (*Satires 7–9*), while also looking back to the use of parody in the first two books (containing *Satires 1–5* and *Satire 6* respectively) and on to cynicism and aloofness beyond the third.

Commentaries on the Latin text of all sixteen satires include those of E. Courtney, *A Commentary on the Satires of Juvenal* (London, 1980) and John Ferguson, *Juvenal: The Satires* (New York, 1979). Accessible commentaries on selected satires include Susanna M. Braund, *Juvenal: Satires 1* (Cambridge, 1996); Niall Rudd and E. Courtney, *Juvenal. Satires I, III, X*

(Bristol, 1977); Paul Allen Miller, *Latin Verse Satire: An Anthology and Critical Reader* (London, 2005), which also contains a selection of representative essays from the 1970s to the 1990s.

For Johnson's imitations of Juvenal, and for other translations and adaptations into English from the fifteenth to the end of the twentieth century, see Martin M. Winkler, *Juvenal in English* (London, 2001).

## XII Lucian

Translations used in this chapter are my own except for the initial one by Paul Turner (*Lucian: Satirical Sketches*, Harmondsworth, 1961); Turner's Penguin has now been superseded by a new one by Keith Sidwell, *Chattering Courtesans and Other Sardonic Sketches* (Harmondsworth, 2004), including a few but not many of the same works. Sidwell's introduction and notes are also very good. There is also an Oxford World's Classics translation by C. D. N. Costa (*Selected Dialogues*, 2005), whose choice of dialogues overlaps with both Penguins.

Neil Hopkinson's *Lucian: A Selection* (Cambridge, 2008) gives a commentary on the Greek text of seven pieces, including *The Dream*; the introduction includes material accessible to those without knowledge of Greek. J. L. Lightfoot's fascinating and learned commentary on *The Syrian Goddess* (Oxford, 2003) is for specialists, but includes many perceptive remarks on Lucian as a whole, particularly when discussing that essay's disputed authorship (pp. 184–208). General books include J. Hall, *Lucian's Satire* (New York, 1981) and R. Bracht Branham, *Unruly Eloquence* (Cambridge, Mass., 1989); both have particularly good chapters on Lucian's 'Aging Deities', as Branham puts it. C. P. Jones, *Culture and Society in Lucian* (Oxford, 1986) explores Lucian's relation to his own historical context. Christopher Robinson's *Lucian and his Influence in Europe* (London, 1979), as the title suggests, is particularly strong on Lucian's later reception: he treats Erasmus at pp. 165–97. Simon Goldhill, *Who Needs Greek?* (Cambridge, 2002) discusses Erasmus in chapter 1 and Lucian in chapter 2, and is particularly good on the subtle indirectness of Lucian's self-projection.

Adam Bartley's collection, *A Lucian for our Times* (Newcastle, 2009), has some good papers: those on topics discussed here include H.-G. Nesselrath on the portrayal of Athens and Rome in, among other works, *Nigrinus*, O. Karavas (briefly) on religion, and especially Maria Pretzler on art criticism. M Çevic (ed.), *International Symposium on Lucianus of Samosata* (Adiyaman Universitesi, 2009), 113-24 is hard to obtain, but contains especially good papers by Mark Edwards on the elusiveness and irony of Lucian's views on religion and by Michael Trapp on *Nigrinus*: there is a downloadable lecture version of the latter at http://www.academia.edu/3066831/Honey_or_Arrows_On_Lucians_Nigrinus. *The Dream* is discussed particularly well by Deborah Gera in *Ethics and Rhetoric: Classical Essays for Donald Russell on his Seventy-Fifth Birthday* (ed. D. Innes, H. Hine, and C. Pelling, Oxford 1995), 237-50.

Greek literature of the Roman Empire has recently attracted much attention, for instance Simon Swain, *Hellenism and Empire* (Oxford, 1996), Tim Whitmarsh, *Greek Literature and the Roman Empire* (Oxford, 2001), both with chapters on Lucian; Simon Goldhill (ed.), *Being Greek under Rome* (Cambridge, 2001) is also an interesting collection. A good introduction to the so-called 'Second Sophistic' is given by Tim Whitmarsh, *The Second Sophistic* (*Greece & Rome: New Surveys in the Classics* 35 (2005)); see also now his *Beyond the Second Sophistic* (Berkeley, 2013).

*Calumny* is discussed extensively in Botticelli scholarship, for instance by Ronald Lightbown, *Botticelli: Life and Work* (2nd edn., New York, 1989), 122-6 and by Andreas Schumacher in Schumacher (ed.), *Botticelli: Likeness, Myth, Devotion* (a sumptuous volume produced by the Städel Museum in Frankfurt to accompany a 2009-10 Botticelli exhibition), 22-6. My personal memories of the 1960s have been supplemented from D. R. Thorpe, *Supermac: The Life of Harold Macmillan* (London, 2011): p. 489 describes the exchange with Paymaster General Reginald Bevins over *That Was The Week That Was*.

# PICTURE ACKNOWLEDGEMENTS

PICTURE ACKNOWLEDGEMENTS

11.1 Times of the Day, Noon, 1738 (engraving), Hogarth, William
    (1697–1764) / Private Collection / The Bridgeman Art Library
11.2 Juvenal Scourging Woman, illustration from 'The Sixth Satire of Juvenal',
    1896 (engraving), Beardsley, Aubrey (1872–98) / Private Collection / The
    Stapleton Collection / The Bridgeman Art Library
12.1 Vicky [Victor Weisz] Published: Evening Standard, 06 Nov 1958
    © Solo Syndication/ Associated Newspapers Ltd./ British Cartoon Archive,
    University of Kent, www.cartoons.ac.uk
12.2 © Photo Scala, Florence—courtesy of the Ministero Beni e Att. Culturali
12.3 wikipedia commons

# TEXT ACKNOWLEDGEMENTS

We are grateful for permission to include extracts from the following translations of classical works in this book.

## Cicero

*Cicero: Political Speeches* translated by D. H. Berry (Oxford World Classics, 2006), reproduced by permission of Oxford University Press.

*Cicero: Selected Letters* translated by P. G. Walsh (Oxford World Classics, 2008), reproduced by permission of Oxford University Press.

*Cicero: On Obligations (De Officiis)* translated by P. G. Walsh (Oxford World Classics, 2000), reproduced by permission of Oxford University Press.

*Cicero: Philippics 3–9* translated by G Manuwald (De Gruyter, 2007), reproduced by permission of Walter de Gruyter GmbH.

*Cicero: The Nature of the Gods* translated by Horace C. P. McGregor and edited by J. M. Ross (Penguin Classics, 1972, 1978, 1984), translation copyright © Penguin Books 1972, reproduced by permission of Penguin Books Ltd.

## Herodotus

*Herodotus: The Histories* translated by Robin Waterfield (Oxford World Classics, 1998), reproduced by permission of Oxford University Press.

## Homer

C. P. Cavafy: lines from 'Ithaka' translated by Evangelos Sachperogolou (Oxford World Classics, 2007), reproduced by permission of Oxford University Press.

*Homer: The Iliad* translated by Martin Hammond (Penguin, 1987, 2003), translation copyright © Martin Hammond 1987, reproduced by permission of Penguin Books Ltd.

*Homer: The Odyssey* translated by E. V. Rieu revised by D. C. H. Rieu (Penguin, 1991, 2003), translation copyright © E. V. Rieu 1946, revised translation copyright © the Estate of E. V. Rieu and D. C. H. Rieu 1991, 2003, reproduced by permission of Penguin Books Ltd.

## Horace

*Horace: The Complete Odes & Epodes* translated by David West (Oxford World Classics, 2008), reproduced by permission of Oxford University Press.

*Horace: Satires* translated by Niall Rudd (Penguin Classics 1973, revised edition 1979, 1987, 1997, 2005), translation copyright © Niall Rudd, 1973, 1979, 1987, 1997, 2005, reproduced by permission of Penguin Books Ltd.

*Odes* 3.30 translated by John Hollander in J. D. McClatchy (Ed.): *Horace: The Odes: New Translations by Contemporary Poets* (Princeton, 2002), copyright © Princeton University Press 2002, reproduced by permission of Princeton University Press.

## Juvenal

*Juvenal: The Satires* translated by Niall Rudd with an introduction by William Barr (Oxford World Classics, 1992), reproduced by permission of Oxford University Press.

## Lucian

*Lucian: Satirical Sketches* translated by Paul Turner (Penguin, 1965): copyright holder not traced.

## Sappho

Sappho fragments from M. L. West: *Greek Lyric Poetry* (Oxford World Classics, 2008), reproduced by permission of Oxford University Press.

## Thucydides

Thucydides: *The Peleponesian War* translated by Martin Hammond (Oxford World Classics, 2009), reproduced by permission of Oxford University Press.

## Virgil

*Virgil: The Aeneid* translated by Cecil Day Lewis (Oxford World Classics, 2008), reproduced by permission of Peters Fraser & Dunlop (www.petersfraserdunlop. com) on behalf of the Estate of Cecil Day Lewis.

# INDEX

3000    1500
.        1500
2000